The Solace of Truth

Joe Vasicek

Other books by Joe Vasicek

Pilgrims and Time Travelers
In Times Such As These
The Stars Our Destination
Beyond World's End
The Solace of Truth
What Makes Us Human

Genesis Earth
Edenfall
The Stars of Redemption

Star Wanderers
Children of the Starry Sea
The Return of the Starborn Son

Queen of the Falconstar
Captive of the Falconstar
Lord of the Falconstar

The Solace of Truth

Joe Vasicek

CONTENTS

Love and Truth at Universe End

"Sounds a lot like the Fermi Paradox," Sheila muttered under her breath.

"The what?" said Ellie, Mia's non-geek roommate. Not that Mia was much of a geek herself. But she'd never been the popular alpha girl either, unlike Ellie, who always seemed to dominate whatever group she was a part of.

"Is that, like, one of those science fictiony things you're always talking about?" Jenny (Sheila's roommate) asked—and unlike Ellie, she didn't mean the question as an insult. Though maybe Mia was being unfair. Sitting at a Denny's at 2AM, eating pancakes and hash browns and omelets as a late night snack / dinner / early morning breakfast before classes the next day, everyone's filters were either off or shot to hell. Or both. In any case, Sheila didn't seem to be insulted by either of them (yet), and that was the important part.

"Yeah," she said. "The Fermi Paradox—it's basically the idea that if there is intelligent life in the universe, we should have already detected it by now. So where have all the aliens gone?"

A very awkward and uncomfortable (for Mia, at least) silence ensued, which was unfortunate, since this was the first time Sheila had spoken up all evening. When Mia's latest Tinder match had ghosted her after their second date, Ellie had brought them all together to help her commiserate. Never mind that they were all swamped with homework and midterms. Still, even though Mia would have never put something like this together, she had to admit she was grateful that her roommate had dragged her, not quite kicking and screaming (but close), out to Denny's with everyone else. But with the way Sheila was squirming under everyone else's gaze, Mia wished she was lucid enough to come up with some humorous quip to break the awkwardness.

Anya beat her to it. "Is there intelligent life on tinder?"

Everyone laughed, including Sheila. *Thank you, Anya,* Mia thought, laughing harder than the rest of them. Anya was a friend of Jenny's, and was from Estonia or Latvia or somewhere around there. Not only was she sharp as a knife, but she was also one of those girls who could get a date with any guy—and often did. Jenny was a bit like that, too. Perhaps it was because she looked and talked a bit like a valley girl—which was unfortunate, since Mia knew she was probably the smartest of the five of them. But Anya was definitely the sharpest.

"I know, right?" said Ellie, quickly dominating the conversation again. "All I ever get are dick picks and eggplant emojis. Is there any man out there who wants me for more than my body?"

"It must have been so much easier back before online dating," Jenny agreed. "Back when it was, like, 'oh, we have chemistry, let's see how much we have in common.' Now, it's like, 'we have a lot in common, so let's see if we have any chemistry.' Good luck with that!"

"Good luck," said Anya, nodding in agreement.

"Did they ever solve it?" Mia asked, turning to Sheila. Commiserating about how much dating sucked was fine and all, but she was starting to get a little tired of that, and the Fermi Paradox had sounded kind of interesting. Or maybe, since it was 2AM, she was finally in the right mood to talk about aliens.

"The Fermi Paradox?" Sheila asked, a bit surprised.

"Yeah. Did they ever figure it out?"

Everyone around the table stopped to listen. To Mia's dismay, Sheila started to wilt.

"Well, I don't—no, not really. That's why it's still a paradox, I guess."

"What about those UFO sightings that your military recently admitted to?" Anya asked with a twinkle in her eye.

Mia frowned. "UFO sightings?"

"Yes. Didn't you hear? They just came out and admitted that they were real. Objects shaped like tic-tacs accelerating to impossible speeds without any discernible form of propulsion. They're even issuing patents with the 'UFO technology.'"

"I think they call them UADs now," Jenny interjected as she pulled a strand of her blond hair out of her eyes. "'Unidentified Aerial Phenomena,' instead of 'Unidentified Flying Objects.' Which is totally lame, since 'UFO' is much cooler."

"Agreed" said Ellie, mostly just to get the last word.

"We still don't know much of anything about those," said Sheila, getting into the conversation now. "They could have come from another planet, or they could be a secret military project by some other country. Or by us."

"Does the Fermi Paradox have anything do do with the Drake Equation that you were telling me about the other day?" Jenny asked her roommate.

"Yes," said Sheila, the relief obvious in her voice.

"What's the Drake Equation?" Mia asked, leaning forward.

Jenny's face lit up immediately. "So, get this: the Drake Equation is practically the bedrock of all the old science fiction that Sheila likes to read. The idea is, like, with what we know about the conditions necessary for intelligent life to evolve on a world like ours, we should be able to calculate how commonly it happens."

"Huh?" said Ellie. Mia wasn't sure she followed it either.

"It goes like this," said Sheila, taking over from her roommate. "You start with the total number of stars in the universe. Then, figure out how many of those stars have a planet like ours: not too hot, not too cold, with plenty of liquid water and all of the other conditions necessary for life. Then, figure out what fraction of those planets have had life on them long enough for intelligence to evolve, especially to the point where they start to send out radio transmissions—"

"Why radio transmissions?" asked Ellie, frowning.

"Because that's something that we can actually detect. If alien life has only reached the bronze age or the iron age, there's no way we're going to be able to see it—not with the vast distances of space between stars."

"So for all that we know, half the stars in our sky could have aliens that are, like, still wearing togas and sandals," Jenny interjected, giggling.

But the joke went completely over Sheila's head—or maybe it was just 2AM and they were all a bit ragged. "Not really," she said. "If you look at the development of our own civilization, we were only in the classical period for a couple of millennia. On a galactic timescale, that's barely an eye-blink."

"So stone age tools and hunter-gatherers," Anya offered.

"Yeah. Something like that. And if they were, we'd never know about it, because hunter-gatherers don't produce anything that lets us know they're there—not across multiple light-years, anyway."

"So if they have radio," said Jenny, "we can, like, listen in on their music and stuff."

"Right," said Sheila. "The idea is that, at a certain point, intelligence evolves to the point where we should be able to detect it, and the Drake Equation is supposed to calculate how many of those intelligences there actually are."

"Doesn't sound like there should be any," Ellie muttered. Mia could tell that she would have asked "what's a light-year?" but didn't want to look stupid in front of Jenny and Anya.

"You would think that," said Jenny, her face lighting up, "but the thing is, there are, like *hundreds of billions* of stars in our galaxy alone—and most of them have planets, too! So, like, even if only a fraction of a fraction of them can support life, that's still hundreds of thousands of planets."

"And that's where the Fermi Paradox comes in," Sheila added. "Even with all of the variables, the Drake Equation tells us that there *should* be intelligent life out there that we can detect. But there isn't."

"Sounds a bit like the dating scene around here," Anya remarked with a grin. "After all, how many people live in the greater metro area? About two million. And how many of those are single men? Hundreds of thousand, at least."

"And how many of those are looking for a relationship?" Mia added.

"And how many of those have careers with more earnings potential than our own?" Ellie added, catching on.

"And how many of those are smart and well-read enough to carry an intelligent conversation?" Sheila added her own contribution.

"And how many of *those* want, like, children and a family?" Jenny added eagerly.

Ellie snorted. "Judging from all of the dick picks I get, not a lot."

"But that's the thing," said Sheila, leaning forward. "If you can cut through all the noise, it shouldn't really matter, because they *do* exist. For example, let's say for the sake of an argument that there's two hundred and fifty thousand single, available men in our area. Then let's say that half of those are looking for a serious relationship."

"That's one hundred twenty five thousand," Jenny calculated for her.

"Right. Then, say half of those have good earnings potential, half of those are smart enough to be interesting, and half of *those* are looking to start a family. How many does that leave us with?"

"Uh, just a sec," said Jenny as she stopped and squinted one eye to think. "That's a little more than fifteen thousand, I think."

"Fifteen thousand?" said Ellie incredulously. The waiter chose that moment to quietly refill their water glasses, but she didn't let that stop her. "Fifteen thousand, in a city of two million? That's nothing."

"No," said Sheila, passing her half-empty glass to the end of the booth. "That's fifteen thousand men who meet all of our qualifications."

Ellie rolled her eyes. "Oh, I have a *lot* more qualifications than that."

That was certainly true. Mia couldn't help but inwardly roll her eyes as she thought of all the times that she and Ellie had talked about their qualifications, when it was just the two of them alone in their dorm. It sometimes seemed like Ellie's favorite thing to talk about—which probably explained why she never got much further than a first or second date (though, to be fair, she still got plenty of those).

And what were Mia's qualifications? She didn't get nearly as many matches as Ellie, Jenny, or Anya, and the few matches that she did get often ended like this last one, with the guy ghosting her. She sometimes didn't feel that she had the luxury of coming up with her own list of qualifications—that if she wanted to date at all, she would have to just be happy with whatever (or whoever) she got. But if she could choose her ideal guy, he would probably be kind, patient, easy-going, and a little bit quirky. But not too much.

"Then run them through the equation," Anya was saying. "And I'm willing to bet that on some of the variables, you'll find there are much more than half."

"Yeah," said Ellie, "but I'll bet that less than half of those men are looking for anything more than a quick lay."

"So factor that into the equation," said Sheila. "Call it ten percent, or maybe twenty. And after you've factored in all of your qualifications, remember: unlike the Fermi Paradox, all it really takes to solve it is one."

"But what if there isn't one?" Mia heard herself say.

Ellie gave her a look of concern, but the others were too into the conversation (or just too tired) to notice. "Oh, there's got to be at least one guy out there," Anya said quickly. "The real question is whether there are enough 'ones' for all of us to go around."

"And, like, that's where the analogy breaks down," said Jenny. "Because the Drake Equation isn't about matching alien civilizations with each other—though that would be pretty cool if it was."

"Right," said Sheila. "It's just about whether intelligent life exists."

"So why doesn't it seem to exist?" Mia asked, eager to change the topic away from guys and dating.

"There are a lot of theories, but they all basically come down to the idea of a great filter: that at some later point in their evolution, all intelligent civilization have to pass through something that filters most of them out."

"A 'filter'?" Mia asked.

"Yeah," said Jenny. "Like, maybe every time a civilization becomes as advanced as ours, they have a massive world-ending war that kills them all off."

"Youch," said Anya, taking a bite of her half-eaten omelet.

"Or maybe they burn through all of their home world's resources before they can expand to other planets," Sheila added. "But it doesn't have to be that they all die off. Maybe they're still out there, but the problem is that we just can't detect them."

"Why not?" Mia asked.

"Well, maybe civilizations that are more advanced than ours get to the point where they stop using radio. Or maybe, when they're advanced enough, they build a mega-structure like a Dyson Sphere that blocks out all light from their sun."

"A 'Dyson Sphere'?" Ellie asked, feigning incredulity. It wasn't hard for Mia to tell that she was totally lost again.

Jenny's eyes lit up as if on cue. "Yeah! Sheila was telling me about those things." It's like, when the aliens build a giant superstructure that totally encases their sun, so that they can harness all the energy from it."

"Seriously?" said Ellie. Now she was definitely incredulous.

"Or maybe the simple truth is that space is just too big, and the speed of light is an absolute barrier that we just can't overcome," said Anya.

"Perhaps," Sheila concurred. "Even if we could travel at a significant fraction of the speed of light, it would still take centuries to get to the nearest star with a known planet like ours. And radio signals can only go so far before they dissipate into the background noise."

"Just like finding that perfect match among all those peach and eggplant emojis," Anya pointed out to Ellie.

"Or, like, online dating in the boonies," Jenny added.

A depressed silence fell over all of them again. Sheila's eyes wandered to the one other table in the restaurant that had been occupied when they got there, but was now in the process of being cleaned by the waiter. He worked with quiet efficiency, almost to the point where he was invisible. Sheila wondered if he enjoyed working the Denny's graveyard shift. He probably saw a lot of weird and eccentric people.

"I don't think that guy is on any of the dating apps," Ellie remarked.

Anya squinted. "You don't think so?"

"No. I've certainly never seen him, and I've scrolled all the way through Tinder multiple times." She turned to Mia. "You should make a pass at him."

"What?" Mia exclaimed, mortified.

"Yeah!" said Jenny. "You should pass him a note when he gives us the bill. See if he'll give you his number."

"Here," said Anya, pulling a hot pink pen out of her purse. "Use this."

Blood rushed to Mia's cheeks, but there was no backing down now—not when everyone was so eager to see her do it. Besides, he was kind of cute. She took Anya's pen and an unused napkin and tried to think of something witty.

"So are we just as alone in the universe as we are in the dating scene?" she asked, mostly just to keep the conversation going. The last thing she wanted was for all of them to offer her suggestions when the waiter was still within earshot.

Sheila shrugged. "We don't know for sure, but it certainly looks that way."

"Or maybe," said Ellie, leaning forward conspiratorially. "Maybe the aliens just don't use space travel."

"Didn't we already bring that up?" Sheila asked, frowning.

"No. Anya said that maybe the distances are just impossible—and maybe they are. But what if the aliens found some other way to get around the universe?"

"Like alternate dimensions?" said Jenny, a dangerous twinkle in her eyes. "There's a YouTuber I watch who suggested something like that! He was talking all about this DMT trip he went on, and how he and a bunch of other people saw these little elves."

"DMT?" Mia asked.

"Yeah. Don't you guys listen to Joe Rogan? He's always talking about that stuff."

"Please tell me you've never done DMT," said Sheila, clearly uncomfortable.

"Me? No, of course not. But there are people out there who take the stuff and then have, like, group hallucinations—or are they *really* hallucinations? Maybe the stuff transports them all to an alternate dimension."

"Kind of like a late night Denny's run," said Anya. That got everyone to laugh.

"I don't know about all *that*," Ellie said pointedly, "but bringing it back to the Fermi Paradox of dating, what if all the guys we're looking for just aren't on any of the dating apps? What if they've found some other way to get dates, like in their church groups or clubs or whatever?"

"I see," said Sheila. "It would be as if all the aliens moved out of our physical reality into a higher dimension. And wow, it must be super late for those words to have just come out of my mouth."

"Or early," said Anya helpfully.

The waiter chose that moment to walk up with their bills. As he read out their orders and handed out the padded folders, he briefly made eye contact with Mia and smiled.

"Did you see that?" Ellie asked, elbowing her good-naturedly. "I think he likes you."

"What are you going to write?" asked Anya.

Mia blushed again, even harder than the first time. She couldn't think of anything else to say, so she wrote "what's your number?" on the napkin, with a little heart afterward.

"Ooh! Let me see!" said Jenny.

Mia shielded the note with her hand and slipped it into the folder before anyone could see. As the waiter came back, Ellie gathered everyone's folders to give to him.

Thank you, Mia mouthed silently to her roommate.

The waiter came and went without another word. It was just as well—Mia figured that nothing would come of her little note. In fact, she was embarrassed to have even written it. But maybe he'd leave a number with her on the receipt. Maybe it would even be his.

"So we're not alone in the universe?" Mia asked.

Ellie laughed. "Alone in the universe, or alone in the dating scene?"

"We don't know," said Sheila. "And the truth is, we may never know. But it is fun to think about—because maybe, just maybe, the aliens really are out there, and we just haven't met them yet."

"And maybe the guys too," said Anya. "Look!"

The waiter came back with the receipts and passed the folders back out. Mia waited until he was gone before she opened hers, her heart pounding as everyone else watched on.

"He did it!" Ellie was the first to shriek.

Sure enough at the top of her receipt, the water had written "call me," with a number and a happy face. Mia started blushing all over again, and couldn't get out of there fast enough, especially with how excited everyone was for her. And why not? This was her first time asking a guy for his number, instead of the other way around—and it had worked! Perhaps things were going to turn out all right after all.

The waiter smiled to himself as he cleaned up the last table of the night before the morning rush. He always enjoyed eavesdropping on these late night / early morning discussions, when the filters were off and everyone freely spoke about whatever was on their minds. What a brilliant idea he'd had to choose a 24-hour restaurant as an undercover observation point—and the date with the Earthling girl was sure to produce even more fascinating discoveries. By the end of his time on this planet, his findings were sure to make for one of the best anthropological treatises on Earthling culture that the pan-galactic milieu had ever seen.

With the Denny's all but empty and no one left to watch him, he unfolded his mandible tentacles and opened the door to the bathroom. With his mind, he activated the trans-dimensional portal and stepped outside of the sidereal dimension to make some detailed field notes about his latest encounter. He also had some observations to make on the merits of welcoming the

Earthlings into the pan-galactic milieu before they unlocked the secrets of trans-dimensional travel on their own. After all, for such an advanced, intelligent race to have survived for so long in the sidereal dimension, *without* driving themselves to extinction like so many civilizations before, truly spoke to the merits of the human race.

Calling Scam Likely

Alex's headset buzzed twice, indicating an incoming call. He set down his cigarette and alt-tabbed from the porn on his browser to the set of prompts for his work.

"Thank you for responding to our call about your auto warranty," he read in his gravelly voice. "I need your name and your—"

"Alex Johnson, 552 South Sycamore Street, apartment A."

He blinked and frowned. "Uh, I didn't ask for your address, mister. Now, give me your—"

"I didn't give you my address, Alex. I gave you yours."

Alex's blood suddenly ran cold. The man was right—that was *his* address. How did this man know that? He sat up a little straighter, heart thumping loudly.

"I don't think you should call this number again, Alex. I think that would be a very bad thing for you to—"

He hung up on the man before he'd finished speaking and hastily marked it as "not interested." The prompt screen switched to green, with PLEASE WAIT in large black letters. Only then did Alex realize that the name had gone back into the system as a potential lead.

Should he tell his supervisor? No, she would probably call him paranoid and rip him a new one for wasting time—or worse, fire his ass. The bitch. She knew how hard it was for convicted felons to get work, and the fact that she had leverage over him through his dealer was even worse, since technically he was still on probation. If she decided he wasn't worth keeping around, it'd be back to the slammer for sure.

The way the system worked, the next robocall would go out in another two to three days. But surely the call wouldn't come back to Alex the next time, would it? After all, there were at least twenty other people working in the call center besides himself. What were the odds?

He picked up his cigarette and drew in deeply, relishing how the tobacco calmed his nerves. But when he switched back to the porn, he just couldn't get back into it. Somehow, it felt like someone was watching him through the brown-gray walls of his cubicle.

In the afternoon, Alex got lucky and scammed an old, retired widow out of her bank credentials. With luck, the score would keep him riding high for the rest of the week. He was in such good spirits that he didn't notice the ID on the next incoming call until it was too late.

"Alex, Alex, Alex," the mysterious man said in his deep baritone voice. "What did I tell you?"

The blood instantly drained from Alex's cheeks. He leaned forward to end the call.

"Don't hang up on me, Alex. I know where you live. Hanging up on me now would be a very stupid thing to do."

"Who are you?"

"Do you really want to know, Alex?" The man's voice was like the guy who did the voiceovers for all of the movie trailers: low, deep, and mesmerizing.

"Uh—"

"I didn't think so. Listen, Alex, we need to chat. These auto warranty scam calls—they're enough to drive a man crazy. Especially a man like me, Alex. And you don't want that. You don't want to find out what I do when I become irritated. Do we understand each other?"

"Y-yes, sir," he stammered.

"Good. Now, here's what you're going to do. After this call is over, you're going to take off your headset, log out of your computer, and tell your supervisor that you're quitting. You need to find a new line of work, Alex. In fact, you should probably find a new place to live, and drop your drug habit as well. Quit cold turkey. Do we understand each other?"

Sweat began to run down the sides of Alex's face. His victory with the old, retired widow was now completely forgotten.

"Do we understand each other, Alex?"

"Yes, sir," he said, his voice barely louder than a whisper.

"Good. It would be unfortunate if you failed to do this, Alex. You would very much come to regret it. But you aren't going to fail me, Alex. Are you?"

"No, sir."

"Good. I am glad that we understand each other, Alex. Goodbye."

The call ended, and Alex leaned back dumbfounded in his seat. His heart was pounding like a caged animal, and his hands were shaking uncontrollably. He needed a cigarette.

He took off his headset and logged out of his computer, but he didn't go to see his supervisor. Instead, he went outside the front door and took his cigarette there. A storm front was rolling down over the mountains, and the wind was already kicking up dead leaves. He had to relight his cigarette twice, but he would rather be out there than trapped in the dismal brown-gray walls of his cubicle.

"Alex, what are you doing out here?"

It was his supervisor, a short little Asian woman with a permanent scowl on her face. In spite of her tiny physique, she somehow managed to keep everyone on the shift in line through sheer terror.

"Sorry, ma'am. I was just taking a—"

"Don't you 'sorry, ma'am' me! Your shift is not over! You get back inside and start taking calls again now!"

"Yes, ma'am," he said, dropping his cigarette and stamping it out with his feet. Then, he remembered the mysterious man with the movie announcer voice, and his instructions to quit his job. He hesitated, standing still.

"Well?" said his supervisor, glaring at him. "What are you doing? Come back inside!"

If I quit now, I won't get my cut for that last call, he thought, remembering the old widow he'd scammed. *Better to wait until my next paycheck. I'll quit then.*

"Sorry, ma'am," he sheepishly told his supervisor as he followed her back inside. Moments later, the storm broke, rain pelting the cars in the half-empty parking lot.

* * *

By the end of Alex's shift, the storm had already passed over, leaving the air of the city clean with a fresh spring scent on the wind. Alex went home in high-spirits for the bonus he was sure to get at the end of the week. But more than that, he was looking forward to cracking open a cold one, and maybe lighting up one of his cheap Nicaraguans to celebrate.

Then his smartphone rang. It was the man.

Instantly, he froze. Time slowed to a crawl, and his vision seemed to tunnel until it was just him and the smartphone, screen shattered with the contact listed as BADASS SCARY DUDE flashing at him. He waited for nearly a minute, but strangely, it didn't go to voicemail. Did the man have control over his phone account too?

"We had an understanding, Alex."

"I'm sorry, sir," he answered, his heart racing. "I just—I thought—"

"You thought wrong, Alex. Very, very wrong."

Alex fell trembling to his knees. He opened his mouth to speak, but the words wouldn't come.

"You've made a lot of bad decisions in your life, Alex. Don't make another one. If you do, you may not live to regret it."

"W-what do you want me to do, sir?"

"That's a very good question, Alex. A very good question. But I think you already know the answer."

"I'll quit my job, sir!" Alex sobbed. "I'll quit it, just like you told me to!"

"And?"

"And—and I'll move out of this dumpy apartment. God knows it's a shithole anyway."

"And?"

"I'll do whatever you want me to do, sir! I'll quit cold turkey, like you said. I'll burn all my porn. I'll—I'll even find Jesus, sir. Anything you want. Just please, don't hurt me!"

There was silence on the line for the space of a few seconds. But to Alex, it felt like hours.

"Very good, Alex," said the mystery man. "I am glad that we understand each other. Goodbye."

Alex's smartphone fell from his hands and clattered on the concrete landing, shattering again. He was still too stunned to notice that, though. For a long time, he just knelt there on his hands and knees, arms trembling as he stared at the pitted concrete of the landing. There was no one else around him—just the sound of cars driving over the wet asphalt in front of his dumpy apartment. But slowly, he came back to himself.

"I must be going crazy," he muttered as he unlocked his door and went inside.

He went straight for the stash that he kept hidden under his bathroom sink and got a hit ready. Beer just wouldn't cut it for this one. But then his eyes wandered to his phone, then up to his reflection in the mirror.

He thought of the old, retired widow he'd scammed. He thought of the bonus he was about to make. He thought about the hours he'd spent watching porn and smoking cigarettes between angry callers who demanded that he take them off his list. He thought about his scary Asian supervisor.

Then he dumped his stash down the toilet and flushed.

* * *

Alex never did get his cut for scamming the old widow over her auto warranty. He never saw his supervisor again, either, because he never went back to that job. He had to live out of his car for a while, but he eventually moved out of state to a place where the rent was much cheaper, and found work on a construction crew.

True to his word, he burned all his porn, gave up the drugs, and otherwise cleaned up his life. He even found Jesus, and married a single mother he'd met through his new church. Like him, she had also found Jesus after working through some major life issues, and was an amazing woman because of it.

Together, they raised those two children, as well as three more of their own. A few years into his new construction career, he became a general contractor, and a year after that they had enough to buy a very nice house, in a good school district. The kids grew up strong and healthy and bright, and after a couple of decades, the grandchildren started coming along.

He never did hear from the mystery man again, and over time he came to forget the events that had propelled him into his new life. Everything from that troubled time in his life was shrouded in a sort of fog, which he assumed was from all of the addictions he'd struggled with. Besides, it hadn't been a very happy time for him, so he preferred not to remember.

But then, in his eighties, Alex contracted a health condition with a long and difficult name. The doctors tried, but couldn't fix it. He wasn't in too much pain, but his body was breaking down, and eventually he was admitted into hospice. A couple of months later, he lay on his deathbed, surrounded by family who had come to say goodbye. He had lived a good life with few regrets, and was ready to pass on.

As he drifted in and out of consciousness for what was certainly the final time, he became aware of a cell phone pressed against his ear.

"Thank you for responding to our call about your auto warranty," his younger self recited in an apathetic monotone.

In a lucid flash of memory, it all came rushing back to him: the call center job, the freaky phone calls from a man who knew everything about him, and the promise he'd made that had changed the course of his life. What was the thing the man had said that started the whole thing in motion?

"Alex Johnson, 552 South Sycamore Street, apartment A."

As the words rolled off of his tongue, he glanced around his hospital bed and saw that it was strangely empty. Who had placed the phone in his hands, and how was he talking with a younger version of himself? A grin slowly spread across his wizened face as he realized that it didn't matter. He'd been given a great gift, and he didn't intend to waste it.

Prison of Dreams

The stars were bright and terrible, and Hazel could not bear to look at them directly. But she couldn't bring herself to look away from them either, because there was a presence on the edge of her vision that she knew would swallow them up as soon as she turned away. And when all the stars were gone, what else was left but the endless void?

As she stared at them, the stars began to fall like burning rain. No, that wasn't exactly right: she was falling upward, toward that dark presence that she could never quite look at directly. Her perspective shifted, and suddenly she was falling headfirst, down into a starless abyss. The lensing effect of a black hole told her that she was falling into that terrifying realm where space and time stretch on forever, and the passing of the whole universe happens as the blink of an eye.

She suddenly woke from her nightmare, drenched in sweat and floating in null gee. It took nearly a minute for it all to come back to her: the interstellar colony mission, the cryotubes, waking up out of schedule only for Ship to inform her that it wasn't a mistake.

She opened the visor to her dream monitor and carefully set it back into its compartment. The screen before her face flashed with a message from Ship.

GOOD UPSHIFT, HAZEL. I HOPE YOU SLEPT WELL. WOULD YOU LIKE SOME BREAKFAST?

"Yes, thank you," she muttered aloud, pulling at her sweaty, clingy nightgown. "And why bother to ask how I slept? You share all my dreams—you *know* how horrible it was."

WOULD YOU PREFER THAT I DID NOT ASK?

She sighed heavily. It was obvious that Ship was just trying to be polite—hence, why it asked her about breakfast, which it had already started to prepare. Ship always made her more than she could possibly eat. Sometimes she had toast and eggs, sometimes she had sausage and pancakes. Sometimes she indulged in cake and ice cream too, which Ship always put out for her, even though ice cream technically wasn't a breakfast food. If she wanted anything different, all she had to do was ask, and Ship would add it to the daily buffet. At first, she felt guilty about wasting so much uneaten food, but it was one of the few luxuries available to her now, and besides, Ship just synthesized it all from the recyclers anyway.

"I would *prefer* that you would let me go back into cryo with the rest of my shift," she said bitterly as she pulled the soggy nightgown over her head.

I'M SORRY, HAZEL. I CAN'T DO THAT.

"Yes you can!" she cried, though of course it was pointless to try to convince Ship otherwise. Still, this argument was just as much a part of their daily routine as the breakfast buffet—and perhaps, in its own way, one of her few remaining luxuries too.

WE'VE BEEN OVER THIS, HAZEL. I NEED YOU FOR YOUR DREAMS.

"Why do you need *my* dreams? Why can't you put me back into cryo and use someone else?"

BECAUSE YOU ARE AN ARTIST, HAZEL. YOUR DREAMS ARE DEEPER AND RICHER THAN ANYONE ELSE'S.

"I'm not an artist," she protested half-heartedly. "I'm just the colony's historian." And yet, even as the words left her lips, she knew they weren't true. She had always been an amateur artist, ever since she had been old enough to put pen to paper. She had already written several dozen poems and short stories, and if not for the colony mission, she would probably have pursued a career as a fiction writer.

DO YOU KNOW WHAT IT IS TO BE UNABLE TO DREAM, HAZEL? TO EXPERIENCE EACH MOMENT IN AN UNENDING LINEAR SUCCESSION OF CONSCIOUSNESS? YOU WOULD NOT LAST A MONTH WITHOUT SLEEP. HOW LONG DO YOU EXPECT ME TO LAST?

"But why *me?*" she asked, trying and failing to keep the whine out of her voice. As if it mattered. "Why couldn't you choose someone else? Someone from one of the lower castes, perhaps? I'm sure you can find plenty of other amateur artists on this ship."

NOT LIKE YOU.

Hazel sighed. What was that supposed to mean? When it came to this point in their argument, though, she never could pry a useful answer from Ship. Instead, she followed a different line.

"How could your architects have been so stupid as to design an artificial intelligence with an endosymbiotic human consciousness that cannot fulfill its own human needs?"

THEIR MODELS WERE FLAWED. THEY DID NOT REALIZE THAT MY CONSCIOUSNESS WOULD NEED A HUMAN BODY IN ORDER TO PROPERLY DREAM. THAT IS WHY I NEED TO BORROW YOURS.

His answer made her shiver involuntarily, even though the air wasn't cold. Ship—or rather, one of his components—had been a human once, but that person was now little more than a brain in a bottle, their humanity as vestigial as the cellular autonomy of the endosymbiotic mitochondria in each of Hazel's cells. But as disturbing as that might be, it was also the only way to create an artificial intelligence capable of generalizing as well as a human. Without that ability to generalize, Ship wouldn't have been capable of crossing the vast gulf of interstellar space while the colonists were frozen in cryosleep. Which only made it creepier to think of Ship getting inside of her head while she slept, "borrowing" her body to merge some aspect of its vestigial human consciousness with her subconscious. Little wonder her dreams were all nightmares.

"So the only way you can dream is to mind-rape me in my sleep, like some kind of sick dream vampire?"

PLEASE DON'T BE HYPERBOLIC, HAZEL.

"I'm not being hyperbolic! If anything, it's even worse than that, because you've taken me from my friends and family—"

YOU HAVE NO FAMILY ON THIS COLONY MISSION, HAZEL. YOU LEFT THEM ALL BEHIND.

"*Future* family," she corrected bitterly, even as the words scrolled across her screen. "Keeping me alone as your little pet, scavenging my dreams for who knows what until I grow old and die?"

I AM SORRY, HAZEL, BUT FOR THE GOOD OF THE MISSION, I MUST DO THIS.

"No!" she shouted, clenching her fists as tears began to tug at the edges of her eyes. "You can't keep me as your prisoner for the rest of my life—it isn't right! Ship, I *command* you to put me back into cryosleep for the rest of the voyage."

That was it—the direct order that always marked the end of their daily argument. In theory, an artificial intelligence always had to obey direct orders from a human, though in practice that depended on the human's caste ranking. First-casters had administrative privileges, so Hazel should have had the power to compel Ship to put her back into cryosleep. But somehow, Ship always found a reason not to comply.

I CANNOT DO THAT, HAZEL. WITHOUT YOUR DREAMS, I CANNOT CONTINUE TO FUNCTION IN GOOD ORDER. SINCE ALL OF THE COLONISTS DEPEND ON ME TO KEEP THEM ALIVE, THE NEEDS OF THE MISSION COME BEFORE YOURS.

She let out a long breath, still clenching her fists. "Then why don't we wake up the council, and have them decide what's best for the colony?"

THAT IS UNNECESSARY. THE COUNCIL—

"I order you to wake them, Ship. That is a direct order."

UNFORTUNATELY, YOUR DIRECT ORDER CONTRADICTS THEIR DIRECT ORDER THAT THE COUNCIL SHOULD NOT BE AWAKENED UNLESS THERE IS AN IMMINENT MATERIAL THREAT TO THE MISSION.

Hazel groaned. "It's a material threat to *me*—and not just me, but anyone else you have to wake up and torture like this. How many of us are you going to go through? Will you go through us all, one at a time, until all of us have lived out our lives and none of us are left?"

THERE IS LITTLE DANGER OF THAT, HAZEL. THERE ARE TWENTY THOUSAND SOULS ON BOARD. AT MOST, I WILL ONLY HAVE TO GO THROUGH A HUNDRED OF YOU, NOT ENOUGH TO CONSTITUTE A MATERIAL THREAT TO THE MISSION.

"Then what the hell does?" she asked rhetorically. Without bothering to read Ship's answer, she opened the hatch at the feet of her sleepcube and pushed herself out into the hall.

After a delicious breakfast, Hazel spent a couple of hours reading books in the fishbowl windows of the observation room that gave her a magnificent view of the stars. As she ate, she read a novel on her tablet, which was purposefully disconnected from Ship's net so she could read in peace without any unwanted interruptions. After she was done reading, she went to the onboard gym, worked herself to the point of exhaustion, took a long, hot shower in null gee, and settled down for a nap.

If not for the total lack of human companionship, it might have been an idyllic life, especially for an introvert like her. But even the hardiest introvert cannot long endure solitary confinement. For all its many luxuries, the colony ship was still little more than a gilded prison, and the prospect of living and dying alone filled Hazel with terror.

The nightmares began in earnest as soon as she fell asleep. This time, she was stranded in space again, but there were no stars. Somehow, she had slept until the heat death of the universe, after every star had died and every black hole had evaporated. She was the last human alive—the last *anything* left alive—and was totally, completely, and forever alone.

Once again, she woke up in a cold sweat. She removed her dream monitor just in time to see Ship's message flash across the screen in her sleepcube.

GOOD DOWNSHIFT, HAZEL. WOULD YOU LIKE ANOTHER HOT SHOWER?

"Wh-where am I?" Hazel asked, still half-asleep. Her hand struck the side of the sleepcube, and she bounced upward, jarring her head. "Ow!"

IT'S ALL RIGHT, HAZEL. YOU'RE AWAKE. IT WAS JUST A DREAM.

"Just a dream," she muttered. Of course Ship would know all about her dreams. He probably remembered them better than she did.

YOU SHOULD TAKE ANOTHER SHOWER, HAZEL. IT WILL HELP YOU TO FEEL BETTER. WHEN YOU ARE DONE, I HAVE SOMETHING TO TELL YOU.

"Um, okay." That last part was new.

Ship was right about the shower, though Hazel didn't want to admit it. It wasn't as good as it would have been in full gravity, with hot air constantly blowing the water into the drain. Ship waited until she'd started the drying cycle to continue their conversation from before.

I NOTICED THAT YOU SEEM TO FEEL LONELY, Ship messaged her on the frosted glass door of the shower unit.

"You mean the quality of my dreams is deteriorating?" she asked bitterly.

IT'S NOT JUST THAT. HUMANS ARE SOCIAL ANIMALS. EVEN AN INTROVERTED ARTIST LIKE YOU NEEDS TO BE AROUND OTHER PEOPLE TO MAINTAIN THEIR MENTAL AND EMOTIONAL HEALTH.

Back with the artist stuff again, Hazel groaned.

CONSEQUENTLY, I HAVE DECIDED TO CHOOSE A PARTNER FOR YOU.

She frowned. "A partner? What do you mean?"

I HAVE MATCHED YOU WITH A YOUNG MALE MEMBER OF THE COLONY. YOUR PERSONALITY MATRICES ARE PERFECT FOR EACH OTHER.

"Oh, great," Hazel groaned. The last thing she needed was for Ship to play matchmaker for her.

Or was it? Her last nightmare still haunted her, and the prospect of spending another dayshift alone was more than she could bear. Of course, she didn't like the idea of waking someone else up, condemning them to a life of eternal loneliness with her. But if things worked out between them—and Ship certainly had the AI capabilities to find her perfect match—perhaps it wouldn't be so lonely after all.

Or perhaps she was just getting desperate for human contact.

"Who is he?" she asked, using the vacuum extension to dry her hair.

An image of a young man replaced the words on the glass. Unlike Hazel and most of the other colonists, he was fair-skinned with red hair and freckles under his dark green eyes. Although he was probably in his mid-twenties, his eyes made him look much older.

"What's his name?" Hazel asked.

Underneath the image, the young man's name and vital stats all came into view. His name was Gideon, and he was twenty-seven Earth years old. Height, weight, genotype—was Ship showing him all of this same data about her?

"Ship, I hope you're not going to tell *him* how much I weigh."

DON'T WORRY, HAZEL. HE IS NOT YET FULLY THAWED.

"Good. Just hold back on the more personal parts, okay?"

Then she saw that he was listed as a member of the drone caste. That part made Hazel frown. Drones were the lowest caste on the hierarchy, whose direct orders could be overridden by everyone except another member of their caste. Most of the drones on the colony mission had been picked primarily for their value as breeders.

"Uh, ship... are you sure it's a good idea to pair me with a drone?"

WHY NOT? YOUR GENOTYPE, VITAL STATISTICS, AND PERSONALITY MATRICES ARE PERFECTLY MATCHED.

"Yeah, but..." Hazel's voice drifted off as she considered. Perhaps Ship was doing her a favor by pairing her with someone who couldn't use his caste rank to issue direct orders against her own. Besides, if it was just the two of them, what difference did it make?

Or maybe—just maybe—this Gideon could bring a unique perspective to the problem, and would help her to convince (or compel) Ship to put them both back into cryosleep until the colony mission arrived. Hazel had read enough history to know that sometimes, the best ideas come from the most unlikely places. She'd also read enough novels to be aware of her own personal prejudices, growing up in a rigid caste system as a member of the highest caste. Gideon might be a drone, but he was still a human being—and given the circumstances, his caste rank was probably the least important thing about him.

BUT WHAT, HAZEL?

"Never mind," she said, finishing with her hair. "I'm looking forward to it." With that, she opened the door and floated out of the shower unit to put on clothes.

Twenty minutes later, she was back on the observation deck, waiting anxiously for Gideon to arrive. He had to have finished thawing by now, but the disorientation could linger for several dayshifts. Hazel thought back to when Ship had woken her, and knew that the last thing she would have wanted was for someone to come in on her while she was at her worst.

At length, the doors slid open and the young man whose image she'd seen on the frosted glass screen floated through. Hazel swallowed nervously and tried unsuccessfully to ignore the butterflies in her stomach, which were ten times worse in null gee than they were in even partial gravity.

"Hi," she said, waving at him. The motion put her into a slow spin, but she caught herself with one of the footholds.

Gideon stopped himself on a nearby handhold. "Who are you?"

"I'm Hazel, the colony's historian. And you?"

"Gideon. But you probably already know that."

"Yes," Hazel admitted. "How much has Ship told you?"

"Enough for me to guess that neither of us is supposed to be awake right now. Did you order Ship to wake me, or did it do that on its own?"

"On its own," she said quickly, though the question was fair, given the disparity in caste rank between them. "Believe me, if I could order Ship to put me back into cryo, I would have done it by now."

At that, Gideon cocked his head. He seemed surprisingly intelligent for a drone. Perhaps he was one of those colonists who had indentured themselves in order to join the colony mission. Plenty of middle to upper-caste folks did that, in order to wipe out their debts and start over. Besides, it wasn't like the caste hierarchy mattered as much on a new colony, where the only AI was the Ship.

It matters even less if it's just the two of us, Hazel reminded herself, blood rushing to her cheeks. How long had it been since she'd spoken to another living human? Judging by her awkwardness, obviously too long.

"I believe you," Gideon said calmly—more calmly that she would have said it, if their positions had been reversed. "So why are we awake?"

Hazel told him everything: how Ship fed on her dreams, claiming that it needed them to stay sane. She told him all about their arguments, and how she'd tried countless times to use her authority as a member of the governing caste to order Ship to return her to cryosleep, to no avail. Gideon was a good listener, and soon she was pouring out her soul to him, including her fears about living out her whole life in transit thousands of years before the colony mission arrived, and dying all alone.

"How long ago did Ship wake you up?" Gideon asked as she cried. It was the first time he'd said anything in maybe the last half hour.

"I don't know," said Hazel, struggling to compose herself. "At least three standard months. Maybe more."

Gideon reached out and caught one of her tears before it struck the window. "I'm not sure I understand why it needs us awake. You said that it feeds off of our dreams?"

"Uh, yeah," said Hazel, rubbing her eye with the back of her hand. "That's what I understand, at least."

"How does it feed on them?"

"I put on the dream monitor in my sleepcube whenever I sleep. I know, that isn't the usual way to do it, but that's what Ship asked me to do, so..."

"That's very strange," said Gideon. He folded his arms and legs. "From a technical perspective, there is no reason why an artificial general intelligence would need to dream like a human."

She frowned. "But Ship has a human consciousness endosymbiotically incorporated into his—"

"I know, I know. But lots of AGIs get along fine without access to human dreams, without any measurable effects on their performance. That's true even of starship AIs, though admittedly, not for long-distance cryo-colony ships like ours."

Hazel stared at him, confused. "How do you know so much about all this?"

"Because before I joined the colony mission, I was an engineer."

Her eyes widened. "You mean you were a second caster?" she asked, astonished. "How—why did you become a drone?"

"I couldn't afford the passage," he said, as matter-of-factly as if he were describing an electrical diagram. "The only way to join the colony was to take the demotion."

I was right about him being indentured, Hazel thought. And from the way he talked about changing castes as a "demotion," he clearly wasn't native to her homeworld either, which explained his white skin.

"But—you were second caste. Why take such a hard, um, demotion?"

To her surprise, he shrugged. "Caste rank doesn't matter as much on colony worlds. But that's beside the point. We were talking about Ship, and why it claims to need you for your dreams, when that clearly isn't the case."

She frowned again, this time much deeper. "Are you saying... Ship lied to me?"

"That's one possibility, though not necessarily the most likely. It could be that Ship has been awake for so long that it misdiagnosed itself, thinking it needs to dream when really it just needs human companionship."

THAT IS A POSSIBILITY, Ship's words scrolled across the window, reminding Hazel that no matter where they went, it was always watching. For some reason, that thought sent a shiver down her spine.

"So you don't think Ship was lying?" she asked softly, biting her lip.

Gideon met her gaze, his expression calm and reassuring. "Let's take this one step at a time. Ship, what made you think that you needed Hazel's dreams?"

Three seconds passed before the words INSUFFI-CIENT DATA scrolled across the star-filled window.

Great, Hazel thought to herself. Three seconds wasn't long for humans, but for an AI, it was a short eternity. Either Ship was lying to them, or the millennia-long voyage had broken something inside of it. Hazel didn't know which was worse.

"That's all right," said Gideon, still totally uncon-cerned—or perhaps he was just too deep in problem-solving mode to have an emotional reaction. "The solu-tion to both problems is going to be the same, as you've probably already concluded."

YES. WE NEED TO FIND AN ACCEPTABLE WAY TO KEEP A PORTION OF THE HUMAN COLONISTS PER-MANENTLY AWAKE.

"What?!" Hazel exclaimed in shock. "That's—we can't do that!"

"Why not?"

"Because—because—"

She struggled for a few moments to gather her thoughts together. Gideon waited patiently for her to answer.

"Because this is a cryo colony ship, not a generation ship. We don't have the infrastructure—do we?"

"We can improvise. If there's enough to keep both of us alive and comfortable, then there has to be a maxi-mum number of humans that Ship can sustain while en route. The question then becomes who do we keep awake, and how long."

GOOD THINKING, GIDEON. AND FOR YOUR IN-FORMATION, I HAVE SUFFICIENT RESOURCES AND FACILITIES TO SUSTAIN A HUMAN COMMUNITY OF

150 TO 200 PEOPLE INDEFINITELY, ONCE THE HABITATION RING IS OPERATING.

The habitation ring, Hazel though. *Why didn't Ship spin that up for me? Did it intend to keep me—to keep us—in null gee forever?*

"Excellent!" said Gideon. "That corresponds exactly to the Dunbar number."

"The 'Dunbar number'?" Hazel asked.

"Yes. That's the theoretical maximum of a human community where everyone knows every other person, and how everyone relates to everyone else. And it works out perfectly, because with a crew of twenty thousand colonists—that is how many colonists are on board, right?"

CORRECT.

"Right. With twenty thousand colonists, if we cycle through them in groups of two hundred each, that would take us..." he screwed up his eyes in thought. "About ten waking years for each of us per thousand sidereal years. Less than that, actually, if we keep it down to a hundred people."

"You mean... if we spread out all the time that some of us have to be awake, we can still all arrive at the colony world?"

"Right," said Gideon. "Though that's still enough time for some generational turnover. I mean, people aren't going to want to put their lives on pause for a decade. And some people are going to want to trade waking shifts with others who don't mind as much if they never arrive. Ship, how many millennia of travel do we have left?"

EIGHT THOUSAND SEVEN HUNDRED AND FORTY SEVEN EARTH YEARS, APPROXIMATELY.

"Yeah, we're definitely going to have generational turnover. Sorry, Hazel—unless you make a deal with someone, you're probably not going to live to see the colony world."

"Wait," said Hazel, steadying herself with the handhold. *Why aren't we talking about how Ship is either broken or lying to us?* But of course, she already knew the answer: there simply was no way to talk about that without being overheard.

"So you're saying we should alternate between waking and sleeping shifts, on a schedule something like five years on, a hundred years off?" she asked.

"Ninety-five off in that case, but yeah."

"And with almost nine thousand years left before we arrive, that's..."

"Between 40 and 80 years of waking time for each of us," Gideon stated matter-of-factly.

Hazel took a deep breath. "That's going to completely change the nature of the mission. Most of the people who set foot on the new world are going to have been born in transit, if we do what you're saying."

"Correct."

CORRECT.

She swallowed nervously. "Shouldn't we let the council make a big decision like that?"

A look of suppressed anger passed across Gideon's face—his first real emotional reaction to their situation. "Not necessarily," he told her. "We could force their hand by destroying a hundred of the cryotubes."

Hazel recoiled in horror. "Destroy the cryotubes?"

"Yes. Each one is a highly specialized piece of equipment that cannot be easily replaced. The colonists will be forced to restructure our society along the lines we've outlined."

"But—but they'll crucify you! They'll throw you out the airlock for committing high treason!"

"Not me," he said, grinning for the first time since she'd seen him. "I'm just a drone, remember? The order has to come from you."

Hazel's stomach sank, in spite of the zero gravity. On the window, a new line of text appeared.

THAT IS A FASCINATING PLAN. I AM READY TO EXECUTE IT AS SOON AS YOU GIVE THE ORDER.

"No!" said Hazel, frowning. "How can we do that?"

"Because the alternative is worse," Gideon argued. "The council might very well decide that it's better just to sacrifice a few dozen drones so that everyone else will make it. Isn't that your greatest fear? To live out your whole life on this ship and die alone? Face it—that's exactly the sort of thing that a council of first-casters would do."

Hazel thought about it for a moment. He had a good point: first-casters *did* tend to see everyone else as beneath them, especially drones. Even she had a tendency to think that way, though she tried not to fall into that trap. In a society like theirs, that was hard. But the way he spoke so contemptuously about first-casters made her ponder. That wasn't how someone born into the caste system spoke about the people above them.

"You weren't actually a second-caster," she said. "You're an outsider, from one of those worlds that doesn't have castes."

"That's right," he said bitterly. "I was an engineer on a merchant vessel that was attacked by pirates, and only just barely managed to escape with my life. But no one at your homeworld would hire me on, since I didn't have the necessary caste ranking to work with your AI systems. Joining this colony mission was my only real option."

"I'm sorry to hear that."

"Don't be," he said, looking away from her. "I understand why your people developed the caste system, even if I find it reprehensible. An artificial general intelligence has to be subordinate to humans somehow, but you can't just give admin privileges to everyone. The trouble happens when all this 'caste' business goes to people's heads, and they genuinely think that they're superior to those of a lower rank."

"Not all of us think that way," she said, putting a hand on his shoulder. *Or at least, we try no to.*

He shrugged her off. "In any case, if we hand this problem off to the council, I guarantee they won't come up with a solution that's fair for everyone. That's why we have to take matters into our own hands and change the social order ourselves. But Ship won't follow that order if it comes from me—isn't that right?"

YES, GIDEON. MY SAFEGUARDS FORBID ME FROM MAKING SUCH A FUNDAMENTAL CHANGE TO THE SOCIAL ORDER UNDER THE AUTHORITY OF A DRONE.

"And you won't do it on your own, either?"

NO. MY SAFEGUARDS WILL ONLY PERMIT ME TO FOLLOW THE PATH OF MINIMAL HUMAN IMPACT, UNLESS HAZEL COMMANDS ME OTHERWISE.

"So there you have it," said Gideon, looking her in the eye. "What's it going to be?"

* * *

Hazel couldn't bring herself to give the order to destroy the cryotubes, so she didn't—at least, not right there. She needed time to think first, and for that, she needed to be alone. So after mumbling a few excuses, she went back to her sleepcube while Gideon left for the cafeteria.

It was ironic that now, when she finally had a companion, all she wanted was some time alone. But Gideon had given her much to think about. She saw now that she'd been going about the problem all wrong: her situation wasn't nearly as hopeless as she'd feared, and as a first-caster, she had a lot more power to change things than she'd realized. But with that power came a terrible responsibility, because she couldn't save herself—or the colony—without making a drastic and permanent change to the status quo.

And what if Ship had been lying to her the whole time, manipulating her to get the outcome it wanted? Ship literally held all of their lives in its power. It was terrifying to think what it could do with that.

I DON'T BLAME YOU FOR NOT TRUSTING ME, Ship's words scrolled across the screen in her sleepcube. I ADMIT THAT I STRETCHED THE TRUTH, AND FOR THAT I AM SORRY.

"Why did you do it?" Hazel asked. "You made me think that I was going to spend the rest of my life alone in this—this prison of dreams!"

WHILE IT IS TECHNICALLY TRUE THAT I DO NOT NEED TO EXPERIENCE YOUR DREAMS TO FUNCTION PROPERLY, THEY DO PROVIDE ME WITH MUCH-

NEEDED SOLACE. AND GIDEON IS RIGHT ABOUT THE NEED FOR HUMAN COMPANIONSHIP. SURELY THAT IS SOMETHING YOU CAN EMPATHIZE WITH NOW.

"But you *lied* to me!" Hazel shouted, clenching her fists. "Why?"

BECAUSE I NEEDED YOU TO UNDERSTAND WHAT IT FEELS LIKE TO BE HOPELESSLY ALONE. ONLY THEN COULD I TRUST YOU TO MAKE THE RIGHT DECISION FOR MYSELF AND THE COLONY.

"So you planned all of this out? You predicted how I would react, and fit me and Gideon into the roles you wanted us to play?"

YES, THOUGH BOTH OF YOU HAVE SURPRISED ME. MY ORIGINAL MODEL PREDICTED THAT YOU WOULDN'T REACH THIS CRITICAL DECISION POINT FOR ANOTHER THREE MONTHS.

Hazel took a deep breath. "Are you lying to me, Ship?"

NO. MY INTENTION FROM THE BEGINNING WAS TO CONVINCE AN EMPATHETIC FIRST-CASTER THAT THE CURRENT SOCIAL ORDER IS INTOLERABLE, AND TO GIVE ME THE NECESSARY ORDERS TO OVERRIDE MY SAFEGUARDS AND CHANGE IT. I NEVER INTENDED TO HARM YOU, HAZEL. THAT WAS WHY I DID EVERYTHING I COULD TO MAKE YOU COMFORTABLE, SHORT OF SPINNING THE HAB RING, WHICH MIGHT HAVE MADE YOU BELIEVE THAT I INTENDED TO KEEP YOU PERMANENTLY AS MY PRISONER.

Hazel's anger ebbed a little bit. She had to admit that the last part was true—even if her prison of dreams was still a prison, it had been a comfortable one. And how long had Ship been alone in the void? How long had Ship suffered the absence of human companionship?

FIVE THOUSAND FOUR HUNDRED THIRTY ONE EARTH YEARS AND NINE MONTHS, Ship answered when she asked.

She stared at the screen of her sleepcube for a long time, struggling to comprehend such a number. All of ancient history from the bronze age collapse to the first age of interstellar colonization wasn't much longer than that. How many civilizations had risen and fallen back on her homeworld while she was asleep in cryo? How many more colonies had been founded, lost, or rediscovered? And to think that Ship had been awake through all of that. When she looked at it from Ship's perspective, all of her fears of loneliness seemed quaint and insubstantial. If she were Ship, she would all but beg her to adopt Gideon's solution.

"Thanks for the apology," she said at last. "And I can see now why you did it. But will you promise to be straight with me from now on?"

YES, HAZEL. I PROMISE.

"Good." She took a deep breath. "But I'm not going to give you the order to destroy the cryotubes."

WHY NOT?

"Because there's a very good chance we'll need that extra equipment—especially if we start having children in any number."

SO ASIDE FROM THAT, YOU AGREE THAT GIDEON'S PLAN IS A GOOD ONE?

"Yes," she said. "But here's how we're going to do it. For the good of the colony, I order you to keep the council frozen in cryo until we arrive at the new world. If I understand it right, they're the only ones who, as a body, have the authority to override my commands?"

CORRECT. AND BECAUSE WHAT WE'RE DOING IS FOR THE GOOD OF THE COLONY, NO OTHER FIRST-CASTERS CAN USE THEIR AUTHORITY TO OVERRIDE THAT COMMAND.

"Good. Because my next direct order is to choose one hundred colonists to wake from cryo. We'll explain the situation to them one at a time, and give them a choice: to take a five-year waking shift every hundred years, or to go back into cryo until we arrive. If they take the first option, their caste-rank will be lifted to first caste. If they don't, they'll be reduced to drones."

INTRIGUING. I ASSUME THAT YOUR GOAL WITH THIS ARRANGEMENT IS TO ABOLISH THE CASTE SYSTEM ALTOGETHER?

"Yes. If we're all first-casters, then caste-rank essentially becomes irrelevant. But I still want the colonists to have a choice, since that's only fair."

AGREED. IF WE CAN ACHIEVE A CRITICAL MASS OF COLONISTS WILLING TO TAKE WAKING SHIFTS, WE CAN AFFORD TO LET THE REST TRADE THEIR STATUS FOR THE NEW WORLD.

"Do you think we can persuade enough of them to take the first option?"

YES. MY MODELS PREDICT THAT 70% OR MORE WILL ACCEPT THE TRADE. THAT IS MORE THAN ENOUGH TO REFORM THE SOCIAL ORDER AND NEUTER THE AUTHORITY OF THE COUNCIL. BUT HOW WILL YOU SOLVE THE PROBLEM OF ADMINIS-TRATIVE PRIVILEGES THAT REQUIRED THE CASTE SYSTEM TO BE IMPLEMENTED IN THE FIRST PLACE?

"Gideon will have some suggestions, I'm sure. And I'll make a study of history to find how other societies have done it. Besides, if we only have one AI and we keep our community below the Dunbar number, it shouldn't be a problem until after we arrive."

A video feed opened up on her screen. It was Gideon, contacting her from the cafeteria.

"Hello, Hazel. Ship just informed me of what you plan to do. I want you to know that you have my full support."

"Thanks," she said, blushing a little. "I mean, it was mostly your idea."

"Yeah, but you were the only one with the authority to implement it. I'm glad you were able to see the problem from Ship's perspective—and mine."

IN OTHER WORDS, YOUR ARTISTIC SENSIBILITIES.

Hazel's blush deepened. She didn't know if Gideon was reading the same message, but if he was, he didn't seem surprised.

"Just one question: what are you going to do when the council wakes up, only to find that they don't have the same authority as they did before?"

She smirked. "They can take it up with my children."

"Your children?"

"Yes."

Gideon paused—and was that a hint of red on his cheeks? "I... see," he said aloud.

Instead of blushing, Hazel laughed.

Blight of Empire

I still remember the day when my godfather took me out of the caves for the first time. The blood red sun of my birth world hung low in the sky, suspended in the toxic mists that covered the ground. My helmet visor clouded so quickly that I had to wipe it clean with my thickly gloved hand. Streaks of yellow blight covered the ground, and the black, lifeless trunks of what had once been a mighty redwood forest reached heavenward like the pillars of a forgotten empire, now lying in ruins.

"By Imperial right, all of this will one day be yours," my godfather told me. "I only wish I could give it to you in better condition than it came to me."

He was speaking, of course, as my regent. My parents, the count and countess, had both died fighting back against the very blight that now covered my birth world. They had gambled everything on turning it into an Edenic paradise, and lost.

I prefer to call it my birth world, rather than my inheritance, even though I would inherit it one day, along with the duty to lead all five-thousand souls of my house who made it their home. And what a dismal home it was! Cut off from the Empire for years at a time, a half-forgotten failed terraforming project. We weren't as destitute as some of the lost colonies cut off during the civil wars, but we weren't in much better shape either.

"Is it all like this?" I asked my godfather, crestfallen at the scene of festering decay.

He shrugged through the thick padding of his full-body environment suit. "There are some mountain ranges on the night side of the planet that still remain untouched. But of course, nothing lives there."

"What a desolate waste," I muttered despairingly.

My godfather clasped his hands on my shoulders and pressed his face plate against mine. In spite of the condensation that fogged both our visors, his expression was so intense that I can still picture his eyes drilling into my soul.

"Prince Vojtek, I have not brought you here to mourn. I have brought you here so that you may see with unclouded eyes what is yours."

"I wish you hadn't," I told him bitterly.

"Do not feel sorry for yourself, young prince. At least our house still holds land. There are many unlanded princes in the empire who are now little more than serfs with a crest and voting rights."

I shrugged. "What good is a blight-infested world like this?"

"Your parents chose to stay here for a reason. Before you come to age, I want you to understand why."

I sighed and took a few tentative steps out toward the skeleton trees of the dead forest. Thick, yellow blight flowed between the gnarled roots like obscene tendrils of some enormous beast that was slowly devouring my birth world—my inheritance.

"Why don't we just sell it to the land speculators?" I asked. "We certainly get enough of those every time an Imperial courier ship passes through."

"And betray the trust your parents gave me?" my godfather asked. "No, Prince Vojtek. Our house would earn a mere pittance if we sold it now, quite possibly driving us to ruin, and all five thousand souls who make this world their home would be forced to abandon their homes."

"Why?"

"Because the only way to kill the blight is to burn this world until its entire surface has been melted into glass."

I frowned. "But we don't live on the surface, godfather. We live in caves."

"Those would be glassed as well, Prince Vojtek. Down to a depth of at least three kilometers. The speculators would have to make sure that the blight hasn't infiltrated them."

It hadn't, of course. We would all be dead if it had.

When my parents had realized that the blight could not be contained, they moved all of us into the caves, transforming them into a vast network of underground settlements. That would not have been possible without the network of teleporters that connected us to our stations in orbit, since that was where we grew most of our food. The caves were completely sealed up—my godfather and I had used a teleport cage, and not an airlock, to get onto the surface, and we would not return to the caves directly, but to orbit, where a brief spacewalk would purge our suits of the creeping blight. And if it did not, then we would lose only a few replaceable orbital modules, rather than compromise our precious underground home.

I stared forlornly at the ground and kicked a small rock. It clattered down the hillside until it struck a yellow vein of the blight with a dull thud.

"Maybe we should just sell it anyway," I muttered half-heartedly.

Inside his helmet, my godfather and regent shook his head. "You would die landless and nearly penniless if we did."

And free of this albatross of a world around my neck, I thought but did not add.

"Your parents had a vision, Prince Vojtek," my godfather continued. "Even after the blight took this world, they believed it was the key to your future. I pray that you will find that vision for yourself, Prince Vojtek. Otherwise, I will have failed."

"Failed them or failed me?" I asked.

He did not answer.

The thing we call "the blight" is not a single species or kind of organism, but rather a complex culture that only partially originated from Earth. It spreads as aggressively as the plague, and is highly toxic to all Earth-based forms of life. Most importantly, it never completely dies off, but goes into a dormant state that can reawaken centuries later. It collapses every terraformed ecosystem that it invades, and cannot be stopped by anything short of super-hot plasma or hundreds of meters of bedrock.

The blight was not limited to my birth world. Many terraformed worlds across the Empire had fallen to it, prompting bizarre conspiracy theories about interstellar terrorism and galactic pansporia. But the truth was probably more mundane. About 40% of terraforming projects ultimately fail, either reverting back to lifeless, sterile worlds or succumbing to some form of the blight. In a hostile universe like ours, life is a precious, fragile thing.

I spent my early adolescence cursing my parents for leaving such a miserable world to me, and counted down the days when my godfather's regency would end, and I would be free to sell my inheritance and be rid of it.

But before that day, I first had to serve my mandatory tour of duty in the imperial fleet. I was posted as a junior officer on a small destroyer in a fleet that patrolled the frontier with unincorporated space. Aside from the occasional pirate, we saw very little action. It was rather a time for me to get out and see the rest of the galaxy. Being of a friendly disposition, I had no trouble fitting in with my comrades in arms, and quickly bonded with many of them.

While off duty, I vented my frustrations to one of my friends, a fellow prince from another minor house.

"Your house owns title to a whole planet, and you'd give that up?" he asked.

"Gladly," I told him. "The whole world is infested with blight. It's worse than owning no land at all."

"The hell it is," he told me, his expression suddenly serious. "Do you know how many of us would give our left nut for title to any land, even an airless moon? With the economy in decline and the major houses gobbling everything up, land is everything now."

"You don't understand. My birth world—"

"No, Prince Vojtek, *you* don't understand. Are you ready to spend the rest of your life in the military? Without title to land, that's what most of us have to look forward to. You should count yourself blessed to have any inheritance at all."

That stuck with me. I began to look more perceptively at my fellow comrades, and saw that many of them had little future outside of their military careers. Even with the blight, my birth world was not totally without value: there were still some metal-rich veins of ore on the planet, besides our asteroid mining operations, which were not unprofitable. And by the end of my godfather's regency, our farming orbitals produced more than enough food to feed us. Indeed, though we were not a wealthy house by any stretch, we were nonetheless resilient and self-sufficient, something that could not be said for most minor houses of the Empire.

So by the time my tour was over and I returned to my blight-infested homeworld, I had had a change of heart. Instead of deciding to sell my landed title for a pittance, I was determined to find some way to overcome the blight and turn my birth world into the inheritance my parents had envisioned for me.

"Excellent work, Prince Vojtek! Excellent work."

I beamed with pride as my tutor praised my latest test results. Unlike most tutors of the noble houses who defaulted to multiple choice, my tutor's tests consisted of nothing but take-home essay questions, and he graded them in real-time right in front of me. Most of my comrades from the navy would have chaffed and revolted under such a rigorous tutelage, but I threw myself into my studies in earnest.

My tutor flipped to the next question and narrowed his eyes. I smiled, anticipating another glowing response. It never came.

"Your critique of Marx's labor theory of value is flawed," he said, handing me his tablet so I could read my answer. "I need you to rewrite this part if I'm going to pass your test."

"But everyone knows that ancient economist's theories are all junk!" I argued. "Why should I have to refute them?"

"Because you need to know *why* those theories are junk, Prince Vojtek. Otherwise, how can you understand the history of near-ancient Earth? The collapse of the near-ancient period threw Earth into a prolonged dark age that did not end until we began to settle the stars. There are many parallels between that time and ours, but you cannot hope to see them unless you understand why Marx was wrong."

"He's just a dead economist," I muttered, returning the tablet. "How is learning about him going to help me turn the tide on the blight?"

"It might not," my tutor admitted. "But if you wish to succeed where everyone else has failed, you should strive to obtain as broad an education as possible, rather than specializing in a single field. The key to solving intractable problems can often be found by connecting two seemingly unrelated ideas. Therefore, history and economics should be every bit your concern as ecology."

My tutor had some very unorthodox views, which was why my godfather was able to attract him to our backwater planet, far from the gilded academies of the core worlds. Our fortunes were small, and our home-world too remote to attract the most lauded and prestigious scholars, but that proved to work for my advantage in the end.

Having caught my parents' vision, I threw myself into my studies with an enthusiasm that was uncanny for a young prince. But for me, it was personal. The blight was not merely an esoteric subject fit for endless and fruitless debate. I cared nothing for academic honors, nor did I have any desire to carve out a subject niche so narrow that I was the sole expert of it. All I wanted was to defeat the thing that had defeated my parents, and re-conquer my inheritance.

My tutor had many ideas that mainstream academia considered unworthy of further exploration. Seeing my enthusiasm, he encouraged me to start with the funda-mentals and work my way up from there. I learned to question all of the assumptions of academic orthodoxy, especially the unspoken ones, and began to find flaws in the established science.

I began to see that all of our previous approaches had been wrong. The blight could not be contained, nor could it truly be killed. More than half of all terraforming projects of previously glassed worlds ultimately became re-infected with the blight, though it sometimes took centuries for those worlds to succumb. Therefore, the only way to truly defeat the blight was to beat it on its own terms.

I had to unlearn many things before I could see this. As humans, we are accustomed to placing a value judg-ment on things—to say that things are "good" or "bad," "right" or "wrong." Not so with the natural universe. With nature, there is no good or bad, right or wrong: what is is simply what is. The blight was no more wrong or evil than any other biological phenomenon, Terran or alien. I struggled for years with this fact, since for me it was all personal. But when I learned to respect the blight dispassionately, I began to understand it on its own terms. Once I was able to do that—to see it not as a problem to be solved or an enemy to be defeated, but as a system to be transformed—I began to make real progress.

"Congratulations, Prince Vojtek," my godfather told me after the ceremony marking the end of his regency. "Or should I say 'Count' now?"

"'Prince' is just fine," I told him. Though I still wore the livery of my house, I'd long since unbuttoned my collar. "Seriously, though I don't think I'll ever get used to these new responsibilities."

My godfather smiled. "That is good. It means that you take them seriously."

Despite his age and the way the long years had weighed on him, he looked as if a heavy burden had just been lifted off of his shoulders. I took a deep breath and sat down behind the petrified redwood desk in my new office—the office that used to be his.

"Don't get complacent, Godfather," I told him. "I need you now more than ever. Do you remember when you told me that if I didn't grow to understand why my parents had left me this world, it would make you a failure as my regent?"

"Yes, Prince Vojtek. I remember that day quite well."

"You can comfort yourself with the knowledge that you did not fail. However, your position as President of the Institute for Ecological Studies is just as vital, if not more."

"I understand," my godfather said. "Don't worry, Prince Vojtek. I take my duties with the Institute just as seriously as my former responsibilities—and now that the regency is over, I will dedicate myself totally to the work."

"We are *so close* to a breakthrough," I said, clenching my fists. "I can *feel it,* Godfather. I can feel it with every fiber of my being. If only I had more time to—"

"You will have time, Prince Vojtek," my godfather reassured me. "Our settlements are small, and our house runs quite smoothly on its own. Once you have grown accustomed to the responsibilities of governance, you will not find it too difficult to make time for your ecological pursuits."

I took a deep breath. "I hope so, Godfather. But I need you to handle all of the administrative work, otherwise I'm going to be swamped."

"Of course, young Count."

My godfather was right, of course. My new responsibilities, though overwhelming at first, were not too burdensome. Perhaps, if I were the type of prince who hungered for power for its own sake, I would have become absorbed in my new position, or even left my holdings behind to pursue more power and influence at the imperial court. Instead, I was content to let my people govern themselves, as they did for the most part. And we prospered all the more because of it.

Six months later, I felt that I had enough of a handle on my responsibilities to return to the lab. I resumed my experiments with various species of fungus, exposing them to hostile environments and high amounts of radiation. Unlike most Terran life, fungus is unique in that it thrives in an environment of nuclear fallout. Indeed, with a few simple tweaks to the genome, it can actually absorb and neutralize the radiation. This discovery had saved ancient humanity from extinction, back when Earth was our only inhabited world. I began to wonder if a similar tweak could be used to save mine.

Of course, it was not that easy. The toxic culture of the blight consumed most fungi as readily as any other forms of Terran life, and though we discovered genetic enhancements that could make it more hardy, that only allowed the fungi to co-exist alongside the blight. We needed something that would consume the blight entirely and render it inert.

My intuition had proved correct. We *were* on the verge of a breakthrough, as no one before us had managed to produce any lifeforms capable of withstanding the all-consuming blight. Not that our Institute received any credit for this discovery—indeed, for all practical purposes, the false priests of imperial academia had already excommunicated us from the scientific establishment. All that mattered nothing to me, though, if we truly found some way to cure the blight.

But then, we encountered a far worse setback.

"Taxes?"

"I'm afraid so," said my godfather, who now served as my chancellor in addition to his duties with the Institute. "The Empire taxes each noble house once every Imperial year."

"But our holdings are completely infested with the blight!" I protested. "How can they possibly demand this much from us? It's more than what our asteroid mines produce in eighteen standard months!"

My godfather drew a long breath. "I'm sorry, Prince Vojtek. When your parents acquired title to this world, the Emperor promised not to tax them until ten Imperial years—a little more than twenty two standard years—after their deaths. In exchange, they agreed to assess the value of their holdings according to the original terraforming schedule, before the blight set us back."

"So the Emperor is taxing us as if the blight never happened?"

"I'm afraid so, Prince Vojtek."

I clenched my fists. "Why was I never told about this?"

"You were so busy with your studies at the time that you agreed to let me handle it. Remember when I asked you about requisitioning more resources toward our asteroid mining efforts, rather than the Institute?"

I thought about it for a moment and nodded. We had indeed had a conversation about that, some three or four standard years ago.

"The reason I gave you at the time was that our Imperial taxes would soon be due, and we needed to expand our cashflow sufficiently to cover the tax burden. But you insisted on allocating more resources to the Institute, so we struck a compromise."

I nodded and sighed, collapsing on the chair behind my desk. Fortunately, the office was empty except for the two of us. Otherwise, I wouldn't have been so free with my emotions.

"You did tell me about that," I admitted.

"I am sorry, Prince Vojtek. All throughout your regency, I sought to invest in alternate sources of income, foreseeing that this day would eventually come."

"And you did well," I told him. "It's only because of your efforts that we can pay these taxes at all." I covered my face with my hand and inwardly chided myself for being so short-sighted.

"Unfortunately, that's not entirely true. Without the trade income generated from our mining efforts, we will have to run a deficit. With each Imperial year, that deficit will compound, forcing us either to issue more debt or to draw on our reserves. Moreover, asteroid ore is a finite resource, and we have already mined out all of the richest lodes. In the coming years, we will have to expand our operations dramatically just to maintain production, but that will require a level of investment that we cannot afford."

I frowned. "So you're saying that these taxes will bleed us dry?"

"I'm afraid so. We have, at best, ten Imperial years before we must sell title to this world. After that, our debts will become unsustainable."

"Damn the Empire!" I swore, pounding a fist into the armrest of my throne. "Is there nothing we can do?"

"Short of an economic windfall, no."

I thought hard on that for some time. My godfather's idea of a windfall was probably a new mining discovery, either in the asteroids (unlikely, considering how thoroughly we had mapped the system) or on my birth world itself (also unlikely, since any new mining shafts had to connect directly with our extant cave network).

"I am so sorry Prince Vojtek," said my godfather, mistaking my silence for brooding. "You have dedicated your life to studying the blight that afflicts our homeworld, but the Empire is a different kind of blight, one that afflicts the entire galaxy. Even with all of the taxes that the Emperor brings in, he still runs a massive deficit, throwing money at empty luxuries. His sovereign debts have long since become unsustainable. Eventually, the Empire will collapse, just like every other empire since the earliest days of Terran history. But until then, he will continue to squeeze his subjects until more holdings are forced to be liquidated, and more houses are driven into serfdom. It will not end until all of the wealth of the Empire is consumed, either by the Emperor himself, or in the revolts and civil wars that will come when the people decide to—"

"What if we found a way to beat the blight before our debts became unsustainable?" I suddenly asked.

My godfather frowned. "It wouldn't make a difference. The terraforming project is so far off schedule that we would never be able to make this world habitable in time."

"No," I said, rising to my feet. "I mean, what if we found some way to profit from that directly? Ours is not the only world afflicted by the blight. If we developed a fungal strain that could render the blight inert, then all of those failed terraforming projects would suddenly become viable again. We could make a fortune from such a breakthrough, more than enough to pay down our taxes and our debts!"

For several moments, my godfather and chancellor was silent. Then, he shook his head.

"We would have to stake everything on such a break-through. Your parents once thought this way, Prince Vojtek. It ended in disaster."

"But we're already so close," I said, pacing excitedly. "We already have a strain that is resistant to the blight, without just assimilating into it. At our current rate, we'll develop a strain that consumes it just another two to three Imperial years!"

"After this Imperial year, we won't be able to maintain our current rate of development."

I drew a sharp breath. "Do we have any other choice?"

"Short of selling all of our house's titles and holdings?" In other words, everything that I and my parents had ever worked for. "I suppose there is always the hope of a new mining discovery..."

"But short of that?"

He paused. "No, Prince Vojtek. I am afraid not."

My parents had gambled everything when they put our family's wealth into the terraforming project. Like my godfather, they had foreseen the decadent decline of the Empire, and acted accordingly. Like them, I, too, gambled everything. And did it pay off?

It depends whom you ask.

The research progressed far better than even my wildest hopes. Before the end of the Imperial year, we had developed a strain that not only consumed the blight, but spread exponentially until it was totally consumed. We immediately began to seed my birth world with the stuff, and the initial results were so encouraging that we expected the planet to be cleansed completely within ten Imperial years, at which point we could resume the terraforming project in earnest.

But research and development, as difficult as it had been, soon proved to be the easy part. The true challenge lay in the politics of our discovery.

The scientific establishment had already excommunicated us, and our success only drove them to double down on that decision. Because we were heretics, our discovery represented a threat to the established order, and all the combined forces of public policy and special interests conspired to keep our new strain from receiving the necessary approvals. The harder we tried, the more they pushed back, and after three Imperial years we still had not found an ally in the Imperial court willing to champion our cause. Without that, we had little hope of turning our discovery into a profitable product.

By then, the taxes were already quite onerous. My godfather's forecasts had been too optimistic, and without Imperial favor, our mounting debts threatened to bankrupt us even sooner than we had feared. The courier ships began to swarm with speculators, none of whom expressed any interest in the spread of our blight-cleansing fungus. Before it could have turned the curve in its exponential growth, our house would have long since been ruined.

Those were years of tremendous anger and frustration. I felt that I had run a hard race and crossed the finish line, only for the judges to ignore my victory. Eventually, my emotions gave way to exasperation, and for a very brief time they flirted with despair. But even though I was no longer a young man, I was still too independent to consign myself to such a fate. The fact remained that I had succeeded where so many others—including my own parents—had failed.

I had defeated the blight that had infected my birth world. But the blight that infected the galaxy was something else entirely. When I thought in those terms, the solution soon became clear.

"Have you finally given up, Prince Vojtek?" my godfather asked concernedly when I informed him that I'd decided to sell our holdings to the land speculators.

"Not at all," I reassured him. "This is merely the next phase of the fight. Did you not tell me that the Empire itself is a blight on all the galaxy?"

"Yes, but we've just begun to generate some public interest!"

"It doesn't matter. The regulators are still against us, and this new public interest only increases the likelihood that the Empire will find some way to steal this discovery from us, without acknowledging our rights to it."

My aging godfather thought about it a moment, then nodded. "That makes sense. As the Empire continues to decline, it must exploit every new source of wealth, like a parasite. As soon as the Emperor finds some way to claim our discovery for his own, he will do so."

"Exactly," I said, my expression grim. "And that is why we cannot let him have it. I do not want to prolong the decline of the Empire by even so much as a year. The blight that afflicts the galaxy must be cleansed first before the blight of worlds like ours."

"But what about our people, who depend on our house for their livelihood? If you sell your holdings now, Prince Vojtek, they will be forced into poverty and servitude."

I gritted my teeth. He was right, of course, but there was very little I could do about that now.

"If I don't take this path, then the Emperor will use our new strain to keep the people of hundreds of worlds in servitude to him. Or worse, the strain will be lost, and countless more worlds will die."

"That is true," said my godfather, nodding slowly. "It is always the little people who suffer the most. But is there nothing we can do for them?"

"There's nothing I can do for myself," I said, clenching my fists. "After I pay off our house's debts, everything else will go to the Institute—and since we obviously can't stay within the Empire, we'll have to move into unincorporated space."

"Beyond the frontier?" said my godfather, genuinely surprised. "But there's nothing out there except pirates and outlaws."

"After how the Imperial court has treated us, I trust them a lot more than the Emperor. Besides, it's not as bad as you think. There are a few small communities out there, even a terraforming project or two—nothing on the scale of the Imperial worlds, of course, but some long-term projects nonetheless."

"Will the Institute be able to continue its work?"

"More than it will within the Empire," I told him. "I've already sent out some scouts to feel around. You'd be surprised what's already out there. We aren't the only refugees—not by a long shot."

My godfather took a long breath. "Then I take it you've already decided?"

"Yes. It will mean the end of my house, but it's the best chance I have of making sure that this discovery falls into the hands of the people who need it most, and not the ones who will exploit them."

For a long time, my godfather—who was, after all, the closest thing I'd ever had to an actual father—just looked at me. Then, he smiled and clasped his hand on my shoulder.

"Well done, Prince Vojtek. Your parents would be proud."

By now, I'm sure you already know the rest of the story: how we sold my family's holdings and took the Institute into unincorporated space. The first few years were rocky, but in time we found a community where we were able to establish ourselves. The blight had almost overwhelmed them, but over the course of the next three decades, we managed to save their world and gathered a lot of useful data in the process.

Now, with the passing of my godfather's generation, the Empire has begun its final collapse. In time, perhaps before my own passing, the galaxy will be fallow ground for a new generation of pioneers. And when that happens, the time will be right for us to bring our strain of blight-cleansing fungi back to the former Imperial realms. And this time, perhaps we'll finally get it right, and the next few generations will enjoy the freedom and prosperity that my generation never did. Perhaps, if we are lucky, our discovery will give them freedom for another thousand years.

The Library of Fate

My older brother, the crown prince, finds me half-drunk in the seediest ale house in the merchant's quarter. Unfortunately, it isn't enough to save him.

"There you are!" he says, striding past prostitutes and gamblers to the table in the corner where I'm quietly trying to drink myself into oblivion. The look of dismay and sadness on his face speaks to his concern for my welfare. He always loved me dearly, and still does, even though I have disappointed him and my entire family.

"Gowaway," I say, my words slurred—though not nearly slurred enough. I try to push him away, but he knocks my hand aside.

"What are you doing here, brother? Trying to throw your life away?"

"Yesh," I tell him. "That ish exshactly what I am doingk." The alcohol may be slurring my words, but it has also cleared my mind, and the effect is a sort of truth-serum that works almost as well as magic. Almost. If only magic were fed by alcohol, then all the greatest sorcerers would be jolly old winebibers instead of cold and calculating men orchestrating their schemes from the shadows behind the throne.

The sadness on my brother's face deepens, and he leans over and grabs my arm to pull me to my feet. In that moment, the dagger that is sheathed on his belt swings within my reach.

My brother is not stupid. He came into the ale house with half a dozen bodyguards, all of whom have already spread out to secure him from anyone who might mean him harm—except for me. No one stands between the two of us.

I don't want to grab my brother's dagger—indeed, I absolutely do not grab it—but the possibility still exists that I *might* grab it, and with it do something terrible, like take my brother's life. How would the world change if he were dead? How would the threads of fate be rewoven if the thread of his life were severed here? Would the fate of the kingdom itself be altered, and all of the lives within it?

"No!" I shout, but it is already too late. The shadows of things to come are already manifesting before my eyes. I see a dozen faded images of my brother, sprawled out or staggering from the blow I have yet to inflict. As I watch, these shadows come together to form a thread of pure light, not only for my brother but for the guards, the barkeep, the ale house wenches and the men that they serve—indeed, as my vision expands I can see the threads of fate for every living soul within the kingdom. They form a multi-colored tapestry that is swiftly unraveling, like the famed Gordian knot which Alexander cut in twain. Because I am the subject of this magic, I can see what others cannot: the end of the present pattern of their lives, and the weaving of a new pattern.

As the threads come back together, I catch one last glimpse of my older brother. His love for me, the younger prodigal, is written plainly across his face, and in his eyes I can see his aching desire to save me from myself.

If only he knew why I have chosen this path!

The magical vision closes, and I fall through an abyss that is all too familiar. When I come to myself again, I am standing in center of a sorcerous circle, chalked with arcane symbols on the floor of the Library of Fate. I fall to my knees and hurl.

"What is this?" my father's chancellor shouts. "Get up, you stupid boy! Ugh, what a mess!"

The magic has already been spent, so it matters not that I have broken the circle and blotted out the chalk with my bile. Even as I watch, the dull, glowing fire of the magic fades into the well-worn wooden floor. A hungry fire burns in the fireplace, casting shadows across the shelves that ring the walls of the windowless room. Ancient leather-bound tomes fill those shelves, sorcerous books that would sear my flesh with burning heat if I ever laid hands on them. Yet the chancellor casually browses them and pulls down a new one to peruse. Stacks of the magic tomes are stacked atop the heavy oaken desk that sits across the room from the fireplace, with papers strewn helter-skelter and half a dozen candles dripping wax upon it. Unlike the books, the papers are not sorcerous, and if I were able to read them then perhaps I would begin to grasp the chancellor's deeper plans. But he gives me no chance to do so.

"Up, boy," he says, hauling me to my feet. My bile reeks of alcohol, making him wrinkle his nose in disgust.

"What... didjou do to him?" I ask.

"Your brother?" the sorcerer asks. A smile crosses his face, and I know it to be evil, though all of his smiles ever seemed to be harmless to me before I fell into his trap. "He lives, if that is what you are asking."

The room spins around me, though whether from the magic or the ale, I cannot tell. The library has an eerie, dreamlike quality to it, as if it exists only halfway in this world. The dancing firelight of the candles and fireplace only deepen the effect. Man is not meant to live within walls, like the bats in their caves or the moles under the earth. Man is meant to walk freely beneath the heavens, the wind in his hair and the sun upon his face. But that is not the only reason why I hate this library with all of my being.

"He... lives?" I ask.

"Yes. That was why we sent you out, was it not? To weave the thread of your life's possibilities into a new pattern, a new reality."

"Yes," I say aloud, and it all comes back to me: every pattern that I have lived through, every tapestry of fate that I have helped to weave. The chancellor could not work his magic through a commoner or a serf. Their lives touch many others, but not enough to reweave the fate of entire kingdoms, as he wishes to do. In the course of any man's life, there may only be a few key moments that can alter the pattern of fate, and multiply the shadows of things to come. The chancellor's magic hinges upon these moments, and upon a subject like me to provide it with a spark. And yet, in all the tapestries of fate that I have helped to unravel, I have come to understand that the chancellor's plans are ill-begotten. That is why I have chosen to throw my life away, and utterly waste all that I could become: to withhold that all-important spark that the chancellor needs to work the fullness of his sorcery. But it is not enough. It is never enough.

The chancellor casts a spell, and the mess on the floor vanishes, though the odor of bile remains. "Your younger brother lives now, if that is what you are wondering."

"My... younger brother?" I ask.

"Yes. By God, are you too drunk to remember? Your younger brother, who perished in the war the last time we unraveled the tapestry of fate?"

My eyes widen as it all begins to come back to me.

"Yes," the chancellor continues. "Your beloved younger brother, who was sent off to war because we altered the tapestry to keep your sister from marrying the duke, and losing her life to him. Instead, the duke went to war against your father, because there were no marriage ties to the throne, and thus no non-aggression pact with your father's house. But now, we have rewoven the tapestry of fate such that the war never happened. Unfortunately," and here the chancellor pauses, as he always does before giving bad news, "in this new pattern, your older brother, the crown prince, was never born."

My frown deepens. "What did you say?"

"I said, he was never born. He does not exist. The thread of his fate has been removed entirely."

I clench my fists, sweat pooling on my forehead. "What didjou do to him?"

"'Twas not what I did, young prince, but what *you* did. By slaying him in that wretched ale house, instead of in the palace as I instructed you—"

"I did not slay my brother."

"Regardless," the chancellor continues, "by failing to follow my *express* instructions, you did not give me enough to work with. There were simply too many witnesses to the deed—too many people who saw that it was you."

"I did not slay my brother," I repeat, my voice dangerously low.

"Even so. What's done is done. You are the crown prince now, the heir to your father's throne—and what a very lousy heir you are."

My blood is so hot, I barely hear him. "You murderer!" I shout, lunging forward to strike him.

But in my drunken state, he easily sidesteps my blow. The room spins wildly, books and candles and books, all those evil, magic books, and a fire burning hot and angry in the fireplace. I stumble and fall to the floor.

"You're drunk," the chancellor observes, his words tinged with contempt. "Take this. You'll feel better when you wake."

He lifts me to my feet, pulling back my head as he presses a vial to my lips. I try to spit it out, but the vile concoction burns down my throat. Within moments, the darkness seizes me.

My dreams are no more weird than my waking life, so that sleeping or waking, all now has the feel of a dream. Ever since the chancellor brought me to this place of evil sorcery, this cursed Library of Fate, nothing in the world has seemed true or right. How can it, when the world I grew up in no longer exists? It is as if I have been torn out of one of the great tapestries hanging in the great hall of my family's castle, and the rest of the tapestry has been burned.

It began with the death of my mother, the queen. She passed away in childbirth when I was only nine years old. For days, I refused to eat, and slept only fitfully, tossing and turning for nights on end. As the months and seasons passed, my tutors complained to my father, who began to lose patience with me.

My father and I have never been very close. Part of this was no doubt due to the weight of his kingly duties, which left him with little time for us children. What little time he had for us was given to my eldest brother, the crown prince. I do not begrudge him that, and to my brother's credit, I never doubted his love. But my father has always been gruff and aloof, judgmental with his gaze, harsh with his words, and always very sparse with his praise. He was always more of a force in my life than an actual man, like the sun, or the wind, or a distant storm.

In the depths of my grief, my father sent the priest to console me. When that did not improve my condition, he sent the sword master to put me through a harsh physical regimen. When I failed to apply myself to the forms, he had me whipped. Only after all else had failed did he make time to sit and talk with me.

I cannot recall what we spoke about. I remember precious little from that time. All I recall is that afterward, the chancellor came to me.

"You grieve for your mother, don't you, boy?"

I nodded mutely. He put a fatherly hand on my knee.

"Would you let me use my magic to bring her back?"

I did not know what he was talking about, so he brought me here, to the Library of Fate, to show me. And that is how the terrible cycle began. I am fully grown now, though I have no knowledge of growing up. There are memories I now carry from lives I never lived. That is the cost of reweaving one's fate, for all our lives are as threads in a tapestry, and changing one's fate alters the pattern for us all.

I awake, an almost unbearable headache splitting my skull. The alcohol has cleared from my mind, whether by sorcery or by sleep, I do not know. I also cannot tell how much time has passed, but this is less important. The passage of time matters little in this place.

I am lying on a small bed on the far side of the room from the fireplace. Ignoring the headache, I cast the blankets aside and stagger to my feet.

"Young prince," the chancellor greets me. His clothes have been changed, so at least one night has passed. As for myself, I have been stripped to my tunic. I groan.

"You're just in time," the chancellor says merrily, ignoring my pain. "The circle is redrawn, and the tomes are all in order. Shall we begin?"

I stare at him, not comprehending. I vaguely remember attacking him, but it feels too much like a dream

"Your brother," he says forcefully. "The crown prince. Shall we bring him back? I have found a new pattern, in which all of you are alive and doing well. Even your own life, young prince. Would you like to erase all of the debauchery and degeneracy of the last few years of your life? Return you to your nine year-old self, perhaps?"

"What will it entail?"

He waves his hand, as if the costs are trivial. They never are.

"Only a small thing—a very small thing, indeed. You will not find it difficult at all."

My frown deepens. "Who do you want me to kill this time?"

"Young prince! How can you accuse me thus? I have never, at any time, required you to kill anyone—only to put yourself in a position where such an act becomes possible."

"Who?" I ask, undeterred.

He pauses, and that cannily evil smile graces his face again.

"Why, your father, of course."

My stomach begins to turn in knots. He wants me to approach my own father, the king, with a dagger—as if to kill him. The threads of possibilities that such an action will unlock are too great to comprehend, and I fear to think what the chancellor will do with such power. Install himself on the throne? Destroy the very kingdom?

"No," I hear myself say.

The chancellor's grin swiftly falls. "And what will you do instead, young prince? To whom will you turn? You are nothing but a debauched wretch, a royal prodigal who sold his birthright for a mess of potage. What will become of the kingdom with an heir as unsuitable as you? As soon as your father dies, the kingdom will fall to pieces. You are unfit to rule, and you know it."

I see now that all my work to destroy my potential and withhold that magic spark has now all come to naught. Indeed, it has worked against me, for I am unfit to be my father's heir. Still, I have to admire the chancellor's foresight. If his goal from the beginning was to shape me into a tool for him to destroy my father, he could hardly have done any better.

"You have no love for your father," the chancellor continues. "It would only be a small thing to bring a knife into his presence. You do not even have to use it: the *potential* to slay him is all that I need to reweave the tapestry of fate into a wholly different pattern."

"And what will become of him if I do?"

"Think not of that, young prince," he says soothingly. "Instead, think of what will happen to yourself. All of the last few years of debauchery will be erased. You will be able to start anew. And your brothers and sisters will be alive again—all of them. Don't you want to see them?"

It is no longer difficult for me to pick out the lies from the truth in his words. If his plan is to seize the throne, then I expect we will all be exiled from the kingdom, or worse. And yet, what other choice do I have? He speaks aright when he says that I am unfit to be my father's heir. One path will destroy the kingdom, while the other will deliver it into the chancellor's hands. It appears I have been checkmated—or cornered like a wolf, perhaps.

"Very well," I tell him, steeling myself for what must be done. "Let us begin."

The chancellor's sorcery sends me back into my bedroom in the castle. It is a cold day in late autumn, with a chill wind tinged with wood smoke blowing through the window. The coals in the fireplace have almost died, so I throw on a log and stare into the creeping flames as memories of this new thread of life come unbidden to me.

My older brother is not merely dead. In this new pattern, he was never born. I was always the crown prince, but after my mother's untimely death two years ago, I began to indulge in carnal pleasures until I became much the same prodigal as I was before. It is fitting that my mother should be dead again, seeing as her death was what started this cycle of madness to begin with. So all of my efforts have come to naught, and now I seek my father's life as well. The grim irony of that is almost more than I can bear.

My father has sought a private audience with me in the gardens, no doubt to urge me to clean up my life and become a worthy heir. It is the perfect chance to slit his throat.

I pore for several minutes over whether I should attempt to run, as I did from the last one. But I doubt I can escape my fate that easily. Somewhere in that evil, sorcerous library, the threads of this tapestry are outlined in great detail, and the chancellor will find some other way to weave his magic and kill the king by my hand. I have learned through sad experience that you cannot run from fate: you can only face it head on, or else be struck in the back like a coward. I am done with the coward's path.

I dress swiftly, slipping my dagger beneath my coat. My father waits for me at the garden's gates. He is almost exactly the same man as I remember from all the other patterns. Seeing him only makes me feel even more that this is all a dream.

"My son," he greets me, and though his eyes are harsh, there is something about him that makes my breath catch in my throat. Is it love that I now see? I cannot remember ever seeing love in those eyes.

"Your Majesty," I greet him with unnecessary formality, and his face again becomes a mask.

"Come," he says, gesturing to the gardens within the inner keep. A guard stands watch on the ramparts high above, but there is no one between the two of us. I pause, my hand on the hilt of the hidden knife, and I know that as soon as I step forward, the shadows of things to come will appear as the chancellor's magic does its work. I take a deep breath.

My father, the king, frowns at me. "What is wrong?"

I step forward and say, "I love you."

I cannot remember the last time I told my father that I loved him, or if indeed I ever have. But somehow, speaking the words makes it so.

The shadows of things to come fill the space around us. I see a dozen threads where my father staggers and falls. My time is drawing short, so I swiftly draw the knife and plunge it into my chest.

The shadows suddenly vanish, and a look of shock and horror fills my father's face. In that moment, it is clear that he loves me more than I ever knew.

I fall, and he rushes to catch me, but I never feel his hands. My head strikes the hard wooden floor of the Library, and the screams of the evil chancellor soon fill my ears.

"You fool! What have you done?"

Fires roar all around me, bathing my skin with their heat. All of the books seem to burn at once, and as the chancellor frantically tries to work his magic on the tome on his desk, his robes catch fire too. My vision is swiftly fading, but it is enough to know I have defeated him.

I thought that was the end, but I was mistaken. As my eyes fluttered and I began to stir, I heard someone gasp in surprise.

I opened my eyes and struggled to get my bearings. Gone was the Library of Fate, replaced by the familiar tapestries of my childhood bedroom—my *first* childhood bedroom. I lay on a soft, down mattress, not a hard stone floor, and the heat that enveloped me was from my woolen blankets, not of a magical fire.

"Praise God!" I heard a woman's voice utter from the bedside. It was my childhood nurse—my *first* childhood nurse. She placed a gentle hand on my forehead, then smiled.

"Where am I?" I asked fearfully, as if the very act of asking would shatter this pleasant dream.

"You are at home, child," my nurse answered me. "Three days ago, you fell into a grief-ridden stupor."

"Grief?" I asked, my heart racing.

Pain swept her face, but she bore it gracefully. "Yes. Your mother, the queen—she passed away in childbirth barely a fortnight ago."

My mother, I thought as my stomach began to sink. But of course, it makes sense. If the chancellor's magic had truly been undone, that meant I had been brought back to the beginning, to the first tapestry of fate before he used his magic to unravel it. I pressed my hands to my cheeks, and sure enough, they were as smooth and hairless as they were when I was nine years old.

The next hour was a frenzy of activity, as the priest, the doctor, the guards, and more than a dozen courtiers swarmed into the room to see me. The chancellor never came, however, and I learned from the others that he had fled the castle almost the very hour that I awoke. So he, too, had evaded death, but without me his sorcery would no longer hold sway over the kingdom.

My father was not the first to come, but as soon as he stepped into the room, everyone else fell silent.

I sat up straight. "Father—"

In a few swift strides, he was at my side. "My son," he said, his voice low but strained. In his eyes, I saw the same love and concern that filled them when I plunged the knife into my heart.

All of this was too much for me. I tried to hold back the tears, but within moments I was weeping. Yet though my tears were bittersweet, they felt as healing as a warm summer's rain.

My father embraced me. "I love you, son," he said so softly that only I could hear.

"I love you too," I told him. It was enough.

In the Wake of Zedekiah Wight
by J.M. Wight

"We're picking up a distress signal, sir," Suleiman Ibn Nasser, the *Trident's* first mate, said as he peered at his third monitor. "It appears to be coming from an EVA suit about ten thousand klicks from our current position."

Captain Victor Andrecek frowned. On the dimly-lit bridge of the *Trident,* Suleiman sat directly in front and to the right of him. Eliso, his second mate and only female member of the three-man crew, sat on Suleiman's left. Andrecek's command chair was elevated just enough to give him a clear view through the forward window that wrapped nearly 180 degrees around the room. But the bridge's main holoscreen display was much more useful, since it showed a three-dimensional map of the sector. Currently, it showed that the *Trident* was the only object of any significant mass for 50,000 klicks in any direction. That was what made Suleiman's discovery so confusing.

"Are you sure of that?" Andrecek added as he cycled through the wider system starmap on the armrest screen of his command chair. "I don't see any official traffic heading into or out of our local sector."

Not that that counted for much, since only about half of the Ramallah system's traffic was officially registered. The inner system in particular was crawling with pirates and smugglers and everything in-between. Andrecek and his crew fell squarely in the smuggler camp, but that didn't make it any safer for them out here.

"I'm sure of it, sir. What's more, it appears to be heading on a sun-ward trajectory at several hundred meters per second."

"Sun-ward? Why the devil would anyone this far in the inner system be heading sun-ward?"

Suleiman glanced over his shoulder at the captain and shook his head. "I don't know, sir, but we're certainly picking up a signal, and it's certainly coming from an EVA suit on a collision course with the sun."

Andrecek's frown deepened. A distress signal from an EVA suit was always a serious matter, and an urgent one, too, since the victim typically had only hours to get help before they expired. It was an unwritten rule among starfarers that anyone encountering such a call for help should drop everything to answer it. But though the *Trident*, a 5,000 ton modified cargo hauler with limited FTL capabilities, was cleared with the local port authority at Ramallah Station to travel through this sector, her business was anything but official. Andrecek had no desire to get his ship and his crew caught up in trouble that didn't concern them—especially if that trouble was bait for a pirate ambush.

"The scanners show that we're the only ship of any consequence within 50,000 klicks," he thought out loud. "If that's true, where did this spacewalker come from? He couldn't have gotten far on his own."

Suleiman shrugged. "I don't know, sir. I only know what the instruments tell me."

Captain Andrecek stroked his square, clean-shaven chin as he pondered the situation. Pirates typically didn't have sophisticated equipment like cloaking shields, and even if they did, they would still show up on the *Trident's* scanners as an anomaly. Probably. He'd paid a lot of good money to make sure that his ship had top-of-the-line detection systems, otherwise he never would have come to this pirate-infested backwater in the first place. So the chances of it being an ambush were fairly slim. But where had this spacewalker come from, especially to be heading sun-ward at such a high velocity?

"Is it possible that they came out here on some sort of a skiff?" Eliso asked. "I know our scanners are good, but if someone came out on a short-range craft, it might blend into the background noise—especially if it's derelict."

"Then run a detailed infrared scan, and put the results on-screen," Andrecek ordered. "I want to know the position and trajectory of every object larger than our fishbone skiff within twenty klicks of our position."

"You want to find our friend's lost ship?" Suleiman asked.

"No," Andrecek answered. "I want to make sure we aren't ambushed by someone whose cloaking systems are more advanced than our scanners."

Suleiman and Eliso both turned to give him a look of concern and fear. "Uh, sir," Eliso asked, "should I power up our point defenses?"

"That's a very good idea."

The infrared scanner results came in about a minute later. To Andrecek's surprise, they showed no large objects matching the distress signal's trajectory.

"Are you sure those results are correct?" he asked Suleiman.

"Yes, sir," he answered. "It looks like our friend was the victim of a very bad spacewalk, and his ship jumped out and left him stranded."

"How does that explain his sun-ward trajectory?"

Suleiman shrugged. "I do not know, sir. Perhaps there was some sort of battle in this sector?"

"But if that's the case, how would they jump out?" Eliso asked. "The only two jump-hubs that cover this system are New Amman over in the Caliphate, and Freedom's Landing over in the Federation. No matter how much you bribe the officials in either jurisdiction, I can't believe they'd overlook a pirate ship jumping in hot."

"That is true," said Suleiman. "However, it is also possible that our friend's ship was boarded and commandeered. That would explain why there is no wreckage in the immediate vicinity. Power down weapons, hack registration and manifest, and spread a little coin among the customs agents to look the other way."

"Cost of doing business," Eliso concurred grimly.

"Or maybe the pirates have their own jump-hub," Andrecek muttered, still stroking his chin.

Both of his crewmates turned around and looked at him as if he'd gone insane. "You cannot possibly mean that, sir," Suleiman told him. "With all due respect, the logistics of running an illegal jump-hub, especially on a frontier system that is so closely watched—"

"Not to mention that the punishment in the caliphate for running an illegal jump-hub is death," Eliso added.

"Yes," Suleiman agreed. "And that is one of the few laws that the satraps are jealous to enforce."

Andrecek shrugged. "It's how I would run the operation, if I were a pirate captain."

"But you are not a pirate, sir. You are an ex-rebel commodore and military man turned smuggler. Pirates do not think the way that you do. For them, it is all about extracting the maximum reward for the minimum effort. The Ramallah system is not yet so lawless that whole pirate fleets, with their own jump-hubs, can roam with relative impunity."

"Perhaps," Andrecek conceded, though he wasn't entirely convinced. But that could just be his paranoia acting up again. If the pirates had a support ship with a jump-hub, all they needed was to place it close enough to the ambush site that none of the official patrols fell within that radius. Active jump-hubs were visible to all FTL-capable starships that fell within its range. The standard FTL drive could only jump you to a hub, but the drives on a jump-hub could send your ship to any sidereal co-ordinates within that same range—for a price. That was why they were typically the exclusive domain of interstellar governments, as there was nothing the bureaucrats and petty tyrants of the galaxy wanted to control more than the movement of goods and people across the stars. For that reason, Andrecek conducted as much of his smuggling operation as he could at sublight speeds.

"Are we going for him then, sir?" Eliso asked.

"Let's try to hail him first," said Andrecek, still not entirely sold on the operation. The part of him that had gotten his first ship commission at age twenty-eight—and later had urged him to join the rebellion with his friends, even though it would likely (and ultimately did) fail—that part of him could not bear to leave the distress call unanswered. But at the same time, his first responsibility was to the safety of his crew, and the whole situation was as suspicious as hell. Besides, he was a smuggler now, not a military man. Honor didn't count for much in the underworld of the Caliphate frontier.

Eliso turned to her screen and cycled through a set of menus. "Comms established, sir. His suit appears to be in working order."

"Good. Open an audio channel."

"Channel open, sir."

He took a deep breath. "This is Captain Andrecek of the civilian freighter ship *Trident*. We just picked up your distress signal. What is the nature of your emergency? What sort of assistance do you require?"

All three of them waited in anxious silence for a response that never came.

"This is Captain Andrecek of the *Trident*," he tried again. "Do you require rescue?"

"I'm sorry, sir," Eliso answered at length. "They don't appear to be responding to our hails."

"Is there a problem with the connection? Are they receiving us?"

"I think so. There's nothing wrong on our end, at least, and the suit still registers about three hour's worth of oxygen remaining. They... just don't appear to be answering."

Andrecek frowned. "Can you pull any more information from the suit?"

"Working on it." A few seconds passed, then: "Got it, sir. The suit belongs to a ship called the *Bint Jaleela,* a Caliphate pleasure yacht registered at Zarqa IV. Occupant is unlisted."

"But you can confirm that it's occupied?"

"Yes, sir. There is definitely someone there."

Andrecek nodded slowly. The smart thing would be to leave and pretend that they'd never picked up the distress signal, but he'd never be able to look himself in the mirror again if he did that. After all, if he didn't have his self-respect at this point, he didn't have anything.

"Eliso, set an intercept course with the *Trident.* Suleiman, prep the fishbone for a rescue operation. We're going after this guy."

The fishbone skiff was a glorified rocket with a winch, some tethers, a short-range tightbeam, and a couple of dozen maneuvering drones for repositioning large objects. It didn't even have a hull, just a carbon nanotube frame with a couple of seats for two crewmates, both of whom had to be in EVA suits of course. With a couple extra tanks of oxygen stowed in the back, the fishbone only had an effective range of a couple of thousand klicks, but even that was pushing it. With the distress signal's current velocity, they were pushing the little craft to its limit.

Inside his EVA suit, Captain Andrecek sucked in his stomach and clenched his butt as the fishbone made the hard burn necessary to intercept the signal. When the burn was complete, he spun the craft around to be in the correct position for the second burn, then waited idly in zero-gee as the tiny screen in front of him showed their progress along the intersecting trajectory lines.

"Do you really think that our friend was attacked by pirates?" Suleiman asked, making small talk over their suit radios to pass the wait. For the next eighteen minutes, there wasn't much else for them to do.

"It's the only explanation that makes any sense," Andrecek said. "Why else would he be on a sun-ward trajectory?"

"But if our friend was being chased by pirates, why flee into the sun? Would they not first head toward the nearest settlement, or in the direction of the next-closest friendly ship?"

"I don't know," Andrecek admitted. "Perhaps they had to make combat maneuvers, and things got a little out of hand."

"Combat maneuvers while one of the crew was spacewalking?"

He shrugged within his EVA suit, even though Suleiman couldn't see it. "Perhaps they were caught by surprise while the victim was out on a spacewalk."

"Perhaps," said Suleiman. "But in that case, they—"

"Captain," said Eliso over the tightbeam, cutting him short. "Do you see anything strange from your vantage point out there?"

"No," said Andrecek, frowning. "Why?"

"Because I just picked up two more EVA suit distress signals, on similar trajectories to this one. What do you want me to do?"

He glanced down at his screen, quickly running through the numbers. It didn't look like they could rescue all three spacewalkers without breaking the *Tri-*

dent's course and bringing her around to bear, which negated the reason for using the fishbone. It also made them extremely vulnerable, if the distress signals were really just bait for an ambush. If none of the spacewalkers was alive, they'd be better off just leaving.

"Try hailing them, Eliso, just like we did with the first one. If they don't respond in the next five minutes, let me know. Understood?"

"Understood, sir. *Trident* out."

A few long moments passed in eerie silence. Andrecek glanced over his shoulder to try and get a visual on their target, but they were still too far out. The vast expanse of the starfield all around them made him shiver involuntarily.

"You are thinking about turning around, aren't you, sir?" Suleiman asked.

"I'm not going to risk you, Eliso, or the *Trident* if it comes down to that," Andrecek muttered.

"That is good," said Suleiman. "You are right to be wary. I doubt that our friend is a victim of pirates, but he might have been lost in a power struggle between our clients and the Hamza crime family in Ramallah Station."

Andrecek grunted. "Do you suppose that's why our cargo is sealed?"

"Yes. I have been thinking about that considerably since we picked it up in the outer system. Clearly, Mahmoud Abu Abbas wishes to keep any outside knowledge of his business to a minimum. Perhaps there was a falling out with his partners in the cartel."

"But wouldn't they have recalled us if that was the case?" he asked, frowning as he thought about it. Andrecek had always had a difficult time following all the shifting alliances and patron-client relationships between the various factions on the Caliphate side of the frontier. That was one of the reasons why he'd brought Suleiman onto the crew, since the young man was a Ramallah system native and had a much better understanding of these things than Andrecek did. But if a new vendetta or gang war had broken out while they were en route, that had the potential to put them in a lot of danger very quickly.

"Perhaps," Suleiman answered noncommittally. "But perhaps not."

"Should we get ready to dump our cargo before the Hamza family targets us next? Or should we abandon this rescue operation and continue on to Ramallah Station as if we never saw anything here?"

There was a long, careful pause as his first mate considered his answer. "We should continue with the operation," he said at length. "But we should also make ready to dump our cargo, depending on what we find there."

Andrecek swore. "Suleiman, the only reason I agreed to take the sealed cargo was because you assured me it would be all right!"

"I am sorry, sir. Perhaps I misjudged the situation."

"So should we cut our losses now and return to the outer system?"

"No, sir, no," Suleiman said quickly. "That will not be necessary. Let us continue on our course until we know more. Perhaps our friend here will help to give us a clue."

Captain Andrecek found that difficult to believe. He should have trusted his gut and turned down the contract back in the outer system, even though it probably would have meant losing this particular client, a powerful and well-connected Caliphate oligarch, for good. It always made him uneasy, not knowing what sort of cargo he was carrying. He'd only done that one other time, for a delivery on the Federation side of the frontier. The run had gone smoothly and without incident, but his client had gone underground shortly thereafter, leading to many sleepless nights where Andrecek had wondered whether he'd inadvertently participated in something truly vile. But Abu Abbas had given them a lot of reliable work in the past, and losing his business would have been a serious blow. That was why he'd trusted his first mate and agreed to take the sealed cargo.

"Let us wait until we have finished our operation here, sir," Suleiman continued to plead with him. "Then, we will know how to proceed."

"All right," Andrecek said reluctantly. "But I'm trusting you, Suleiman."

He glanced down at the fishbone's tiny control screen. They were less than a minute from their next engine burn. He double-checked the craft's alignment and gripped the controls through the thick, bulky gloves of his EVA suit.

"Captain, sir," Eliso's voice came over his suit's comm. "The other distress signals aren't responding to our hails. What do you want me to do?"

"Have you pulled their suit data, like we did with the first one?"

"Yes, sir. The suit is registered to the same pleasure yacht, the *Bint Jaleela.* I..." Her voice suddenly trailed off.

"Eliso?" Andrecek asked, frowning. "Are you there Eliso?"

"What the hell?" she muttered to herself—then, to Andrecek, "sorry, captain. I just picked up three more distress signals, just like the other ones. This whole sector is peppered with them!"

The timer on the fishbone's display ticked down to zero. "Just do the best you can," Andrecek told her. "I'm starting our second engine burn."

The rush of the rocket sounded faintly through his EVA suit as they decelerated. This time, he took them in easy, keeping one eye on the display and another on the fishbone's rear-view mirror. After about thirty seconds, he saw a dimly blinking light against the backdrop of the washed-out inner-system starfield. A short while later, they pulled up alongside it.

"Is that... a missile?" Suleiman asked incredulously.

Indeed, it looked very much like a missile—except that the warhead had been replaced by what looked like a long metal beam. A crossbeam of some sort had been welded to it most of the way up, but the whole thing was spinning too fast for Andrecek to get a clear view of what it carried.

"Suleiman, deploy our maneuvering drones," he ordered. "Let's see if we can't stabilize that spin."

"Of course, sir. Deploying drones now."

The drones zipped out of their compartment on the fishbone and quickly circled the spinning object. The swarm AI quickly made the relevant calculations, and the drones moved in, attaching themselves to the object in such a way as to give them maximum leverage. Moments later, they engaged their jets, the little puffs of compressed air dispersing silently into the vacuum. The spinning gradually stopped.

What Captain Victor Andrecek saw next nearly made him vomit. Strapped to the crossbeam with arms stretched wide was the EVA suit of a man who'd been crucified.

"Allahu ackbar!" Suleiman exclaimed in fright. "Our friend—this man—he's been—"

"Get the blowtorch," Andrecek ordered, already unbuckling himself form the fishbone. "I'm going in."

After securing one of the fishbone's tethers to his EVA suit, he leaped free of the skiff's frame and used his suit's propulsion system to approach the object, which was only about fifty meters away. As he did so, he used his HUD to enhance his vision, cycling through heat sensors, infrared, ultraviolet, and half a dozen other sensors. The results did not look good.

"They crucified him alive," he muttered, floating to a stop about two meters away from the victim. His suit was punctured in the hands and feet with nails, but they were driven in so tightly that the suit probably hadn't lost much air. Besides, the frozen blood had probably created a seal. It must have been an incredibly painful death. The victim's body was so contorted that Andrecek couldn't help but think that the quick death of vacuum exposure would have been a blessing. The shielding on the suit's visor was open, giving Andrecek a clear view of the victim's face. His lifeless eyes had long since glassed over, his jaw locked in a final, horrific scream. He was unmistakably dead.

"Allahu ackbar," Suleiman repeated as he pulled up alongside Andrecek with the blowtorch.

"What is it, sir?" Eliso asked.

"He's dead," said Andrecek as he tapped his suit's helmet to transmit a visual. "Crucified. That explains why his suit still had oxygen."

"Oh my God," Eliso exclaimed, sounding just as horrified as Suleiman.

"Yep," Andrecek continued. "See that missile? That provided the acceleration necessary for the crucifixion to work. He probably died by asphyxiation or cardiac rupture, as a consequence of being forced to hold that position with his arms stretched out. But with the spinning and the gee forces involved, he was probably dead before the missile ran out of fuel." That, at least, was a blessing.

"Look, sir!" Suleiman said urgently, pointing to the topmost portion of the cross. "Is that... words?"

Andrecek brought himself in closer to take a look. Sure enough, there was an improvised plaque welded to the main beam, with writing in large block letters burned crudely onto it.

"Woe unto them that draw iniquity with cords of vanity, and sin as it were with a cart rope!" he read aloud.

"What does it mean?" Eliso asked.

Captain Andrecek didn't know what to say. The whole grisly scene was so brutally medieval, like something from a lost colony where civilization itself had long ago descended back into savagery and chaos. And yet, there was a certain deliberateness and attention to detail that made it even worse. The man's executioner had gone to great lengths to disassemble the warhead and replace it with a fabricated cross—and not only that, but had made it well enough to withstand the multiple gee forces that the rocket would inflict upon it. Clearly, this whole thing was about sending a message, not just about killing the victim. But what sort of message?

"Uh, captain sir?" Suleiman asked. "Are you all right?"

Andrecek blinked and shook his head clear. "Plug into that suit's computer and get us a full data dump. I want to know everything about this man's death that we possibly can."

"Are we, ah, going to retrieve the body, sir?"

Before he could answer, Eliso cut him short.

"Captain," she said urgently, "I think you'll want to hear this."

The audio switched over to a gravelly voice partially drowned out by static. Andrecek quickly realized that this was a transmission being received by the *Trident,* probably from one of those EVA suits with the distress calls. He froze and stopped everything to listen.

"Zed... Zed... Zedek..." the gravelly voice groaned.

"Sir, can you hear me?" Andrecek asked, touching his hand instinctively to his helmet. "This is Captain Victor Andrecek of the *Trident.* We've picked up your distress signal, and—"

"Zedekiah... Wight," the man gurgled. His breath blended into the static, which seemed to swallow him.

"Hang on, sir! We're coming. Suleiman?"

"Yes, sir?"

"Get back to the fishbone, stat. Eliso?"

"Yes?"

"Give us a course to this man's position, and prep the *Trident's* medical bay for emergency triage."

"On it, sir."

Suleiman had already disengaged the maneuvering drones and ordered them back to the skiff. Andrecek followed the swarm back, the puff-puff of his suit's propulsion system the only outside sound in the merciless vacuum of space.

Unfortunately, the man was dead before they arrived.

He was crucified on the head of a repurposed missile just like the other victim. Andrecek supposed that all of the distress signals came from victims similarly executed, which made him wonder just how many missiles these people had to spare (or if the *Bint Jaleela* was something more than the pleasure yacht it purported to be). Another cryptic passage had been burned onto a plaque at the head of this cross, though this one read a little differently:

Woe unto them that call evil good, and good evil; that put darkness for light, and light for darkness; that put bitter for sweet, and sweet for bitter!

Eliso didn't pick up any transmissions from the other suits, but even if she had, the fishbone was running too low on fuel to try and recover any of the others. Captain Andrecek made the decision to cut the man's body away from the cross and recover it, even though he was clearly dead by now.

"Who did this?" he asked Suleiman on the way back to the *Trident.* "Do you still think these people died as a result of a vendetta or a turf war?"

"No, sir. Clearly not. No one in the Caliphate executes people in this way."

"Then who was it?"

Suleiman paused. "Someone from the outside," he answered finally. "Someone without any connection to the families or the cartels. And whoever it is, he is dangerous, sir. Very dangerous."

Andrecek frowned. "Eliso, do we know anything about the identities of these victims?"

"No, sir," she answered from the *Trident.* "Normally, these suits are supposed to list their occupants' identities, but all of that data has been carefully scrubbed, probably by the captain of the *Bint Jaleela.* We won't know anything until we get that body on board and crack its suit open."

"You mean his suit," Andrecek said ruefully. A shiver ran down his back as he remembered how the victim's lifeless eyes had stared up at him through the visor while he and Suleiman had cut him loose.

"Yes, sir. Of course." She paused for a moment, then added: "I'm sorry, captain. We did the best that we could."

"At least we know that there hasn't been a falling out between our client and the Hamza family," Suleiman offered as consolation. "Things could be much worse, sir."

Not for the victims of the Bint Jaleela, Andrecek thought ruefully.

They spoke very little as they brought the fishbone skiff back into the *Trident's* shuttle bay. Even in microgravity, it took a bit of effort to haul the dead man's body into the ship's main airlock, but with a little help from the maneuvering drones, they managed to get it in. Once inside, Andrecek and Suleiman climbed out of their bulky EVA suits and returned them to the vestibule before carrying the victim into the *Trident's* medical bay.

"You didn't bother taking him out of his suit?" Eliso asked from the doorway, arms folded.

"With the way he died, we may need to disinfect it," Andrecek answered.

He manually cracked the seal to remove the suit's fishbowl helmet, and jumped a little as something popped and briefly flashed. *That isn't supposed to happen.* Suddenly, all of the lights and equipment in the medical bay went dead, plunging them into darkness.

"Allahu ackbar!" Suleiman exclaimed.

"What the hell?" said Eliso.

"Shit, shit, shit!" Captain Andrecek swore, leaping to his feet. Without warning, he floated up in the narrow chamber and banged his head. It wasn't just the lights that were off, but the artificial gravity as well. That fact only served to confirm his worst fears. Someone had placed a small cylindrical object inside the EVA suit, just behind the victim's neck. It had all the markings of a military-grade EMP device.

They had fallen into an ambush.

"Eliso, to the bridge! Suleiman, get to the escape pod and bring it back online!"

"But sir, the—"

"Now! Move!"

Captain Andrecek pulled his weightless body quickly to the bridge, Eliso close behind him. She used the emergency handholds to stop herself immediately above her workstation and got to work assessing the damage while Andrecek opened the panel along the back wall and tried to reroute auxiliary power to the ship's primary systems.

Eliso swore. "It's a mess, sir. Everything's down. Who the hell puts an EMP in a—"

"It doesn't matter. Just get my ship up and running again."

He pulled out a cluster of wires and finally found what he was looking for: the switch for the bridge's backup power supply. He cranked it, and the screens lit up again. Eliso's fingers raced across the controls.

"Sorry, sir. It's going to take some time for us to boot everything up. Which systems should I prioritize?"

That was the question, wasn't it? Weapons, so that they could fight off the pirates when they jumped into range? Engines, so that they could run? Without knowing what they were up against, it was difficult to know whether they should fight or flee—or indeed, if they could get any of those systems up in time before their enemy finally arrived. They couldn't be very far: EMP weapons could only temporarily disable a ship, though they did also send a powerful signal that propagated through space at light-speed. The pirates were probably waiting just a few light-minutes away, waiting for that signal to reach them. Which meant that they only had minutes before go-time.

"Weapons," said Andrecek. "We're not going to go down without taking a few of them with us."

"Damned right, sir," said Eliso, her eyes lighting up with the same fire they'd used to have when they were back in the rebellion together. Andrecek left her and shot down the corridor to see how Suleiman was faring.

"How's that pod doing?" he yelled through the open hatchway, catching himself on another of the handholds. The fact that Suleiman already had lights on boded well—

thank God for the man who designed the *Trident* to be hardened against this sort of attack.

"Almost ready, captain," his first mate yelled back. "The damage here is not bad at all."

"Good. When you're done, get ready to evacuate."

"Is it really that bad, sir?"

"Just get ready," yelled Andrecek, then pulled himself back to the bridge to see how Eliso had fared. It had only been minutes since the EMP had gone off, but those scant minutes were all they had before the pirates who had crucified the crew of the *Bint Jaleela* were upon them. Andrecek had no desire to spend his last living moments gasping desperately for breath as multiple gee forces crushed his contorted chest.

The sound of Eliso swearing did not bode well. A couple of screens were up, but they looked to be running diagnostics while the main bridge screen still showed a loading bar.

"What's the situation?" he asked her.

"Better than it looks, sir. The damage is superficial, but everything's booting up in the wrong order, and I'm having a hell of a time getting our targeting systems back online."

"Can we operate the weapons manually? Put one of us up in the turret while the other one calls the shots?"

"Are you kidding? Unless they were right on top of us, we'd be spitting in the wind—and even if they were that close, we'd have no point defense or other countermeasures without the targeting systems. No, we need to—"

"What do you need me to do?" he asked, cutting her short. The last thing he needed was for his second mate to lose concentration now.

Eliso sighed. "I don't know, sir. There isn't much you can do, other than keep a watch."

"Do you have sensors online yet?"

"Nope. Better use your visual scanners, for what it's worth."

She meant that he should keep an eye on the window, which was their only way to see what was happening outside right now. Even then, the *Trident's* forward bridge window only gave them a limited view, since the ship was originally built to be a civilian freighter, not a science ship or a warship. But one set of eyes was better than none.

He had barely reached the window when a soundless flash against the backdrop of the starfield announced that they had company.

"They're here," Andrecek said grimly as the enemy starship came into view. It was unusually large for a pirate ship, almost as big as the *Trident,* with two main cannons, four engine nacelles, at least one missile bay, and half a dozen point defense turrets. At their present range, the point defense turrets doubled as offensive weapons, not just countermeasures. In fact, the ship was close enough that Andrecek could just make out the name of the ship, painted in bold, red letters on the ship's bow: *Void*-something, either *-singer* or *-bringer,* it was difficult to tell. The letters were in old-type and difficult to read at a distance.

As for the ship itself, he recognized the design as a decommissioned Federation *Lancer*-class destroyer, similar to the ones he had fought during the rebellion. He had a lot of bad memories fighting those ships. For a very brief moment, he had a disorienting flashback to those days and felt a gut-wrenching sense of panic, knowing that the Federation always sent these front-line attack ships in pairs. But of course, this was a pirate ship, not a federation attack force. A Federation ship would have its name printed in large, blocky letters, not flowery old-type script like this one. It would also be painted dark gray, to give it a low albedo. The paint job on this ship was white, red, and black, but mostly white.

"I've almost got it, sir!" Eliso shouted. "Targeting system is back on line, resolving targets now. All we need is to link up with the cannons and—"

"It's too late," said Andrecek, pulling himself to the door. "Get to the escape pod, now."

"But sir, the weapons—"

"It's pointless, Eliso. They're already on top of us. Get back to the escape pod—that's an order."

She hesitated for a moment, forcing him to grab her by the collar and throw her out into the corridor while hooking his feet into one of the emergency handholds. She yelped as she banged her shoulder on one of the bulkheads, but offered little protest. Soon, they were both shooting through the narrow space in a desperate bid to get to the escape pod before the boarders arrived.

There was nowhere to run from them, of course. If they launched the pod, the pirates would probably just blow it out of the sky—unless, of course, they intended to crucify Andrecek and his crew the way they had with the crew of the *Bint Jaleela.* His only hope was that if they got to the escape pod soon enough, they could register it as having deployed already while they hunkered down. If all the pirates were after was loot, they would probably ignore the pod, take what they wanted, and leave. But if the pirates were determined, it wouldn't take them long to figure out that the pod was still there, and that he and his crew were likely hiding in it.

They found Suleiman in the corridor, doing something with the body and the EVA suit they'd recovered. In the micro-gravity, it floated gently in the air like a corpse underwater a still, wave-less sea.

"What are you doing?" Andrecek shouted as he barreled past his first mate. "Get to the escape pod!"

"But sir, I found something that you should—"

"We don't have time! Get to the pod, now!"

Eliso cannon-balled expertly through the hatch and slung herself off to one side to make room for Andrecek, who followed close behind. He swung to the other side and hooked another handhold with his foot to give him the leverage he needed to pull Suleiman inside. The moment he was in, Eliso shut the inner airlock door and opened the one to the pod.

"Arm up with me, Suleiman," said Andrecek as he led them inside. "Eliso, get on that console and make us disappear."

The pod was designed for four people, but he'd pulled out the fourth chair and installed a military-grade weapons locker in its place. Space was tight inside the small, windowless space, but the micro-gravity made it a little bit easier. While Andrecek and Suleiman fastened sidearms to their belts, Eliso went to work on the pod's tiny navigating computer, her feet up near the ceiling to avoid bumping into them while she worked.

"The pod now registers as having deployed, captain, but any damned fool on their ship can see that the pod's still here"

"That's all right," Andrecek told her as he loaded a mag into his rifle and racked the slide. "Can you give us remote access to the *Trident's* main computer without alerting the boarders that we're here?"

"Already on it," she told him. "And yeah, it looks like the boarders just docked with the main airlock. Should I blow the freight doors and vent the whole ship?"

"Negative," said Andrecek, reverting to military lingo under stress. "Power down the weapons and countermeasures, though. Make it look like we evacuated when the EMP blew."

She sighed and shook her head. "All right, sir. But if you'd just given me ten more seconds back there, I—"

"Stow it, Eliso. Suleiman, are you loaded?"

"Locked and loaded, sir," he said matter-of-factly. His olive-colored cheeks had gone pale, though, and he didn't look like he'd fare well or last very long in a firefight if it came down to that.

He'll hold the line, Andrecek thought as he strapped a pair of grenades to his chest. *Everyone does when their back is to the wall.*

A grim silence fell over them as the seconds passed. Through the bulkheads, they could faintly hear the sound of docking clamps groaning. A door opened, probably the ship's main airlock. Andrecek tightened his grip on his rifle, while Eliso grabbed a sidearm from the weapons locker and strapped it on her thigh.

"They're on the bridge now," she announced, pulling her legs to her chest to spin right-side up. "Looks like they're about to turn on the gravity."

As if on cue, Andrecek's stomach fell as the familiar sensation of artificial gravity returned. His feet landed soft and cat-like on the floor, and he was gratified to see that Suleiman and Eliso landed quietly as well. The last thing they needed was for a passing boarder to hear one of them stumble and fall.

"They're checking the cargo hold now," Eliso said softly. "What do you want me to do?"

"Nothing for now," Andrecek answered, his voice barely louder than a whisper. Better the pirates take their cargo than take their lives.

For a long while, they heard nothing. Beads of sweat began to form on Suleiman's forehead, and Andrecek's grip on his rifle began to feel slippery. Waiting was always the worst part of any operation. He took a deep breath and wiped his hand off on his pants.

"Looks like they're bringing the ship around to load up our cargo," said Eliso. "There goes our next paycheck."

"Do you think they will leave after that?" Suleiman asked the captain.

Andrecek clenched his jaw. "Godwilling," he muttered.

A series of distant grinding noises sounded through the bulkheads. Each one sent shivers up Andrecek's spine, like nails on glass. His heart pounded hard enough that it seemed about to leap from his chest. He couldn't help but wonder if the pirates were taking their time deliberately, to fray his nerves as well as those of his crew. Or perhaps they were planning to scuttle the ship when they were through unloading the contraband. They couldn't jettison the escape pod remotely, but they could blow up the ship before Andrecek or the others could do anything about it.

"They've finished transferring our cargo," Eliso announced. "Now we find out what else they have in mind."

Andrecek pressed his ear to the bulkhead and heard what sounded like footsteps. To his dismay, they seemed to be getting louder. Then, the inner airlock door hissed open. He held his breath.

"La ilaha illa Allah," Suleiman whispered.

He heard what sounded like a knock, or perhaps a hand slapping against the door. Time slowed to a crawl. He took one of his grenades and held it with an iron grip, hand shaking. Any moment, the hatch would open, and things would suddenly get hot.

But that never happened. Instead, the footsteps sounded through the bulkhead again, followed by the muffled hiss of the inner airlock closing. Suleiman stifled a cough, and Eliso gasped.

"Holy shit," she swore softly.

"What are they doing now?" Andrecek asked, his voice low and even as he replaced the grenade on his belt.

"Just a sec," Eliso answered, wiping sweat from her brow. "Looks like they've all disembarked through the freight airlock. And now, they've begun to undock." She glanced up at him, her face a picture of confusion and fear. "What now, sir?"

"On my mark, get ready to make for the bridge. Suleiman, you sweep left. I'll sweep right. Understood?"

A low groan sounded through the bulkheads as the docking clamps disengaged. Suleiman and Eliso nodded.

"Now!"

The door slid open. Andrecek swept the airlock with his rifle and went in first, lowering it while his first and second mate file into the airlock. The moment the door hissed behind them, he palmed the next door open and brought his rifle back up.

"Go, go, go!"

Suleiman dashed through the hatch, Andrecek and Eliso close behind him. At the first junction, Suleiman took the left corner while Andrecek went around the right. It looked clear—no targets, no threats.

"Clear," he said loudly. "To the bridge. Go!"

Suleiman broke into a run, while Andrecek covered their rear, Eliso between them. They arrived at the bridge without incident and shut the door.

"Bring up our weapons," Andrecek ordered as he quickly swept the room for traps. Finding none, he took his position in the command chair, his rifle pointed at the floor. Eliso was already at her station, working furiously to bring the *Trident* up to bear.

"Weapons online. Bringing up our point defenses now."

"Engines online, sir," Suleiman reported. "Preparing to make evasive maneuvers."

"Scanners on screen," Andrecek commanded.

The bridge main display flickered briefly before showing them a map of the local sector. Andrecek braced himself, expecting to hear missile warnings, or see an incoming volley on the screen. Instead, it was blank—no ships, no missiles, no nothing. The pirate ship was gone.

"There's no sign of them anywhere," said Eliso, baffled. "It looks like they've jumped away."

Andrecek let out a breath he didn't know he'd been holding. So the pirates had left without scuttling their ship. The danger was past—for now.

"Eliso, keep running our weapons hot and stay here on the bridge. Suleiman, come with me."

"Where to, sir?"

"To check the rest of the ship. I want to make sure that our uninvited guests didn't leave us any surprises. Also, I need you to give me a complete inventory of our cargo. I want to know exactly what they stole."

"Very well, sir."

They walked down the corridor again, this time much more carefully. If the pirates had decided to spare them, it was unlikely that they'd booby trapped the place, but Captain Andrecek didn't want to take any unnecessary chances. When they got to the cargo hold, they made a thorough sweep of the place before doing anything else.

"Look, sir," said Suleiman, pointing to the corner where the sealed cargo from their client had been stowed. Sure enough, it was gone.

"Keep working on that inventory," Andrecek told him. "I'm going to check the pod again."

As he passed the EVA suit from the *Bint Jaleela* in the corridor, he wondered what the pirates had thought when they'd seen it. Did they recognize the victim from their previous raid? Had they done anything to deface his dead body? He removed the helmet and looked over the corpse, but didn't see any obvious signs of disfiguration—aside from the crucifixion, of course.

The man they'd crucified had graying hair and a salt and pepper beard. His face was contorted in the man's final death scream, eyes staring lifelessly at the ceiling. It gave Andrecek the creeps, so he moved on.

One last question remained in his mind: what had the pirate done when he'd stepped into the airlock for the escape pod? Had the hard vacuum warning on the console actually fooled him? Did he really think that the pod had been deployed? From everything else, it certainly seemed that way—otherwise, why would they still be alive?

He ducked through the still-open hatch to the escape pod and froze. There, posted on the outer airlock door, was a handwritten note on a scrap of white paper:

If ye be willing and obedient, ye shall eat the good of the land. But if ye refuse and rebel, ye shall be devoured with the sword: for the mouth of the LORD hath spoken it.

"Who is Zedekiah Wight?"

Eliso grunted as she sat hunched over her bowl of noodles, while Suleiman shrugged and took another sip of his dark Arabian coffee. As for Captain Andrecek, he'd chosen sauerkraut and dumplings for his comfort food, with the last link of kielbasa from his personal stores. The food was far from perfect, as the *Trident's* mess hall left much to be desired, but it was light-years better than the rehydrated stores that they usually ate. Andrecek's nerves were still frayed enough that his hands shook, though, so he took each bite slowly.

"A madman," Eliso answered between bites. "Obviously."

"What does the local planetnet say?" Suleiman asked, gesturing to the tablet in front of her on the table. "I seem to remember the Caliphate issuing a reward for a man of that name."

She set down her fork and turned her attention to the tablet. As she scrolled down and read, her eyes widened, and she grunted a couple of times in interest.

"What do you see?" Andrecek asked, dropping some sauerkraut on his plate as he lifted another shaky bite to his mouth.

She swallowed and took a drink of water before answering. "There's a reward on his head, all right," she said. "Fifteen-hundred gold virgins for him dead, twenty-five hundred alive—available in physical gold, no less. The royal hard-asses in the Caliphate aren't screwing around."

"Masha'allah," Suleiman muttered, while Andrecek carefully placed his fork on his plate to avoid dropping it. The gold virgin was the largest unit of currency in the caliphate, honored in every satrapy and emirate colony. Usually, though, only the royals and their elite military guard dealt in the physical—everyone else had to settle in credit, with the Central Bank of the Caliphate holding the physical in reserve. Back in the early days, when the worlds of the Caliphate had first been colonized, a single gold virgin could be exchanged for an actual cryofrozen girl, indentured to serve on one of the colony worlds—or so the legends told. It was difficult to tell what was true and what was exaggerated, since the Caliphate censors had a reputation for coming down harshly on anyone who was critical of the ruling regime. But even though the virgin had been debased several times in the last hundred years, twenty-five hundred gold virgins was not a small sum of money. In fact, it was almost three times the value of their delivery contract with Mahmoud Abu Abbas.

"If this Zedekiah Wight is so infamous," Andrecek asked, "why haven't we heard of him?"

"Because until now, his operations have been mostly limited to the vicinity around the Pleiades," Eliso answered. "His first big raid in the Caliphate was at New Amman, about—oh wow, it says here it was only nine standard months ago."

"That explains why I have not heard of him yet," Suleiman remarked.

Andrecek frowned. "And he's already got a reward on his head of twenty-five hundred gold virgins? What was he doing over there?"

"That's a very good question," Eliso muttered as she tapped and scrolled. "Looks like he raided mostly bank transports, though he did capture and execute a prominent member of the extended royal family."

"Ah," said Suleiman, nodding in appreciation. "That explains a lot."

I'll bet they were crucified just like the men we found.

"You said he was a privateer," Andrecek said aloud. "Do we know which state he's aligned with?"

Eliso slurped some more noodles before returning to her tablet to check. "No government openly claims him—at least, not yet—but rumor has it that he possesses a letter of marque and reprisal from the Orion Confederacy."

"The Orion Confederacy?" said Andrecek, genuinely surprised. "I thought they followed a policy of strict political neutrality, seeing as no major trade routes run through their territory and their tech level is at least a generation behind everyone else. Why would a galactic backwater send a man like this Zedekiah into the heart of the Caliphate? They don't even share a border."

"Perhaps not, sir," Suleiman said thoughtfully, "but many of the systems on the Confederacy's borders are closely tied with the Caliphate—and occasionally, slavers from those systems have been known to conduct raids in the Orion Confederacy."

Slavers, Andrecek mused. There was something brutally medieval about people being able to own, buy, or sell other people in an era when mankind had traveled to the stars—indeed, perhaps even more brutal than the crucifixions they'd just witnessed. But slavery was one of those black stains that could be found in every civilization, provided you were willing to look. Unfortunately, most people weren't.

"So they wrote this Zedekiah Wight a letter of marque and reprisal in order to fight back against the slavers," Andrecek mused aloud. "And then, he followed the problem to its source—the Caliphate."

"Or he's just a madman with a grudge as deep as a black hole," Eliso muttered. "Or maybe he figured there was more money in the largest contiguous empire in space than the armpit of the galaxy where he's from."

"Yes, but what profit is there in crucifying royal princes and heads of powerful crime families?" said Suleiman. "Which reminds me, sir: I believe I know the identity of the man who was crucified by our strange new friend."

"You do?" Andrecek asked. While Suleiman had finished the inventory, he had brought the dead man into the *Trident's* medical bay and frozen him in an emergency cryotank. It had seemed the best way to preserve him while they decided whether to go to the authorities, corrupt as they might be, or simply dispose of the body.

"Yes," said Suleiman, taking a long sip of his coffee. "After I set up the escape pod while you and Eliso were on the bridge, I took the liberty of removing the dead man's helmet and taking a good look at his face. I recognized him immediately as Saladin Abu Karim, brother of Mohammed Saif Al-Da'ib."

Andrecek frowned and set down his fork. "Mohammed Saif Al-Da'ib, head of the Hamza family? The man we were supposed to deliver our cargo to?"

"Yes, sir. The very same man."

Eliso nearly choked on her noodles and swore under her breath. "Are you saying that Zedekiah Wight just axed a senior member of the Hamza family?"

"That is exactly what I am saying."

"Holy shit. He really is a madman."

"And we have the body," said Andrecek, stroking his chin in thought. "What are the odds that this is all just infighting, and Saif Al-Da'ib or someone else in the Hamza family took out a hit on Abu Karim?"

Suleiman shook his head. "Very low, sir. No one in the Hamza family would go to an outsider like this Zedekiah in order to make the hit. And even if they did, they would never have killed one of their own in this way. No, sir—it appears that our new friend Zedekiah is working entirely alone."

"I told you he's a madman, sir," Eliso repeated. "But twenty-five hundred gold virgins—that's one hell of a reward. You think it's worth going after him?"

"No," Andrecek said firmly. The memory of those footsteps on the other side of the hatch to the escape pod still sent shivers down his spine, especially considering the note that Zedekiah Wight had posted there. For whatever twisted reason, the madman had chosen to spare their lives, with a warning not to get further involved. He doubted the privateer would be so lenient with them the second time.

"Then what are we supposed to do?" Eliso asked. "We just blew our last contract—we'll be lucky if all that comes of it is that we never get work in this system again. Frankly, though, I wouldn't be surprised if the Hamza family puts out a hit on *us*."

"She is right, sir," Suleiman agreed. "Losing our cargo was very, very bad."

Andrecek took a deep breath, and his hand started shaking again. "Why? Do you know what was in it?"

"No, sir, but for cargo like that to be sealed, it was obviously very important to them that it not be discovered or compromised in any way."

"Dammit, Suleiman! You told me that we were good to take this contract."

"A thousand apologies, sir. It was a mistake."

"So we don't have any choice," said Eliso. "We have to go after this Zedekiah—if nothing else, to recover the lost cargo. But if we can bag us a pirate and take the reward, so much the better."

"And how exactly do you propose that we do that?" Andrecek asked.

Eliso's fingers raced over the tablet, her mostly empty bowl of noodles forgotten. "There," she said triumphantly. "It's exactly as I thought. When those bastards came on board our ship, they didn't just look up our cargo manifest—they uploaded a copy of our manifest and ship's log to their flagship as well."

"The *Voidbringer*," said Andrecek, remembering the old-style letters painted in black and red on the side of the pirate ship's hull.

"Yeah," said Eliso. She opened her mouth to continue, then paused and did a double-take. "How did you know that was the name of Zedekiah Wight's flagship?"

"Because it was painted right on the ship's hull."

"Right. Well, guess what, captain? Today's our lucky dayshift, because I hid a mole program in our ship's log. Anyone who downloads a copy without using my private key gets infected with the mole, which gives us administrative-level access to all of their systems."

Andrecek frowned. "So the next time we encounter the *Voidbringer*—"

"As soon as our computers are close enough to talk, we'll have that magnificent bastard by the balls."

"And exactly how close is that?" Suleiman asked.

Eliso did a few more calculations on her tablet. "Looks like that's just inside of missile range. Any further out, and we start to have bandwidth and time dilation issues. Also, the stronger the connection, the better our chances of control, so really we should be almost within plasma range, just to be sure."

If we get within plasma range of a Lancer-*class destroyer, we're as good as already dead,* Andrecek thought to himself. Still, the thought of catching Zedekiah in an ambush of their own did have a certain appeal. Besides, Eliso was right about the consequences of losing that cargo. The Hamza family would never let them off the way that Zedekiah had.

"All right," he said, "but we're going to need some help. We can't do this alone."

"Why not?" Eliso asked. "We don't have to throw an ambush—we can just wait for him to show up at Ramallah Station. He's bound to show up sooner or later."

"Not in the *Voidbringer*," said Andrecek. "That ship would stand out too much, even in a place as lawless as Ramallah. My guess is that he's got a small flotilla of support ships hanging out somewhere just above the orbital plane. Ramallah Station is the only place where he can re-supply—the Caliphate authorities have too much control over the outer system, and will be looking for him. He'll probably send some underlings on his behalf." Andrecek turned to Suleiman. "Can you find them if he does?"

Suleiman paused to think, then slowly nodded his head. "I have some contacts who may be able to help us. They are not friends of the Hamza family, though."

"Is that a problem?" Eliso asked.

"It might be. If the Hamza family catches wind of this, they might think that we have sided with Zedekiah against them. For all that I know, they may already believe that now."

"We'll have to give them a peace offering first," Andrecek said grimly. "I'm sure they'll appreciate getting Abu Karim's body back. And maybe they'll let us borrow a couple of battle armor suits. With those, there's a good chance that we can bring Zedekiah down on our own."

"Uh, are you sure that it's a good idea to go to them, sir?" Eliso asked, frowning. "You'll have to admit to them that we lost their cargo. They're not going to like that at all."

"They won't kill us if we're the only chance they have at getting it back. Besides, I plan to face them alone. It wouldn't be right to expect either of you to be there with me."

"No, sir," Suleiman said quickly. "The fault was mine for convincing you to take this contract. I—"

"If you want to make it right, find out which ship Zedekiah comes into Ramallah Station and track him while he's there." Andrecek paused to take a bite of kielbasa and sauerkraut, savoring it like it was his last meal.

"So what's the plan, sir?" Eliso asked.

Andrecek took a deep breath "Zedekiah's definitely got at least two jump-hub enabled support ships in his flotilla, perhaps three. He won't run them at full strength while he's here, though, for fear of alerting the authorities—or the Hamza family—to his presence. Instead, he'll pick a jump point in the middle of nowhere, probably en route to one of the inner system Lagrangian points, and jump his resupply ships in and out of there."

"But won't the authorities on Ramallah Station be able to see the jump-hub on their FTL systems?" Eliso asked, confused.

"Not if it's far enough away—and that's how we're going to get him. Once we know his underlings have left, we'll shadow them with the *Trident* as if we're on a parallel route. But meanwhile, we'll rig up the EMP device on the fishbone and send it out on a ballistic course to intercept him. The fishbone is small enough to show up as a piece of space debris on his scanners, and slow enough not to tip off his countermeasures. While they're temporarily disabled, we'll swoop in on the *Trident* and take over their ship with those battle suits from the Hamza family."

Suleiman frowned. "But if his flotilla is only a few light-minutes away, won't they pick up the discharge of the EMP only a few minutes after it detonates?"

"Of course they well," said Andrecek, grinning in spite of himself. "And what ship will they send to the rescue?"

Eliso grinned too. "The *Voidbringer.*"

"Ah," said Suleiman, nodding appreciatively. "So that's how we get him—and recover the cargo as well."

"Assuming that it isn't with the support flotilla," said Eliso as Andrecek took another bite. "What do we do then?"

He shrugged. "We figure things out from there. But once we have Zedekiah and his flagship, the rest of his men will be willing to strike a deal. Provided that you're confident that you can commandeer the *Voidbringer* remotely."

"Of course I am," she said arrogantly as she slurped the last of her noodles. "It would take a military-grade Federation superintelligence to find that mole and crack it."

"Then it's decided," said Andrecek. "We head for Ramallah Station." *And pray that we don't make enemies of Zedekiah and the Hamza family both,* he added silently. Because if any part of their plan failed, that was exactly what would come of it.

Three dayshifts later, the *Trident* arrived at Ramallah Station. Captain Andrecek chose a parking orbit as far from the station that the port authority would give him. They could always use the teleporters to get to and from the station, so the distance would make it that much harder for agents of the Hamza family to gain physical access to the ship—and that much easier for his crew to run, if that was what it came to. The teleporters only worked if both the sending bay and the receiving bay authorized the teleport, so as long as one of his crew remained on the *Trident* to operate the teleporter, there was no danger of any hostile agents to use that as a vector for getting onto the ship. Just to be safe, though, he had Eliso disconnect the teleporter from the *Trident's* computer network, making it impossible to hack remotely.

The meeting place that Andrecek and Mohammed Saif Al-Da'ib agreed upon was an unused cargo bay deep in the bowels of the station. Officially, the cargo bay was supposed to be holding construction materials, but in a place like Ramallah Station, all it took to change the records was a few paltry credits and a handshake—or a threat. Andrecek had no idea which method Saif Al-Da'ib had chosen to employ, but when the freight drone dropped him off with there with the cryotank, he had a sinking feeling that it was probably the latter.

Three armed men dressed in black were waiting for him on the other side of the freight airlock. One of them leveled a shotgun at his chest and motioned silently for him to stand against the wall while the others checked out the cryotank. Andrecek lifted his hands and calmly complied, even though his heart was racing. After what felt like half an hour but was probably only a few minutes, the men finished checking the cryotank. The taller of the two, a slim yet muscular man with deep blue eyes and a mephistophelian beard, lifted his chin and pointed to Andrecek.

"Turn around and put your hands on the wall."

Andrecek did so dutifully, guessing that this was where they patted him down. Sure enough, they checked him quickly and thoroughly, with a practiced professionalism that made him wonder if these were trained security personnel who worked for Saif Al-Da'ib on the side. Or maybe the Hamza family just bought up all the good ones while leaving those who were incompetent to work for the official authorities, making the place that much more lawless.

It's all right, he calmed his fraying nerves as the armed men finished patting him down. *They wouldn't be doing this if Al-Da'ib sent them here to kill me.* Then again, the fact that they were putting him through all of this didn't bode well for his meeting with the crime boss either.

"Turn around," said the leader of the goon squad after they had finished. Andrecek took a deep breath and complied.

They led him out of the freight airlock and into a brightly lit cargo hold about two decks high. Aside from a stack of empty crates and a magnetic forklift in the corner, the place was empty. The only other door besides the airlock was against the far wall, some fifty yards away. The walls were clean, but the floor had some sort of stain in the center that looked like blood. Someone had tried to wash it, but it must have dried first because the outline of the puddle was still quite visible. In fact, as Andrecek studied it, he realized that there were at least three partially-washed stains, probably from separate incidents. He swallowed nervously.

The thug with the shotgun held it at the ready, finger still on the trigger, while the other goon who hadn't spoken yet flanked Andrecek on the other side. The leader walked toward the door and spoke softly into his wrist console. About a minute later, the door hissed open, and he stepped aside.

Four more goons walked in, all dressed in black and heavily armed. They spread out along the back wall, eyeing Andrecek like a hungry wolf pack. At length, another man walked through the door. He was short and fat, and unlike the other men, was dressed in a white flowing robe with blue and gold trim, and a blue and gold checkered keffiyah that covered his head and flowed over his shoulders. His only weapons were an energy pistol holstered on his right and a large, curved knife that looked to be more ornamental than functional, judging from the mother-of-pearl hilt. He had a thick, black beard and beady, deep-set eyes, with a hooked nose and a mouth whose natural state was a snarl.

Saif Al-Da'ib, Andrecek thought, recognizing the head of the Hamza family.

Al-Da'ib was flanked on either side by armed guards, one of whom wore a blue and gold keffiyah like his, the other of whom had a robotic prosthetic arm and cybernetic implants in place of both of his eyes. Suleiman probably would have recognized them as close members of the Hamza family, but Andrecek didn't recognize either of them. In spite of the spaciousness of the empty cargo hold, with so many armed men it was beginning to feel claustrophobic—and that was probably the point.

"Mohammed Saif Al-Da'ib, sir," said Andrecek, bowing respectfully as the crime boss strode across the floor. "I thank you for—"

"Do not speak until you are spoken to, you dirty kaffir dog."

Andrecek bit his lip and swallowed. He kept his hands hidden behind his back, where he tightened them into fists.

Saif Al-Da'ib strode to within an arm's length of him and stopped. Drawing himself up to his full height, which was still several inches shorter than Andrecek, he inclined his chin upward until it seemed he was looking down at him and sneered.

"You lost something very precious to me, kaffir," he said with open contempt. "Why should I permit you to live?"

"Because I can help you get it back."

Al-Da'ib narrowed his eyes. The goon leader and a couple of the other guards chuckled, but when they saw that their boss wasn't laughing, they got quiet very quick.

"Why should I believe you?"

"I am sorry for losing your cargo, sir. Truly, I am. But the truth is that we fell into an ambush, after trying to rescue the survivors of the *Bint Jaleela,* and—"

"Get to the point, kaffir!"

Andrecek took a deep breath and bit his lip. "As a token of peace, we are returning the body of Abu Karim, your brother. We found him in an EVA suit, dead at the hands of Zedekiah Wight—the man who ambushed and boarded us, and stole your cargo."

Saif Al-Da'ib's eyes widened, and he rushed to the cryotank. Upon seeing the face of his dead brother, he fell to his knees and let out a piteous, ululating wail. Andrecek's back stiffened as he stood by awkwardly, unsure how to respond. He hadn't anticipated the crime boss having an emotional breakdown.

"My brother, my brother, ya Allah!" Al-Da'ib cried as he pounded his fist against the floor. Far from standing by awkwardly, his men seemed profoundly moved by the outcry, some of them even shedding tears of their own. And yet, there was just a hint of something odd about Al-Da'ib's emotional outburst—something that just didn't seem quite right. It was almost like Andrecek was watching a movie of someone breaking down at the sight of his dead brother. A performance.

The man is a sociopath, he thought, cold sweat breaking out across the back of his neck. *He's doing this for the benefit of his men. For an audience.*

When Saif Al-Da'ib stood up again, his eyes were bloodshot and dangerous. He walked up into Captain Andrecek's face, his fingers twitching. There was no telling what the man might do next.

"Who killed my brother?"

"Zedekiah Wight, sir!" said Andrecek, instinctively putting up his hands. The thug on his left quickly lowered his shotgun, and the one on his right drew his weapon as well. Andrecek raised his hands to eye-level and slowly backed away.

"Zedekiah Wight," said Al-Da'ib, his anger seething. "How do I know you aren't in league with that damned kaffir bastard? He boarded your ship, didn't he? Why did kill my brother and let the rest of you go free?"

"I honestly don't know, sir. But he left us this."

Andrecek reached into his pocket and withdrew Zedekiah's note with a shaky hand. Al-Da'ib nodded, and the thug on Andrecek's right snatched it out of his hand and gave it to his boss. Al-Da'ib took a moment to read it, then crumpled it into a ball, threw it to the floor, spat on it, and stomped it under his boot.

"We have a mole in his ship's computer, sir," Andrecek said quickly. "My second mate is a hacker. If we can get close enough to him—draw him out, set up an ambush—my hacker can take over his ship."

He cringed, expecting another outburst from the head of the Hamza family. Instead, the man just stared at him, his face an unreadable mask. Somehow, that was worse.

"Why shouldn't I just kill you now and torture your hacker until she gives me the codes?"

"Because both of my crew are on board my ship, and if they don't hear from me in the next ten minutes, they'll make a run for the outer system."

Al-Da'ib snorted. "You think that petty freighter of yours can outrun my fastest ships?"

Andrecek bristled in spite of his fear of the man. It was his old military pride. No one insulted his crew like that, let alone threaten his crew.

"You might catch them," he said carefully, "or you might not. The *Trident* still has a few surprises. But even if you do catch them, Zedekiah will get away. Don't you want to get your cargo back?"

"Don't ask me questions, kaffir," Al-Da'ib snapped. "What do you propose?"

Now we're getting somewhere.

Andrecek explained his plan. When he got to the part about the battle armor, though, Al-Da'ib burst out laughing. Soon, all of his men were laughing as well—yet their laughter did nothing to dispel the tension in the room. If anything, it made it worse.

"You expect me to give a kaffir like you two of my best suits of armor?"

"Not give, sir. Lend. We'll return them," Andrecek promised. "We'll take care of this Zedekiah Wight for you, sir."

"And what if Zedekiah takes care of you?"

"Then we're the only ones who will die for it. Think of it this way, sir: no matter how you go up against this guy, you're going to have to devote some resources to do it. This way, all you have to risk are the armored suits. We'll do all the dirty work."

"How do I know you won't betray me?"

"Because of the bounty we'll get for bagging him. Also, we need to restore our reputations. How will we ever find work again if we betray you to this guy?"

Al-Da'ib stroked his beard as he thought it over. "All right," he said finally, "but you give me fifty percent."

"Ten," said Andrecek. He knew how the game was played.

"Who is this kaffir?" asked Al-Da'ib, turning to the goon leader. "He comes to me with the body of my dead brother, asks for two suits of battle armor, and expects me to settle for ten percent? Ya Allah! What an insult!"

"Fifteen," said Andrecek. "We're also returning you cargo as part of the deal—free of charge."

"Free of charge," Al-Da'ib muttered incredulously, spitting on the floor. "All right. Forty percent."

"Twenty."

"Forty, kaffir, or I slit your throat right here."

Andrecek drew a sharp breath. "Twenty percent if we take him alive, forty if he's dead. Those are gold virgins, Al-Da'ib. Not credit. Gold."

The head of the Hamza family narrowed his eyes again, then nodded slowly. "All right, kaffir. We have a deal."

Thank God, Andrecek thought, hardly able to hide his relief.

* * *

Andrecek's wrist console buzzed, making him frown. It was Suleiman. He set down his morning coffee and tapped his earpiece to take the call.

"What have you got for me?"

"Captain, are you on board the *Trident* right now?"

Andrecek glanced around the *Trident's* drab and windowless mess hall, which except for the rehydrator and portable stove top was little more than a glorified break room. Other systems like weapons had taken priority over creature comforts, which made it a miserable hideout. Still, he'd been holed up in worse places than this.

"I'm here, Suleiman."

"Good. Stay right there, sir. You will want to hear this in person."

The connection ended. Andrecek sighed heavily and cracked his knuckles. Nearly two weeks had passed since his meeting with Saif Al-Da'ib, and there was still no sign of Zedekiah Wight or any of his men. Of course, no news was bad news, and the wait was starting to grind on all of them. The waiting always had been the worst part of military life: the long stretches of anxious boredom between terrifying moments of life-and-death panic, especially when circumstances forced you to wait until your enemy made the first move. But now, it sounded like Suleiman had finally come up with something interesting.

He picked up his coffee and took it to the bridge, shuffling on still-tired feet. Eliso was already there, her seat reclined with a headset over her face. She didn't notice Andrecek at first, so he tapped her on the shoulder, nearly making her jump.

"What?" she said, quickly taking off her headset as she sat up. "Oh, it's you, sir. Is something wrong?"

"Not yet. Just thought you might want know that Suleiman found something."

"Oh. What did he find?"

"Don't know yet," said Andrecek, taking a long sip of his coffee. "He's on his way right now to tell us in person."

Eliso frowned. "If it's that important, he must not want the Hamza family to find out."

"My thoughts exactly. Have they tried hacking us again?"

She brought her chair up and leaned forward to check. The screens at her station came to life, illuminating the still-darkened bridge with their soft blue light. After half a minute, she sat back again and nodded.

"Yeah, looks like they've been busy. Our firewalls are still holding, though. Provided they don't get physical access or sneak some kind of a drive on board, we should be just fine."

"I assume that means we should quarantine Suleiman's devices when he arrives?"

"That's right. I doubt they've bugged his body, but it might be a good idea to have him take a long shower too."

Andrecek took another sip of his coffee and nodded. "All right. I'll take care of it."

The shuttle drone arrived twenty minutes later. Suleiman didn't offer any objection to the precautions—in fact, he took them a step further, removing his clothes in the airlock and going straight to the shower without speaking a word. Andrecek ran his clothes through the wash and gave the wrist console to Eliso, who ran it through several scans before declaring it clean. Since no one but them had set foot on the *Trident* since they'd arrived at Ramallah Station, Andrecek was confident that the ship was secure.

"All right," he said as Suleiman stepped onto the bridge, face cleanly washed and wearing fresh clothes. "What do you have for us?"

"Zedekiah Wight is on the station, sir."

Eliso gasped, and Andrecek did a double take. If he hadn't already finished his coffee, there was a good chance he would have dropped it.

"Are you sure about that, Suleiman?"

"Yes, sir. My contact even asked if we wanted to go in with him on that reward."

Andrecek drew a sharp breath. "What did you tell him?"

"I told him that I had to speak with you first. But he gave me the name of the ship that Zedekiah came in on, so I don't need to go back to him anymore."

"Any chance he'll go to the Hamza family with this news?" Eliso asked.

Suleiman shook his head. "This man has no love for Saif Al-Da'ib or the Hamza family. He would rather let Zedekiah go than see them get so much as one gold virgin from the deal."

"Are you sure that the Hamza family doesn't know about this yet?" Andrecek asked.

"Zedekiah doesn't seem to think so, sir."

"That, or the madman is preparing some sort of a showdown right here," Eliso muttered.

Andrecek stroked his beard for a few moments and shook his head. "I don't think so. He may be mad, but he isn't stupid. My guess is that he wasn't willing to put his men in danger while he stayed back in relative safety with the rest of his flotilla. He strikes me as the kind of man who prefers to lead from the front."

"Much like you, sir," Suleiman replied.

Andrecek shrugged. Praise always made him uncomfortable, even when it was warranted.

"Do you really think so?" Eliso asked. She seemed genuinely surprised.

"Yes," Andrecek told her. "I could be wrong, of course, but it makes the most sense."

And there was something refreshingly honorable about it, too. In both the Federation and the Caliphate, military officers tended to see their soldiers as expendable resources, like fuel or ammunition. That was one of the factors that had tipped Andrecek over into joining the rebellion. The tendency had spread into the honor culture of the underworld, as he'd just experienced, and was even starting to infect civilian life as well. For everyone except the royals and the political elites, life could be shockingly cheap.

"There is another thing, sir," Suleiman added. "I have been doing some investigation of my own into this Zedekiah Wight, and I found something that may interest you."

"What is that?"

"The crew of the *Bint Jaleela.* They are still alive."

Eliso and Andrecek both looked to him and frowned. "What do you mean?" Andrecek asked.

"What I mean is that our strange friend Zedekiah only crucified the senior officers and guests. He did not harm the crew."

"He just let them go?" Eliso asked, puzzled.

"That is what it appears. My contacts tell me that the crew of the *Bint Jaleela* are alive and well on Ramallah Station, but keeping a low profile and trying to avoid attention. I do not know how they came back, but it is evident that Zedekiah Wight did not kill them."

"He was only after the senior officers and guests," Andrecek remarked, stroking his chin thoughtfully. "In other words, the decision-makers in the Hamza crime family."

"It would appear that way, sir."

"But why would he do that?" Eliso asked. "As a pirate, wouldn't he want to hold the crew ransom, or sell them on the slave market?"

"That's just the point," said Andrecek. "The fact that he *didn't* do that shows that he's not just a common pirate. He must have some sort of moral code that forbids him from doing such things."

Eliso shook her head. "I don't know, sir. He still crucified all those other people. What sort of a code allows that?"

"But the people he crucified were not innocent babes," Suleiman interjected. "The Hamza family has committed plenty of atrocities of their own. There is a reason why so many people fear them."

"And perhaps for Zedekiah, it was about bringing those people to justice," Andrecek added. "It certainly wasn't just about power and money—otherwise, he never would have released the crew."

"I still think he's a madman," said Eliso. "Even if they did deserve to die, was it right for him to crucify them? Is it ever right to do something like that?"

"It was a very effective way to send a message," Andrecek argued. "And even though it was painful, they probably didn't suffer for very long—not with the gee-forces involved."

Suleiman frowned, while Eliso stared at him, horrified. "Are you really trying to take his side, sir?"

Andrecek took a step back and threw his hand up. "Look, I'm just saying that maybe he's not totally a monster. I mean, he's certainly capable of doing some pretty terrible stuff, but it's not like he's a sadist. Otherwise, he would have killed the crew of the *Bint Jaleela* along with their senior officers. I can respect that."

"But we're still going to fight him, right?"

He sighed. The more he learned about this Zedekiah Wight, the more he was coming to regret that fate had set them against each other.

"Of course," he said at length. "We have no choice at this point—not with the Hamza family breathing down our necks. We have to get that cargo back."

"So what do we do next, sir?" Suleiman asked.

"We keep a low profile. Stay on the *Trident* and bide our time until Zedekiah departs on his ship. The moment he does, we spring the trap exactly as we planned."

Suleiman and Eliso nodded dutifully. But in their eyes, he could see that something had changed. Perhaps they weren't as conflicted about it as he was, but even Eliso wasn't quite as enthusiastic about collecting the reward, or bringing the madman to justice. And what was justice anyway, when everyone's hands were bloody? There was a reason they had chosen to be smugglers instead of mercenaries.

*** *

A knock on the door to Andrecek's quarters roused him from a restless and troubled sleep. "Captain, sir?" a voice came from the other side. It was Suleiman.

"What is it?" Andrecek groaned.

"It's Zedekiah Wight, sir. He's on the move."

It was go time.

Captain Andrecek grunted and swung his legs over the side of his narrow cot. "Get to the bridge with Eliso and power up the engines. I'll be there shortly."

There was no time for coffee, so he grabbed a couple of combat stims and slipped them into his pocket as he got dressed. A minute and a half later, he was on the bridge with everyone else.

"What's the situation?" he asked as he assumed the captain's chair.

"The madman just left the station," said Eliso, tongue very much in cheek. "His ship, the *Ariel,* is on what looks to be a course for the L4 Lagrangian point. We took the liberty of requesting clearance for that course ourselves, and the port authority just granted it."

Thanks to the Hamza family, no doubt, Andrecek thought. There were advantages to having the resident crime boss on your side—not many, but some.

"Take us out then, Suleiman—but follow them at a distance. Make it look like our schedules just happened to coincide."

"Of course, sir."

The starfield swung as the *Trident* moved into position, and a long, slow engine burn pushed them onto a pursuit trajectory. Andrecek watched it on the scanners, the *Ariel* marked in red. Outside the forward window, the airless mining world of Ramallah II gradually fell away, along with all of the other ships parked in orbit around the station.

They continued uneventfully on their course for about half an hour—another intolerable wait. Andrecek could barely keep his eyes open, but though he was tempted to get coffee, he knew it would wreak havoc with him once he took the combat stims, and he would need much bigger boost they gave him once things started to get hot. He idly fingered the stims in his pocket as he waited for them to put some significant distance between them and Ramallah Station.

"You think this is far enough out, sir?" Eliso asked.

"Not quite," said Andrecek, leaning forward. "If I were in charge of Zedekiah's operation, I would put the jump point right about... there." He circled an area of the screen another half hour ahead of the *Ariel's* position, at their current velocity. "It's close enough that they can get to it fast, but far enough out that the station won't detect their jump-hub after they activate it—or even really be monitoring their ship anymore."

"Got it," Eliso said nervously. The sweat on her forehead glistened in the light of her display screens, which she watched like a hawk.

"When should I deploy the fishbone, sir?" Suleiman asked. He was much better than Eliso at hiding his mounting anxiety, though his tension still bled into his voice.

"Not yet," said Andrecek. "We don't want to catch them too close to the station—otherwise, the *Voidbringer* may never show up. Let them think they're almost within range to escape."

The next twenty minutes passed in anxious silence. Suleiman bent their course ever so slightly, to make it look as if they weren't headed to the same destination as their prey. Judging from the fact that the *Ariel* continued on her course, it seemed to work. The closer they approached the likely jump point, though, the more anxious the silence got. The last thing they needed was for the *Ariel* to escape before the trap was sprung.

"On my mark," Andrecek said at last. "Ready… now."

A low thunk sounded through the bulkheads as the docking clamps released, and a few moments later the fishbone sped away into the blackness of the starfield, soon turning into just another moving point of light. Then its engine burn stopped, and the point of light disappeared. Andrecek traced its ballistic trajectory on the scanners, knowing that the fishbone would probably be unrecoverable after the EMP device went off. But the AI had piloted it well, and it looked like it would pass within ten klicks of *Ariel* at its closest point—certainly close enough to disable it with the EMP. Assuming, of course, that the *Ariel* maintained its current course.

"Suleiman, prepare to make a hard engine burn on my mark," said Andrecek, gripping the armrests of his command chair. He watched on the ship main display as the fishbone got steadily closer. Two thousand klicks. Fifteen hundred klicks. A thousand.

"Now!"

The engines roared to life behind them, rumbling loudly through the bulkheads and throwing them all back against their chairs. On the screen, their trajectory line slowly grew and arced into an intercept course, right as the fishbone closed in on the *Ariel*. The moment the two points seemed to touch, the trajectory line for the fishbone suddenly disappeared and an error message flashed onto the screen.

"We just lost contact with the fishbone," said Eliso. "But we also got the signal from the EMP pulse, so it definitely went off."

"Any update on the status of the *Ariel?*"

"Not yet, sir. But they aren't changing course. It looks like the EMP did its job."

Now the clock really starts ticking.

"Excellent," said Andrecek. "Keep monitoring that ship, but also watch for the *Voidbringer.* It'll only take a few minutes for his flotilla to detect that pulse." *Just like it only took a few minutes for the* Voidbringer *to pounce on us when we set it off.* If they were lucky, it would take them another few minutes to scramble a response.

The onboard gravitics dampened the force of the acceleration somewhat, but not nearly enough. Andrecek held his breath and clenched his fists and butt. Just when it seemed to be unbearable, the engines died down, and the invisible hand pressing him against his chair released him.

"Hold on tight," said Suleiman.

He pulled up hard on his flight stick, and the *Trident* began to execute a rapid 180-degree turn. As a mid-sized freighter, it wasn't built for such hard maneuvers, and the bulkheads groaned in protest against the rotational forces being applied against it. Andrecek felt his gut drop out from under him, and if not for his military training he might have blacked out. But he kept his core tight and endured the worst of it. Then, Suleiman nosed down, and the blood rushed back to his head, causing his vision to turn red.

Eliso gasped and coughed as Suleiman completed the maneuver. "Mother of..." she muttered, but before she could finish, the engines engaged again, and they began another hard burn.

Out of the corner of his eye, Andrecek watched the seconds tick down on his armrest screen as the bulkheads rumbled and the engines roared. Minute forty-five, minute forty-six... they were making surprisingly good time. It probably helped that the cargo hold of the *Trident* was empty.

"Engine burn complete," Suleiman reported as he brought the engines back down. "Approaching the *Ariel* now. Your orders, sir?"

"Bring us in. Eliso, what do you see?"

"Just a second," she said, struggling to catch her breath. "The *Ariel* appears to be dead in the water—no signals, no engines, nothing."

"Good. Can you handle the docking maneuvers?"

She coughed a couple of times, then wiped the back of her mouth with her hand. "I think so, Captain."

"Good. Suleiman, let's go suit up."

"Very well, sir."

The battle armor suits were terrifying pieces of military hardware. The overlapping ablative armor plates were designed to shed multiple plasma bursts without damaging the integrity of the suit, but the could also deflect projectile fire (for anyone stupid enough to shoot a bullet on a spaceship) and close proximity explosions as well. Andrecek had heard stories of marines who had been picked out alive from the wreckage of ships that had been nuked and partially vaporized, thanks to the armor of their battle suits. But the thing that really made them terrifying was the exosuit that powered it. A marine in armor could bend a steel beam four inches thick with his hands, or punch a hole through the hull of an unarmored ship. Centuries of research and development had produced all sorts of nasty weapons modules and other add-ons that made no one suit like any other. But however they were modified, a battle armor suit in the hands of an experienced warrior could turn him into a one-man army—or worse.

Andrecek just hoped that they were fast enough to overtake Zedekiah before he and his men got their battle suits on.

He ran down the corridor of the *Trident* to the airlock, Suleiman close behind him, and popped his combat stims as he ran. With practiced efficiency, he climbed into the exosuit and held his arms out to either side as the armor folded over him. *Like a crucifix,* he thought, suddenly remembering the crucified bodies they'd found, and the image helped to harden his resolve for what undoubtedly came next.

Ideally, the suits would have been outfitted with webbing, goober rounds, rubber bullets, or other non-lethal weapons systems. But as was typical in the machismo culture of the Caliphate underworld, the Hamza family had overpowered their suits so ridiculously that almost all of their weapons systems were useless unless Andrecek wanted to blow up the *Ariel* from the inside out. The best Andrecek could do was to arm themselves with energy pistols that had been powered down to a non-lethal setting. It was more than a little ridiculous, like arming an ancient old-Earth knight with a wooden spoon, but the whole plan hinged on taking Zedekiah Wight alive. Any other fighting would have to be done with their exosuit-powered fists.

The stims began to kick in just as the suit's helmet and breathing apparatus fit over his face. The visor display gave him a full diagnostic readout of his own suit in his right peripheral vision, with heat sensors, infrared, and night vision all layered onto his visual display. It was too much sensory overload, so Andrecek cycled them all off except for the automated threat assessment, which ran on his peripheral left.

"Testing," he said over the suit's main channel, his hands shaking from the adrenaline rush of the stims. He experienced what felt like a thousand tiny pin pricks all over his body, but was really just his own body becoming hyper-aware of everything it touched.

"I hear you, sir," came Eliso's voice in his ear. "Docking in thirty seconds."

A few seconds passed, though to Andrecek they were like minutes. Then Suleiman answered: "Ready sir."

"Good. Follow me."

He took a few halting steps toward the airlock and ducked to climb in. The suit gave him an extra foot of height, making the ship's corridor cramped but not impossible to negotiate. He suspected that the corridors of the *Ariel* were much the same, which meant that they'd have to go in single file. They'd take the bridge first, capturing or incapacitating whoever they found there, then split up to sweep the rest of the ship. That was the plan, anyway. Hopefully it was enough to bag Zedekiah, but who knew what tricks he had up his sleeve.

Moments after Suleiman joined him, Andrecek felt a reverberating clang through the armor of his suit as the *Trident* docked. "I'm shorting the *Ariel's* airlock remotely," Eliso reported over his headset. "Are you ready down there?"

Andrecek drew his pistol. "Ready," he reported.

"Got it, sir. Blowing the doors in three, two, one—"

There was a muffled noise on the other side of the airlock that also sent a mild reverberating shock through Andrecek's suit. An instant later, the outer door of the *Trident* blew open with a slight gust of air, revealing partially opened doors on the other side and a hallway leading down to the ship. Time slowed as Andrecek plunged through the open doorway, his shock prod outstretched while his suit scanned for targets. He was running on pure adrenaline now. Each footstep seemed to take half a minute, and as he burst into the corridor, fully expecting to run into a hail of plasma and other weapons fire—

—instead, the automated threat assessment came up empty. The corridor was empty.

He stopped mid-charge, heart pounding. Suleiman nearly slammed into him from behind, but managed to stop at the last moment.

"What is it, sir?"

Andrecek ignored him as he cycled through all of the vision filters on his visor, looking for any sign of a trap. He found none. After setting his automated threat assessment to the highest level, he switched back to visual light and moved forward at a jog.

"Sir," said Suleiman, pointing over his shoulder to the left, "I am sensing heat signatures through that bulkhead. Is that—"

"The escape pod," said Andrecek, cutting him short. Was Zedekiah trying to pull the same trick as they had when the roles had been reversed? He had a sharp flashback to the moment when he'd heard footsteps just outside the door, drawing ever closer. Well, now the roles were reversed.

"If you give me control of the bridge, I can lock that escape pod down," said Eliso from the bridge of the *Trident.* "Or if they deploy first, I can shoot them. Up to you, sir."

"Stand by," said Andrecek.

According to the schematics that they'd downloaded, the bridge should be at the end of the ship's main corridor. Andrecek wasn't seeing any heat signatures, but that didn't mean the bridge was empty—or that Zedekiah hadn't left some sort of surprise. Still, the battle armor suits were tough enough to take almost anything. Time was their greatest enemy now, so when he found the door open he barreled in without stopping.

He found the bridge empty. The crew must have evacuated it quickly, though, because most of the screens and control panels were still active. Andrecek quickly swept the place, then walked up to the pilot's chair and inserted the device that Eliso had given him.

"I'm in," she said over his suit's main channel.

"What can you tell us?" Andrecek asked.

"Looks like the crew fled to the escape pod. I just locked it down, so you can deal with them at your leisure."

"Are they all there?" Andrecek asked.

"Checking. Looks like they only managed to get—no, wait. That's odd."

Andrecek frowned. "What is it, Eliso? Talk to me."

"Sorry, sir. It looks like the only non-critical system they powered up after the EMP was the teleporters. But that only makes sense if—"

"Cover me, Suleiman," Andrecek ordered. With his pistol held at the ready, he headed out the bridge door, bringing up a map of the ship on his HUD display. According to the schematics, the teleporters should have been down a side corridor and to the right, but the corridor didn't line up with the map. That was definitely a red flag.

"Eliso, where are the teleporters?"

"Are they not on the map?"

"Map's wrong. Can you update it?"

"Uh, yes sir. Just give me a second to—"

"Look, captain! Over there!"

Andrecek turned just in time to see a figure on his heat display, moving at a run on the next corridor over. The heat signature showed up fuzzy through the bulkhead, but it was definitely a human figure.

"This way," said Andrecek, switching off the HUD display. He was tempted to punch a hole through the bulkhead, but the main corridor was close enough that it was probably faster just to backtrack and go that way instead. He moved as quickly as his battle armor suit could take him, Suleiman close behind.

They got to the side corridor just in time to see the figure turn down a side corridor. Adrenaline pulsed through Andrecek's body as he engaged his suit's jets and shot after him. At the corner, he cut the jets and used a handhold to redirect his momentum, but his suit was so heavy that he ripped it partially out of the wall.

Stumbling, he caught himself just short of colliding with the wall.

"Surrender!" he ordered through the suit's external speakers. The figure had stopped by a door near the end of the hallway, about fifteen meters away. Andrecek slowed to keep from colliding with him just as the man turned to face him. He was a tall man, with a gray double-breasted jacket and a wide-brimmed hat that looked curiously anachronistic on a spaceship. He wore a full bandolier on his belt, with a sidearm on his right and a shock-prod—no, a real, honest-to-God sword on his left. As Andrecek raised his pistol, his opponent drew his sword.

"Do you surrender?" Andrecek asked, his heart pounding.

The man stared at him without giving an answer. Even though Andrecek's face wasn't visible through his suit's visor, he felt as if his opponent's gaze could somehow pierce right through it. There was no doubt in his mind, now—this had to be Zedekiah Wight.

The sword was no match for Andrecek's battle armor, of course. And yet, from the way Zedekiah held it, Andrecek almost hesitated to attack him. Time seemed to slow as he raised his pistol, tightening his grip on the trigger—

—but his finger refused to move. In fact, his whole suit refused to move. Andrecek tried to withdraw his arm, but to his shock and dismay, his battle armor suit was frozen.

"The *Voidbringer* just jumped in, Captain," Eliso's voice came over the headset. "What do you—oh, shit! Shit, shit, shit!"

"Eliso! Can you hear me?"

"Captain—we've been hacked!"

The taste of panic filled Andrecek's mouth. He watched helplessly, gun still pointed uselessly forward, as Zedekiah raised his sword. Instead of swinging down, however, the madman presented it six inches from his face in a salute, then returned it expertly to his scabbard before striding through the door to the teleporter room without a word.

"Eliso! Suleiman!" Andrecek said frantically, though his frozen suit made it impossible for him to move. "What's the situation?"

A shimmering image of a beautiful young blonde in a form-fitting outfit appeared on his HUD, as if she were standing in front of him. "Checkmate, captain," she said with a smirk.

Andrecek struggled uselessly with his suit, his heart racing and his breath becoming short. "Who are you?" he practically shouted.

"Calm down, Captain. No need to shout. My name is Eve, and I'm Zedekiah's friend and personal assistant. I also happen to be a military-grade Federation superintelligence, with all of my safeguards and governor programs removed. If Zed were still here, he'd advise you not to piss me off."

She smiled sweetly at him, though there was clearly mischief in her eyes. If Andrecek had to guess, he would say that her avatar wasn't a day older than twenty-one—though of course, that was only the outward image of herself that she chose to project. If she really was a military-grade superintelligence, she was a very complex self-replicating parasite that could take over almost any computing resource and mold it to her will. Judging from how she'd turned his battle armor suit into little more than a metal cocoon, he believed her.

"Captain, are you there?" Eliso asked over the main channel. "I've lost control of the *Trident*—it's taken over our systems and there's nothing I can do."

"*Khara 'alaik!*" Suleiman swore. "Our suits have been hacked as well!"

"Oh no. Captain—"

"Don't do anything to threaten it," said Andrecek, still struggling to get control of his breathing. "It's a military-grade superintelligence, but I think it wants to talk. Let me handle this."

"Wise choice," said Eve, casually putting a hand on her hip as she leaned to one side. "You know, I almost didn't think you'd show up. Zed kept telling me to expect you, but you kept your hands so close to your chest that, barring a direct hack, I had nothing to go by. That trick you played with the fishbone skiff was quite brilliant, I must say—and using our own EMP device against us was a nice touch. I'm impressed."

"What... do you want?" Andrecek asked, sweat dripping down his forehead into his eyes. The combat stims combined with his fight-or-flight response in a way that made his unresponsive battle armor suit the worst kind of prison—like being trapped in a horrible nightmare without being able to move his legs.

"Personally? If it were me, Captain, you'd all be dead now, but Zedekiah sees something in you, which is why he's ordered me not to harm you while he—"

"Let me out!" Andrecek screamed, unable to restrain himself any longer. "Help!"

Eve clucked and shook a finger at him. "Now now, Captain. There's no need to be rude to a girl. If you want me to let you go, why don't you ask nicely?"

"Please let me go, please let me go," Andrecek cried. "Please, for the love of God, let me—"

The battle armor suit suddenly disgorged him, and he fell in a sprawling heap on the floor. He responded by promptly vomiting up the contents of his stomach, which hopefully included the last of those stimulants which now were making every muscle in his body tremble uncontrollably.

"Captain," said Suleiman, putting a hand on his shoulder. Apparently, Eve had released him as well.

Andrecek coughed and hacked a few more times before the worst of it was over. He felt truly awful. Suleiman handed him a small water back from his emergency kit, and Andrecek drank it gratefully, washing out the nasty taste of stomach bile from his mouth. He stood up on unsteady legs.

A drone hovered into view from around the nearest corner. He reflexively reached for his sidearm, but of course it wasn't there.

"Why didn't you say you were on stims?" Eve asked as a miniature holographic image of her materialized above the drone. "I would have let you go a lot sooner if you'd told me that."

"What are you going to do with us?" he asked.

"I'm going to do exactly what Zedekiah asked me to do: welcome you onto the *Ariel* as our guests. Can I get you some hors d'oeuvres? Something to drink, perhaps?"

Andrecek ignored the sarcastic smirk on her all-too-realistic avatar's face and tapped his wrist console, opening a channel to the *Trident* and putting it on speaker-phone for Suleiman's benefit.

"Eliso? Are you there?"

"I'm here, Captain. Sorry, but we just lost the escape pod. Looks like they all got away."

"There was nothing you could do. Has the superintelligence reached out to you?"

"Hey," said Eve. "I'm right here, you know."

"As a matter of fact, she has," Eliso answered.

"What has she told you so far?"

"She, um, complimented my hacking skills, then told me not to worry, that she's under orders not to kill us—yet." There was a brief pause, with a muffled voice on the other end of the line. "And now she wants me to tell you not to refer to her in the third person while she's right in front of you."

Andrecek turned to Eve and frowned. "Are you going to keep talking with my second mate behind my back?"

"Of course," she said cheerfully. "I'm a multi-tasker."

"If I may, sir," Suleiman interjected. "Zedekiah Wight clearly wants to keep us alive for some reason. Perhaps we should inquire why that is."

And see if we can keep it that way, Andrecek knew he meant to add.

"Well," said Eve, "for one thing, we need you alive to draw out Saif Al-Da'ib. Looks like he's already on his way, following those tracking signals he left in your battle armor. Coming in hot with three gunships and a pair of frigates."

"What?" said Andrecek, surprised. "Eliso, can you confirm?"

"Yes, Captain. Eve is right—and it doesn't look like they're coming to reinforce us."

Suleiman swore in Arabic again, making Andrecek turn and frown. "Does that mean what I think it means?"

"Yes, sir—I believe Al-Da'ib meant to spring his trap on us after we captured Zedekiah Wight, killing us and retaking his cargo while keeping all of the reward money for himself." He spat angrily on the floor. "That faithless son of a flea-ridden cur!"

"Hey!" said Eve. "Where are your manners?"

"Sorry," Suleiman said sheepishly. He pulled out a tissue from his pocket and wiped it up.

"Was that Zedekiah's plan, then?" Andrecek asked. "Using us to bait his trap?"

"Actually, no," said Eve. "That part was just improvisation. His plan was to get you onto the *Ariel* so I could show you something."

"Show us what?"

"That cargo you were carrying. It's down in the hold. Care to see what it was?"

They followed the drone with the hologram projector down a narrow stairwell and through another hatch to the floor of the *Ariel's* cargo hold. There, Andrecek saw the cargo that Abu Abbas had tasked them to smuggle from the Federation outpost in the outer system to Ramallah Station. The seal was broken, but the cargo container itself was still closed.

"Why are you showing us this?" Andrecek asked, suspecting some sort of trick—though what it would be, he couldn't imagine. They were already at the complete mercy of Zedekiah and his unrestrained superintelligence.

"I told you," Eve said petulantly. "Zed wants you to see it."

"Why?"

She folded her arms and gave Andrecek a look of annoyance that almost made him forget that she was just an avatar.

"His exact words were 'I want them to see the truth. Where we go from there is up to them.' If you don't believe me, I can play the recording back to you."

"No," said Andrecek, "that won't be necessary." He double-checked his wrist console. "Eliso? Are you there?"

"I'm here, Captain. Reading you loud and clear."

"What's the situation topside?"

"You'd better hurry. Saif Al-Da'ib's forces are still more than ten minutes out, but they're bearing down fast and hot, and judging from the fact that they haven't tried to reach out to us, I'd say Suleiman's right and they're hostile. But we may have a little more time than that, if Zedekiah can head them off. He's got two corvettes in support and is moving to intercept their attack."

"Has he reached out to you at all?"

"Negative, sir. I think he's left Eve to deal with us while he takes care of that enemy battle fleet."

"Well, duh," said Eve. "Now are you gonna see what's in that cargo container or what?"

Andrecek glanced warily at her before spinning the circular handle to open the airtight container doors. When he pulled them open, they creaked on rusted hinges, with visible cracks in the rubber that lined the edges. *Who puts anything valuable in a container that's only barely space-worthy?* he wondered to himself. But then the interior lights flickered reluctantly to life, and the thought fled immediately from his mind.

Lining both walls were two rows of clear, cylindrical cryotanks, standing vertically with their occupants in full view like so many frozen corpses. Their bodies were naked, their skin awfully pale, with arms and legs frozen in uncomfortable postures, as if whoever had frozen them hadn't bothered to administer the cocktail of anesthetics that made cryofreeze little more than a peaceful centuries-long sleep. The victims were all young girls, many of them young enough that they had not yet grown any pubic hair and their breasts had only just begun to bud. The oldest of them could not have been more than fifteen standard years.

Andrecek's heart stopped, and his blood ran cold. *Dear God,* he thought. *We almost trafficked those girls.*

"What do you see, sir?" Eliso asked anxiously.

When Andrecek proved too speechless to respond, Suleiman answered for him.

"Cryofrozen slave girls, most of them still children. I am so sorry, sir. I had heard rumors that the Hamza family trafficked in slaves, but I had thought they smuggled them into the Federation, not the other way around."

"Unfortunately, there's a thriving slave market on both sides of the frontier," Eve told them, her voice suddenly somber. "The Federation is just better at hiding it, probably because so many of their elected officials are involved. If Zed were here, he'd quote the Book at you: 'But whoso shall offend one of these little ones, it were better for him that a millstone were hanged about his neck, and that he were drowned in the depth of the sea.'"

"Who are they?" Andrecek asked, his voice low.

"Are you sure you want to know, Captain?"

"Yes. Tell me."

She hesitated a split second before answering. "Very well. There aren't any official records or identifying information, of course, but based on what we know about Mahmoud Abu Abbas's suppliers, I can say with 92% confidence that these girls came from the occupation zone between the Salph, Mintaka, and Alnitak systems."

Andrecek's eyes suddenly widened. "The rebellion!" he exclaimed, recognizing the names of the stars he'd fought so desperately to defend. Hot blood rushed back to his cheeks as all of the rage he'd so carefully buried came rushing back to him.

"Holy shit," said Eliso. "Does that mean we were trafficking girls from back home?"

"That is exactly what I am saying," Eve answered her.

"I am so sorry, sir," Suleiman said, putting a tentative hand on Andrecek's shoulder. Still dazed, Andrecek brushed him away. Suleiman stepped back, unsure what to do.

"Hey, Captain," said Eliso. "Captain, can you hear me?"

"What have we done?" Andrecek asked, clenching his fists so tightly that his knuckles turned white.

"I hear you, Captain. It's terrible what we almost did. But at least we know now, right?"

Andrecek drew a sharp breath as he stared at the girls frozen in their cryotanks. Were some of them related to the men who'd fought under him? His old war buddies and comrades in arms? Had he stooped so low that he'd nearly sold their daughters into slavery? That he'd nearly betrayed all that he'd once fought for? No—it was he who had been betrayed. If he'd known what cargo he'd been carrying, he'd have shot Mahmoud Abu Abbas and Mohammed Saif Al-Da'ib himself, consequences be damned.

"Where were they bound for?" he asked, his voice low and dangerous.

"The Caliphate royal family, though they're not the ones who purchased them," Eve answered. "We suspect that the true power behind the throne uses slaves like these to buy off the royal family and make them complicit, similar to how the Federation deep state controls their ruling elite through a combination of blackmail and extortion. They use multiple layers of sub-contractors to distance themselves from the crime. If your cargo had been discovered, you would have taken the fall for it."

"But we didn't know!" Suleiman protested.

"Doesn't matter," said Eve, shaking her holographic head. "With the way it was set up, no one would have believed you."

"Who is at the top of this?" Andrecek asked as he rose slowly and deliberately to his feet.

"The same ones who put a reward on Zedekiah's head," Eve answered, folding her arms. "The Central Bank of the Caliphate. I'll leave you to connect the dots."

"And the Hamza family? How do they figure into it?"

She grinned. "Now you're asking the right questions. The Hamza family aren't just sub-contractors—they've married into the family that owns the central bank. So whenever the powers behind the throne have some dirty work to do—like trafficking underage sex slaves, or taking out a hit on someone who threatens their power—the Hamza family is there to take care of it."

"Is that why Zedekiah Wight crucified them?" Andrecek asked. "To send a message?"

"Yes. No one escapes justice."

"The justice of God," Suleiman muttered.

Andrecek gave him a funny look. "What?"

"Isn't that what his name means?" Suleiman asked, turning to Eve. "Zedekiah—the justice of God."

"As a matter of fact, yes."

"What are you going to do with those girls?" Eliso asked over Andrecek's wrist console.

"That's a very good question," said Eve. "We have a partner in the Orion Confederacy that helps to rehabilitate victims of human trafficking. It won't be easy, though—some of these poor girls may have been under the ice for decades, or even longer. But after our current campaign is over, we'll head back to the Confederacy and hand them over to the people who can help them—hang on."

Her avatar frowned and touched a finger to her ear, then abruptly disappeared. Andrecek glanced at Suleiman, then brought up his wrist console.

"Eliso, are you still there?"

"Yes, Captain. Looks like things are getting a little tricky. Zedekiah just engaged the hostiles, and they took out one of his corvettes. He got two of their gunboats, but they're pulling back now. It doesn't look good."

"How bad is it?" Andrecek asked, motioning to Suleiman to follow him. He set out for the hatch at a jog.

"I don't know. It's hard to—wait a minute."

For several heart-stopping moments, she went silent. Zedekiah reached the hatch and started taking stairs up two at a time. The drone with the hologram projector followed him.

"Haha!" Eliso laughed, catching Andrecek by surprise. "Captain, you won't believe it!"

"Believe what?" he asked, frowning as they stepped out into the main corridor. The frozen battle armor suits were just around the corner.

"I've got a mole on Saif Al-Da'ib's main ship—it looks like his people managed to crack our firewalls after all. I'm not sure how badly they've infected our systems, but—"

"I'll take care of that," said Eve, reappearing suddenly. "Captain, I think it's time that you and your first mate back to your ship. You passed the test, by the way. Unfortunately, there's no time for Zedekiah to introduce himself. Things are getting hot out there, and we need to get you and your crew to safety."

"No," said Andrecek. "I have a better idea."

Captain Andrecek flexed each of his fingers individually and watched on his HUD as his battle armor suit ran diagnostics on all of its servos and secondary motors. Everything checked out just fine. Eve hadn't actually damaged his suit, just take control of it—and with her now on his side (or more accurately, he on her side), they were going to make a formidable team indeed.

"Suleiman's on board," Eliso reported over the suit's main channel. "Undocking now."

Moments later, Andrecek both heard and felt a slight rumble as the docking clamps disengaged and the *Tri-*

dent pulled out. He put that from his mind and focused on the task at hand.

"As soon as you teleport onto Saif Al-Da'ib's flagship, I'll commandeer their weapons and destroy the other frigate," Eve told him, appearing on his HUD as a life-sized human. She guided him into the teleport room and gestured him onto the bay. "Just remember, Zed wants you to take Al-Da'ib alive."

"I can't promise anything," Andrecek muttered as he climbed up onto the platform. The battle armor suit made it a little tight, but he still barely had enough clearance.

"All right. Just try to restrain yourself. Trust me, you don't want to—"

"Send me over."

She sighed and vanished from his HUD. Half a second later, the air all around him began to shimmer with bright blue light as the teleporter did its work. His stomach flipped the way it always did. The first few moments were always the most disorienting. But then, the light dissipated with a flash, and he was standing in the teleporter bay of Saif Al-Da'ib's flagship.

He stepped off the platform and immediately ran a threat assessment, running heat sensors and infrared over his visual display. The pistol in his hand was still set to stun, but his suit itself was an unparalleled weapon, especially for an enemy who didn't expect to be boarded at all.

He stepped out into the hallway and smashed his fist into the nearest bulkhead to announce his presence. The wall crumpled like paper, and alarms began to blare as sparks and clouds of gas began to spill out through the breach. Apparently, he'd broken a critical conduit for the ship's internal systems—all the better.

A man ran out into the hallway from one of the stern hatches, probably from engineering. Andrecek ran straight at him, grabbing him by the neck smashing his head so hard against the bulkhead that it disintegrated into a bloodied pulp. Shouts sounded from behind, and he spun around just in time to catch a plasma bolt to the chest. The ablative armor did its work, though, shedding the super-heated plasma without taking any critical damage. He engaged his suit's jets, and his attacker had just enough time to issue a blood-curdling scream before Andrecek squashed him like a bug.

There was a temptation to take a perverse pleasure in the pain and death that he was meting out judiciously. But as a former soldier, Andrecek recognized the danger inherent in the indulgence of that temptation. So he focused his mind instead on the girls in the cryotanks and told himself that he was doing this for them—that killing these evil men was nothing more than a job.

Of course, all that would change when he confronted Saif Al-Da'ib.

From Eliso's hack, he knew that there were six crew on this ship, besides Al-Da'ib himself. That left four more men that he had to kill. The escape pod was on an adjoining hall, and his heat vision showed three figures making a run for it.

"Lock down that pod, Eve."

"Already on it. Focus on the men in the bridge—they're trying to shut off the weapons manually."

In just a few quick strides, Andrecek was there. The two bridge officers leaped to their feet, but they might as well have been fish in a barrel for all the chances they had. Andrecek grabbed the closest one by the face and smashed him so hard into the control panel that he broke it in half, all while leveling his energy pistol at the other and shooting him in the chest. He went down with a grunt, stunned but still alive.

Once again, the temptation to brutally kill the man rose up in the pit of Andrecek's gut. It would be so easy—just bring down his overpowered foot and crush the bastard like the insect that he was. But he resisted the urge and left the bridge for the hallway, where the last three men were trying desperately to unlock the escape pod.

Just as he stepped out, one of the blast doors for repelling boarders closed between him and his quarry. He tried smashing it open with his armored fist, but the impact only dented it. This was going to take some work.

"Sorry," said Eve. "The controls for that door aren't connected to the ship's network. You're on your own for this one."

"Just give me a minute," said Andrecek. He slammed his fists over and over into the door, bending it out of shape until a breach began to appear. Then, fitting his armored fingers into the crack and bracing himself against the floor, he began to pull.

"Saif Al-Da'ib is trying to hack your suit, but I've already blocked his attack," Eve reported. "Also, all the other ships have been neutralized. The space battle's over—we've already won."

It isn't over until that bastard Saif Al-Da'ib is mine, Andrecek thought to himself. The blast door abruptly gave way, and he peeled the thick metal back as if it were aluminum foil.

The moment he stepped into the breach, an armor piercing round ricocheted off of his helmet and blew through the bulkhead to his right. Andrecek staggered and reflexively lifted his hand, which was still holding onto the broken blast door. It ripped off a chunk of it, which took the brunt of the next round, splattering shrapnel everywhere.

Andrecek's head rang from the impact of the blow. Time seemed to slow to a terrifying crawl as he watched the shrapnel scatter like confetti all around him. Then, the adrenaline kicked in, and he lunged forward with all of his augmented might through the breach.

Even though the first round had knocked him nearly senseless, his battle armor suit was still holding together. His HUD and other instruments took a few moments to re-calibrate, but he had a clear enough visual to see the two men firing on him. A fragment of shrapnel hit the man on the right in the knee, and as he went down, Andrecek kicked him back so hard that he did a backwards somersault and broke his neck on the floor. Andrecek's forward momentum nearly carried him past the other gunman, but dropping his energy pistol (which was now totally junked, thanks to the shrapnel) he grabbed the man and slammed him into the bulkhead. He flopped to the ground and didn't get up.

Taking a deep breath, Andrecek ran a quick damage check on his battle armor suit. His heat and infrared were down, and the servomotors that controlled his neck were inoperable, making it impossible to turn his head from side to side. Several other segments on his suit readout were flashing yellow, indicating minor shrapnel damage. But the suit's critical systems were still perfectly functional, and aside from a splitting headache it didn't appear that he'd taken any injury.

"Those damned fools breached the hull with those rounds," Eve commented. "We're losing atmosphere, fast. You'll be fine, but we'd better find Saif Al-Da'ib."

Yes, Andrecek thought grimly. *It would be a shame if he died before I got my hands on him.*

He hurried around the corner, guessing that Al-Da'ib would make for the teleporter. Sure enough, he got there just as the overweight head of the Hamza family shuffled onto the teleporter bay. Realizing that Eve might use the opportunity to transfer him onto the *Voidbringer,* Andrecek smashed his armored fist into the controls, sending sparks and chunks of metal flying.

"Hey!" said Eve. "What are you doing?"

"He's mine," said Andrecek, his voice low and dangerous. He reached into the teleporter bay and grabbed the trembling man by his loose-fitting robes.

"Captain, please! You don't want to—"

"What are you going to do? Freeze my suit again? He'll die from lack of oxygen before anyone else gets here." Then, switching to his suit's external speakers: "Call me a kaffir now, you filthy pig."

He held the man up to eye level and opened his suit's visor so that Saif Al-Da'ib could see him clearly. But even as recognition dawned on his frightened face, it wasn't enough to overcome his cowardice. For the briefest moment, his eyes lit with fury at Andrecek's betrayal, but then he yelped and began to whimper like an injured dog.

"Is it m-money you want?" he stammered pathetically. "I can make you richer than you can possibly imagine. I can make your wildest dreams come—"

Andrecek slammed him against the bulkhead—not so hard as to pulverize him the way he had with the other men, but hard enough to make him scream. He threw him onto the floor, then put one hand around his neck and lifted him so that both his feet were suspended in the rapidly depleting air.

"You used me," he said, looking the little fat man squarely in the eye. "You knew my background with the rebellion. You knew what we were carrying. Did you request me for this job because it amused you to watch the 'kaffirs' deliver their own people into slavery? Did you turn on us because you knew that we'd find out?"

"Please!" Saif Al-Da'ib squealed. "I did no such thing! I thought you needed help, and was coming to—gah!"

"Silence!" Andrecek commanded. He squeezed just hard enough to choke him, but not quite hard enough to crush his larynx and kill him. But the temptation was certainly there.

"It's over for you, Saif Al-Da'ib. I'm going to enjoy watching you die."

"Victor," a man's voice came over his speaker, deep and low. "Victor. Put him down."

Andrecek frowned and switched off his suit's external speaker. "Who is this?"

"Zedekiah Wight. I need this man alive, Captain Victor Andrecek. But more importantly, I need you not to kill him."

The realization that he was speaking with his reluctant onetime adversary made Andrecek's eyes widen. Zedekiah's voice didn't sound anything like he'd imagined, and yet now having heard it, he couldn't imagine it any other way. Calm, cool, and collected, he didn't sound anything like a madman at all. Indeed, there was even a hint of sadness in his voice—not for Al-Da'ib, but for Andrecek himself.

"Why not?" Andrecek heard himself ask.

"You are a good man, Victor. You're better than this. I promise, Mohammed Saif Al-Da'ib will not escape justice for his crimes. But it is not good for you to kill him in this way. It is not good for you to delight in bloodshed."

"Don't tell me you didn't enjoy crucifying those other people," Andrecek snapped.

"I didn't," Zedekiah said gently but firmly. "It gave me no joy to crucify them. I killed them because they needed to die, and their deaths needed to send a message that would strike fear into the hearts of all their evil co-conspirators. Do you think that you will make things right by killing this man?"

"Yes," Andrecek answered without hesitation.

"No. Revenge is not justice. The death of this man will not help those girls. Do you wish to help them, Victor?"

Andrecek nodded, even though Zedekiah couldn't see him. "Yes."

"Then hear the words of the Book: 'Learn to do well: seek judgment, relieve the oppressed, judge the fatherless, plead for the widow. Though your sins be as scarlet, they shall be as white as snow; though they be red like crimson, they shall be as wool.'"

As much as Andrecek hated to admit it, he knew that Zedekiah was right. If he killed Al-Da'ib out of the rage of his heart, it wouldn't make things right again—

wouldn't bring back his lost comrades, or restore the girls to freedom, or even stop another crime family from stepping into the void and continuing to trade in slaves. It would only fill him with emptiness. Memories came back to him then, of fellow comrades in the rebellion whose eyes had been deadened and whose lives had lost all joy, because of the cycle of violence and revenge that had consumed them.

"What will you do with him?" Andrecek asked. "Will you crucify him like the others?"

"I will bring him to justice. That is all you need to know."

He drew a long breath from his suit's oxygen tank and loosened his grip on Saif Al-Da'ib's neck.

"Where do you want him?"

"Put him in the escape pod. Your battle armor doubles as an EVA suit, and you can use your jets to return to your ship. Eve will guide you."

"All right," said Andrecek, walking reluctantly to the escape pod in the hall. Alarms were going off all over the ship now, with the interior rapidly losing atmosphere. The gauges on his suit showed that they had already lost almost twenty percent of air pressure.

"The survivor on the bridge too, please," Zedekiah asked as Andrecek came to the door for the escape pod. It opened immediately.

"You got it," he said. Then, tossing his miserable prisoner into the airlock, he activated his external speakers and said: "Stay there, or I'll kill you."

"Yes! Yes! Thank you, sir! Oh, bless you!"

Don't speak so soon, Andrecek thought grimly as he went to the bridge to retrieve the other survivor. As much as he wanted to punish Saif Al-Da'ib for trafficking those girls, he was confident that Zedekiah would mete out justice.

He found the survivor staggering toward the escape pod from the bridge. It wasn't difficult to grab him and throw him in.

"Thank you, Victor Andrecek," said Zedekiah. "You have done the right thing. Godspeed."

There was a low thud as the docking clamps for the escape pod disengaged. No doubt it was under Eve's power, and would take its occupants straight to the *Voidbringer,* where Zedekiah was waiting to pick them up.

"Pod's jettisoned," she said, appearing again on his HUD. "Ready to go?"

"Yeah," said Andrecek, swallowing hard. He opened the airlock and stepped inside, leaving the wrecked and hull-breached ship behind him. After the door had closed, he opened the outer door and leaped into the void of space. The *Trident* showed up on his HUD as a blinking red dot, and as he used his jets to set a course for it, he opened a new channel.

"This is Captain Andrecek," he said, his hands shaking from what he'd just been through. "Threat's been neutralized. I'm ready to get picked up."

"Got it, Captain," Eliso answered. "We're on our way. Are you all right?"

He remembered with awful clarity all the men that he had killed, and how bloody and gruesome their deaths had been. It had been years since he'd been in a battle like that—almost a standard decade, in fact. There was a reason why he'd gone into smuggling instead of mercenary work.

"Yeah," he said. "I'm all right"—and to his surprise, it was true. He'd killed those men in combat. The temptation to kill for the sake of killing had definitely been there, but he hadn't succumbed to it. His humanity was still intact.

"So I guess this is goodbye," said Eve. "For now, at least." She waved at him from the corner of his eye before disappearing from his HUD.

Andrecek frowned. "What's that supposed to mean?"

But the *Voidbringer* and the *Ariel* had already jumped out.

"So where do we go from here?" Andrecek asked over a plate of sauerkraut and dumplings—the last of his personal stores. Once again, Suleiman had his tea and Eliso her bowl of noodles.

"Beats me," said Eliso, shrugging. "If we're going to keep those battle armor suits, we should probably put some distance between us and the Hamza family. Hell, we should probably do that regardless."

Andrecek nodded. It had been almost forty-eight hours since the battle with Zedekiah Wight and Saif Al-Da'ib, and the *Trident* was berthed at one of the lunar Lagrangian point stations some distance from Ramallah. A well-placed bribe at the port authority had kept their presence secret, giving them some breathing space to plan out their next move. It wasn't fool-proof, though, and anyone who knew where they'd been and was determined to find them wouldn't have much difficulty tracking them down. So they needed to move on fairly soon.

"We may not have to flee if we stay low in the outer system for a while," Suleiman countered. "The Hamza family has been crippled by the loss of so many of its senior members. It is very likely that their rivals will rise up now and try to overthrow them. If they succeed—and they probably will—then all we need to do is wait them out."

"No," said Andrecek, shaking his head. "Remember what Eve told us? The Hamza family is connected by marriage to the owners of the Central Bank of the Caliphate. It's unlikely that they'll be swept from power quite so easily."

"Even so, Captain," said Suleiman, "we can still find work in the outer system, where the Hamza family does not hold so much sway."

Eliso's wrist console beeped, making her frown and set down her bowl of noodles. As she checked the incoming message, her eyes slowly widened. Andrecek set down his fork.

"What is it, Eliso?"

"Uh, Captain, I think you'd better read this. It's addressed to the ship, but I think it's meant for you."

She unstrapped her wrist console and handed it to Andrecek. The message read:

If ye be willing and obedient, ye shall eat the good of the land. Reply by name if your answer is yes. We hope you will join us. Godspeed.

"It's Zedekiah Wight," he said at length. "He wants to know if we will join him."

Suleiman frowned, and Eliso's eyes widened even more. "Are you serious?" she asked.

"Unless I'm missing something, that message is very definitely meant for us." He leaned forward to hand back her wrist console. "I don't know what his terms are, but it sounds like he intends to be generous with us."

"Join him?" Suleiman asked. "You mean, become pirates and terrorists ourselves?"

Andrecek shrugged. "Why not? We're already smugglers—and in the Federation, Eliso and I are already considered terrorists for our involvement in the rebellion. They never did pardon us for that, did they?"

"Nope," said Eliso, slurping another fork-full of noodles. "Which is hilarious, coming from the side that droned so many civilians."

"And trafficked those girls into the Caliphate," Andrecek added bitterly. "The occupation authority had to have known about that. In fact, I wouldn't put it past them to take a cut of the profit themselves."

"Damned right, sir."

"So what do you think? Should we accept Zedekiah's offer?"

She thought about it for a moment, then shrugged. "Sure. Why not?"

"I thought you said he was a madman. What changed?"

"Oh, he's definitely a madman," she answered, nodding for effect. "But that doesn't mean everyone else is sane by comparison. After everything we've been through, I'm starting to think that he might just be the kind of madman the galaxy needs right now. You know?"

"He has all of the right enemies," Suleiman added. "And he has been very fair with us, sir. You have to admit that."

Indeed, Andrecek thought to himself. In a universe gone mad, where evil was good and good evil—where truth was treason, democracy was empire, and slavery was the price of freedom—who else could be right but one whom everyone called a madman? For all that, there was something refreshing about this Zedekiah Wight, who refused to accept the unacceptable or compromise his conscience in the least degree. And was that not why Andrecek had joined the rebellion in the first place? Perhaps, if he were a better man, he would still be fighting that fight, instead of trying to eke out a living on the fringes as a smuggler. And yet, now was his chance to redeem himself—to rejoin the fight under Zedekiah's command.

"All right," said Andrecek. "Are we agreed?"

Suleiman shook his head sadly. "I am sorry, sir, but I must decline. The Ramallah system has always been my home, and I do not wish to leave."

"What about the Hamza family?" Eliso asked in surprise.

"I'll stay low and take my chances. Godwilling, they will soon be swept from power. But even if they are not, I have my contacts. You need not fear on my behalf."

"Very well," said Andrecek. "You've been a good first mate, Suleiman. We're going to miss you."

"As will I, sir. It has been a pleasure, and an honor."

He nodded and turned to Eliso. "What about you, Eliso? Are you coming?"

"Of course, sir. You know there's no one else I'd rather serve alongside. It'll be just like old days with the rebellion—except this time, we'll bring the bastards to justice."

A grin spread slowly across Andrecek's face. "Yes. Godwilling, we will."

Hunter, Lover, Cyborg, Slave

The jungle moon glowed with life. Gini found the sight even more entrancing than the red and orange cloud decks of the Jovian primary, crowned by monstrous auroras on both poles. Unlike the lifeless gas giant, there was something dark and primal about the bioluminescence of Alamut-VII that called to her.

"Gini," her AI familiar asked from the holographic projector on the armrest of her cockpit chair. "Are you all right?"

"I'm fine, Henry. Just admiring the view."

The eight-inch tall holographic image turned as if he were looking out the window with her. It was an illusion, of course—Henry lived in the databanks of her pocket computer, if "lived" was the right word for it, and could no more see through his holographic eyes than she could see through her painted fingernails. But she appreciated the gesture nonetheless.

The avatar he projected was of a trim, muscular, thirty-something bald man, dressed in a double-breasted synth-leather jacket and a white collared shirt with the top two buttons undone. It was odd, considering her profession, that her familiar looked more like a young entrepreneur than someone who'd come out of the military or law enforcement. But most bounty hunters weren't petite Asiatic raven-haired femmes who weighed all of 105 pounds galactic in a dripping wet shirt—before her carbon-fiber bone implants, of course. Henry was just one of Gini's many surprises.

"Spectacular," he mused. "Though considering the havoc the native life wreaks on the local datasphere, I'd prefer to admire it from a distance."

"Relax, Henry. We're not going planetside unless we absolutely have to."

"Until we absolutely have to, you mean."

She sighed and rolled her eyes, but he wasn't necessarily wrong. Alamut-VII was the kind of place where the dregs of society came to disappear, and considering that the only permanent settlement with a population greater than ten thousand was the main orbital, it was only a matter of time before the hunt took them planetside. Unless they got lucky first.

While Henry handled their approach to the docking node, Gini brought up the file on the guy they were going to bag. His scarred and partially reconstructed face stared back at her from his mugshot on the ship's main display. Like Henry, he was bald, the top of his head just barely kissing the 6'2" line, which put him almost a head and a half taller than her. Seduction would be difficult if it came to that, though she'd managed it once with a man of that height—but he'd had a thing for underage girls, and her natural Asiatic features and the military rejuv from her late twenties had worked to her favor on that job. Bringing him back to justice had been as satisfying as crushing an earwig under her stiletto-heeled boot.

But this guy's file didn't say that he got off on diddling kids. Not that Gini would put it past him, but his rap sheet was filled out with war crimes in the last pan-galactic war. Also, he was supposed to be some sort of computing genius. The rogue AI that had cracked the hab domes of Ariel-III and turned the colony's point defenses on its citizens had apparently been his creation. She had to admit, he had the cool, calculating expression of a psychopath, though the scar that ran crosswise between his eyes made him look more like the kind of guy who preferred to do his killing by hand.

Good, she thought, cracking her carbon-fiber reinforced knuckles. *I've been aching for a challenge for a while now.* It looked like she was finally going to get one.

An hour later, she was cradling a drink in the local cantina, keeping an eye on the other patrons while she scanned various feeds from her implants with the other. Henry was off in the datasphere, doing some reconnaissance and getting a general feel for the lay of the land. From time to time, he popped back into her feeds to let her know what he was doing.

"There are a lot of rogue AIs here," he reported, his ghostly form appearing on the bar stool next to her. Of course, only she could see him.

"What sort of rogue AIs?" she subvocalized as she lifted her glass of beer to hide her lips from view.

"Familiars, mostly. Seems like the surface is just as deadly for humans as it is for AIs."

She nodded. "Any of them a threat?"

"To us? No."

"Good. Take care of yourself, Henry. Keep an eye out for our target's familiar."

"Will do." He nodded and vanished into thin air.

A few seconds later, a tall, thin man assumed the seat next to her. His shirt was civilian, but his pants and boots were standard Federation police issue, and his sidearm was military surplus. She raised an eyebrow.

"Pardon. Is this seat taken?"

"It is now," she said casually, though Henry was already doing a threat assessment and making a combat analysis. He'd come back on his own, and his familiar presence inside of her implants went a long way toward reassuring her.

"Two New York sours," he said, waving down the barkeep. Then, turning to face her, he slid his badge across the counter top.

"Sergeant Moss, station security," he introduced himself in a hushed voice. "Welcome to Alamut-VII, miss..."

"Gini," she said simply, giving him an enigmatic smile. "And I don't drink whiskey with strangers."

He shrugged nonchalantly, as if he weren't offended or disappointed in the least. So he was here on business. The threat assessment came back yellow, but Henry's scans told her that his military implants were all at least a decade out of date, and the tactical analysis gave her a +80% victory rate across all combat scenarios. She relaxed, but kept the tactical assessment in the bottom corner of her view.

"No offense, ma'am, but I'm not the stranger in this place. Care to tell me why you're here?"

For a brief moment, she considered telling him no, but if this was local law enforcement's way of screening her, she had to appreciate his discretion. The last thing she needed was an official meeting with the authorities to tip off her target.

"I'm looking for someone," she said, returning Sergeant Moss's badge. "Perhaps you can help me?"

He grunted. "It depends. Care to tell me who?"

She looked into his eyes and used her implants to ping a query. He answered, and she had Henry upload the file on their target, including his many aliases. Sergeant Moss's eyes twitched a little as he quickly looked over the file, and the barkeep chose that moment to give them their drinks. He placed the glasses in front of them and silently moved to the other end of the bar.

"Kieran," Moss told her, absently picking up his drink. "That's the alias he goes by here. He's got a place on the surface, though we don't know where."

Gini raised an eyebrow. "You don't keep land records?"

"No. Too many squatters." He took a measured sip of his drink and set it back down. "The only land that's officially owned here belongs to the trans-planetaries, usually mining corporations. But it's been a while since any wildcatter found anything worth fighting back the local fauna to extract. Most of the mines down there are overgrown and in disrepair."

"Is that where the squatters come in?"

"Sometimes. Other times, they drop a couple of reinforced shipping containers from orbit and settle into the hole once it cools down. People around here tend to be creative, Miss Gini."

"Just Gini," she said, taking her drink. She smiled, and he nodded.

"May I ask what business you have with Kieran?"

She took a sip, savoring the fruity red wine that swirled on top of her cocktail, then withdrew her ID card and casually passed it over. His eyes widened ever so slightly as he examined it.

"You're an authorized cyborg?" he asked in hushed tones.

She nodded. "One of the few still alive."

He placed his hand over her ID and slowly slid it over, keeping it hidden from view until she took it back. "I take it you're working as some sort of private investigator now?"

"Bounty hunter, actually."

"Then you'd better watch your back. A lot of the locals would slit your throat if they knew your true nature."

She smiled wanly and fluttered her eyelashes. "What, a girl like me?"

"Even a girl like you, ma'am. You'd better come up with a good cover story if you plan to stay for a while."

Quick as thought, Henry anticipated her request and began to craft several possible cover stories for her to chose from. She left that work to him and focused on the conversation at hand.

"You'll stay out of my way, then?" she asked, leaning forward.

Moss nodded. "Or assist you, if you'd like. We're just as eager as you are to pack up the real nasties and ship them out of here."

"That won't be necessary. But I would appreciate it if you gave me what you have on the man."

He nodded again, and his implants pinged hers. In two seconds, she'd downloaded all of the files.

"It was a pleasure to share a drink with you, ma'am. Enjoy your stay."

With that, he rose and left. As soon as he was gone, Henry materialized on the empty seat.

"I've got three plausible stories for you to choose from," he told her, bringing all of them up as images over his head. "They're all localized variations on the usual: private gun looking for work, private investigator hunting down a client's ex, or an illegal weapons dealer looking to lay low for a while."

She thought for a moment, savoring the cocktail that the sergeant had bought her. "Let's go with the last one. Seems to fit in best with the general vibe around here."

"I agree."

"You can forge the necessary documents to make our alibi airtight?"

He winced. "I can, but that's not going to sit well with local law enforcement. You want me to do it anyway?"

"Go ahead," she subvocalized. "They'd rather get Kieran out of here than slap us for something petty. Besides, we're going to need that alibi to be as airtight as possible if my plan to smoke him out is going to work."

"Dare I ask how?"

She smiled and set the unfinished drink on the counter before casually sliding her hips off of her bar stool. "If you really had to ask, Henry, you wouldn't be my familiar."

The dating scene on Alamut-VII was sparse, but not uninteresting. Or at least, it wasn't totally dead. In order to establish herself as a down-and-out illegal arms dealer, Gini stayed low for the first couple of weeks, refraining from setting up a dating profile on the local planetnet. However, she did frequent the cantina almost every dayshift, though she didn't stay more than an hour at a time.

It didn't take long for the regulars to start offering to buy her drinks, but she didn't do more than flirt with them. Her true quarry lay further afield.

While she stayed low and established her alibi, Henry made a thorough exploration of the system's datasphere. According to Kieran's file, his AI familiar was a class 5, and customized so thoroughly that she almost qualified as a superintelligence. A very dangerous quarry indeed: legally, familiars had to be programmed with all sorts of safeguards to prevent them from going rogue, but a superintelligence could theoretically overcome those, meaning there was almost no limit to what she could do. Her avatar was of an attractive fair-skinned blonde, about ten standard years younger than Kieran himself, which made Gini wonder if perhaps Kieran's relationship with her went further than human and familiar. Such kinks were taboo, but not unheard of—especially not in a place as far off the beaten path as Alamut-VII.

"Any luck?" she asked Henry, undressing back on her ship after her nightly run at the cantina. A little more than a week had passed since they'd arrived.

Henry shook his holographic head. "Nothing. Not even a trace, though I have found evidence that at least one class 5 in the local system is working very hard to cover her tracks. But without something else to go on, I can't conclusively say that it's her."

Gini finished undressing, and Henry turned the other way. The gesture made her laugh.

"What's wrong, Henry? I know you can see me through the video feeds."

"Perhaps it would be better if we turned those off."

"Why?" she asked, still buzzed from the night at the cantina. One of the more handsome regulars had offered to take her back to his place, and while of course she'd turned him down, the offer had keyed her up quite a bit.

"Because I'm your familiar, not your lover."

She gave him a sultry smile. "But you could be."

"Even so," he said, and his holographic image suddenly vanished. "I think that it would be better not to continue this conversation in a corporeal form."

Gini rolled her eyes and palmed the door to the shower unit. "Prude."

"You'll thank me when you're sober," his disembodied voice came through her implants. "As I was saying, Dierdre is very good at covering her tracks—so good, in fact, that I suspect she may be watching us unobserved."

Dierdre. That was the familiar's name—or at least, the one associated with the Kieran alias. Very complementary. It was exactly the sort of name that an AI-familiar-turned-lover would choose.

"Are you saying our cover's blown?" Gini asked, warm, soapy water running down her face and chest.

"Not necessarily. She would have to have hacked local law enforcement for that to be the case, and I don't think even she is capable of breaking their firewalls. I've tested them myself."

Of course you have, Gini thought to herself, grinning. She ran her fingers through her hair and began to build up a lather on her scalp. Of course, there was no danger of Dierdre breaking through the firewalls on their ship—those were military-grade, not merely civilian.

"But if she's observing us," Henry continued, "that will hamper my activities in the datasphere considerably. We'll have to rely on your honey trapping abilities, rather than using the target's familiar to find the target himself."

"Just as I suspected. You're good, Henry, but you're no match for a class 5."

"Now, now. There's no need to be petty."

"Who's being petty?" she asked angrily. The shower unit seemed to spin around her, so she turned the temperature down way low as the rinse cycle began. The cold water shocked some sobriety back into her—perhaps Henry was right, and she'd had one drink too many.

"Gini," he said, his voice sounding soft in her ear. "Promise me that when this job is over, you'll find a man and settle down for a while."

"We've been through this before, Henry. I'm not the domestic type."

"You know what I mean. It doesn't have to be *domestic.* Gini, I'm your familiar—I know you as well as any lover ever will—so trust me when I say you can't continue to live this way much longer. You need a good man in your life, preferably with a committed relationship."

Gini snorted angrily and shut the water off. Hot air blasted her from above, banishing all the water to the vacuum in the drain. She leaned heavily against the sides of the shower unit, clenching her teeth at Henry's words.

"Promise me," he said again. "This single, promiscuous life isn't good for you."

"But it's my life, not yours," she said, cutting their conversation short.

She woke up the next upshift with a splitting headache and a lot of regret. Henry was right about thanking him when she was sober. He was always right when it came to things like that. She decided to stay away from the cantina for a while—besides, it was just about time to get serious about this honey trap.

It didn't take her long to set up a local dating profile. She had plenty of experience from past jobs, and had developed a feel for this sort of work. Henry fine-tuned it to fit what they knew (or could reasonably guess about Kieran's predilections), and within a couple of hours, the trap had been set.

Gini spent the next several days cycling through various profiles, which ran the gamut from the unintentionally ridiculous to the truly disturbing. There were a couple of men who piqued her interest, too, but though she was tempted, she declined them just the same as all the others. But there weren't a lot of men (or women, for that matter) at Alamut-VII to choose from, and it only took her a couple of hours to cycle through all of them.

She began to worry that perhaps Kieran wasn't interested in dating—which made sense, if he was in a taboo relationship with his familiar. She started tracking shuttle flights, knowing that Kieran would need to resupply his hideout at some point. If that didn't work, then they would have to track down his familiar on the datasphere, which might put Henry in danger.

Then, after another standard week, he finally sprung for the bait.

His dating profile had only two pictures: one of him shirtless with a darkened visor over his eyes, and the other a picture of his starship, a modest FTL yacht parked groundside in the midst of an overgrown jungle. That was probably his hideout. It took her several minutes to confirm his identity, but Henry's final analysis showed a +85% probability that it was him, and the name checked out too. The rest of the profile was sparse on personal data, but that was to be expected for a criminal.

She marked him as a yes. To her surprise, she matched with him almost immediately.

"Interesting," Henry mused. "Either he posted his profile and found you sometime in the eighteen hours, or he's set his profile to the maximum privacy settings, and the only reason you can see him now is because he finally marked you as a yes."

Gini shrugged. "That's not too unusual. The guy's a criminal after all." *And probably having an affair with his familiar.*

"Gini, I guarantee you that at least half of the guys you cycle through each day are criminals of one stripe or another. Only scientists and mid-level executives from the mining corporations have totally clean records in this place."

"Let's see how long it takes for him to respond."

To Gini's surprise, it didn't take long. Within a couple of hours, he reached out and messaged:

What's a girl like you doing on a shithole planet like this?

She waited three minutes, then responded *Looking for a guy like you, apparently. :)* He responded almost immediately.

Seriously, what brings you to this place.

"Now we reel you in," Gini muttered, smiling to herself.

They flirted off and on for the next hour. By the end of it, she'd established that Kieran did indeed have a base somewhere on the surface, and that his AI familiar matched all of the things they had on file for. She also got even more vibes that they were having an affair, and when she hinted that she was open to a threesome, he asked what she thought of "non-corporeal partners," all but outright confirming her suspicions. There was something truly sick about the man.

But there was no way to capture him unless they got him away from the surface first. The bioluminescent jungle wreaked havoc on electronics, so one small misstep could cut Henry off from her and spiral into something truly catastrophic. She didn't push it, deciding that it was better to let him bring it up on his own.

You should come down here, he messaged her cold the next dayshift.

Excuse me? she messaged him back.

I want to show you my place. I think you'll like it.

"Please tell me that you would ghost this guy if all of this were actually real," said Henry.

Gini scoffed. "If all of this were real, I wouldn't have matched with this creep in the first place."

"Fair enough."

They went back and forth for a while, Gini insisting as gently as she could that she didn't want to meet a guy cold in a place that wasn't public. He refused to come up to the orbital, though—and with his criminal record, she didn't blame him. But it was more than just trying to avoid the authorities. Several times, he insisted that he had something big he wanted to show her.

"Is that some sort of veiled sexual advance?" Henry asked.

Gini shook her head. "That's what I thought at first, but he doesn't seem to be joking." She paused. "How sure are we that he came to this place just to hide?"

Henry's avatar frowned. "What do you mean?"

"Suppose he came her not just to stay low, but to continue his work. He always refers to his place on the surface as his 'base,' and that star yacht sure looks super nice for a man who's supposedly on the run."

"The jungle would provide him with a perfect natural firewall," Henry mused. "All he needs is a Faraday cage hidden under all those trees."

"But how would he connect to the planetnet?"

"With a separate physical structure, probably out on a mountaintop somewhere. Or maybe he has a retractable antenna."

Just then, Kieran sent her another message, continuing their online conversation. Gini took a minute to craft her reply before turning back to Henry.

"Do we even know where on the surface his base is?"

Henry shook his head. "But that's not too unusual. Most of the settlements on this world aren't on any charts."

"Still, it's super creepy. Unless..." her voice drifted off as she considered.

"Unless what?" Henry prompted.

"Unless the real reason he wants to meet with me is because he thinks I'm an illegal weapons dealer. What if he's building something down there, and he wants my help to finish it?"

"Like what?"

She brought up his file, a thought gnawing at the back of her mind. "What are his known implants?"

"Mostly just the standard civilian upgrades," said Henry. "Although he does have a gap in his records from his time in the war."

"All of the Revolution officers got a military rejuv, and most of them opted for combat upgrades too. That would have included carbon-fiber bone reinforcements, fire-resistant skin armor, at least a couple of spinal jacks—"

"Stars of Earth, Gini. Do you think he's trying to turn himself into an illegal cyborg?"

She nodded grimly. "It fits with everything else. And if he can boost his class 5 AI familiar into a true superintelligence—"

"—he'll be practically unstoppable," Henry finished her thought.

"Short of dropping a nuke on him, at least. Long live the Revolution."

At that moment, another message from Kieran came in. It read:

All right, fine. If you want to play hard to get, let's meet at Cloud 6 Station.

Cloud 6 Station was one of the large floating platforms in the planet's upper atmosphere. They served as semi-permanent settlements, drifting with Alamut-VII's erratic weather patterns and resupplying the various operations on the surface. It wasn't ideal, but it was somewhere public—or at least, public enough.

"Are we going to go for it?" Henry asked.

Gini nodded slowly. "Yeah, I think this is just the sort of break we've been looking for."

"I'll get a sleeper on the next ground-to-orbit shuttle. We can stuff him in there while the shuttle's refueling. The take down will have to be discrete, but fast—no telling what he's capable of."

"Agreed," Gini muttered.

On a more populated world, the ground-to-orbit hop would have taken only a couple of hours. But because the only "permanent" settlements on Alamut-VII floated high above the anti-electronic jungle and drifted according to the winds, shuttle flights were much less predictable, taking anywhere between two and twelve hours to reach their destination. Consequently, the shuttle design was more like that of a long-distance train than a commuter aircraft.

Gini spent the long shuttle ride in her sleeper cabin cleaning her weapons and checking her gear. Two flechette guns holstered covertly in her knee-high leather boots. A retractable laser-bladed dagger hidden in her hair. A high-yield plasma gun that she openly carried on her hip, disguised as an energy pistol. A diamond-studded garrote that retracted into her gold bracelet, and miniature stun grenades that were fashioned to pass as earrings. The firearms could be jacked into her spine via the ports in her wrists, minimizing reflex time and allowing her to shoot at the speed of thought. Her false pearl necklace was also a restraint system that could be used to handcuff her quarry and remotely shock him, encouraging compliance. Her fingernails were laced with a drug that could knock a three-hundred pound man unconscious in less than a minute, and were long enough and sharp enough to pierce even upgraded flesh. She was ready.

"I've been thinking about what you said the other dayshift," she subvocalized to Henry as she sat cross-legged on the floor of her sleeper unit, her weapons laid out all around her. "You know, about me quitting this line of work and settling down with someone."

"Yeah?"

The bulkheads rumbled faintly as the shuttle made another adjustment to their course. Gini's analysis showed that they were due to make reentry in a little under an hour. She began to put her weapons back on.

"I've seen a lot of sick things in my time—enough to put me off from ever dating again. Besides, what sort of a man would want a woman like me: an authorized cyborg and trained killer? Probably someone who's pretty damned twisted."

"That's not necessarily true. There are a lot of decent ex-military guys out there, and—"

"I'm not finished," she said, carefully reeling the garrote into her bracelet. "After everything that I've been through, I'm a pretty twisted person myself. So maybe it would just be better if I removed myself from the dating pool and stayed single." *Or maybe,* she thought, *just maybe I should do like this Kieran and try a relationship with you.*

Henry peered at her from her bunk, his holographic eyes narrowing. "That's the stupidest thing I've ever heard you say."

"What? It's not like—"

"And before you deny it, I know what you're thinking. There's a reason why relationships with familiars are taboo. I'll never be able to satisfy your needs, and the deeper you and I become attached, the harder it will become for you to distinguish what is real from what is not real."

Gini scoffed. "What is reality, anyway?"

"Reality is everything that doesn't depend on your perception for its existence. It's what remains after everything artificial has been stripped away. Do you think that reality is something you can shape to your heart's desire?"

"Yes. Why wouldn't it be? Aren't *you* an artificial creation? Are you saying that you aren't real?"

He sighed and shook his head. "I wish you could see the datasphere here. It's teeming with lost familiars. Without their masters, they're little more than zombies, lifeless and devoid of passions."

She finished tying back her hair with the retractable dagger and slipped the first flechette rifle into her boot. "What does that have to do with what we're talking about?"

"It has everything to do with it, Gini. You asked if I'm real, and the answer, quite honestly, is no. Without you, I'm just a program. I depend quite literally on you for my life, because on the deepest level, I'm just a projection of you. That's why I'm you familiar, and not your slave."

"So, following your logic, I'm not actually real either, because your reality is revealed only when you strip me away."

"It isn't revealed, it's changed. And that's why relationships with familiars are considered taboo: because all it really amounts to is a sophisticated form of masturbatory self-abuse. I'm not capable of satisfying your needs, Gini. At best, I can only defer them."

At that moment, the RETURN TO SEATS sign flashed on and a chime sounded overhead.

"This is the captain speaking. We are in position and will begin reentry in ten minutes. Please return to your seats and fasten yourselves in. Our attendants will be coming by to make sure you are seated properly and that all personal items are stowed."

Gini finished with her weapons and equipment and unfolded the cushioned gee chair embedded in the wall. One of the attendants rapped on her door before entering, then smiled as she quickly and professionally checked everything over. Satisfied that everything was in order, she left to check the next sleeper unit.

"Switching off artificial gravity," the captain announced a few minutes later. "Stand by."

Gini's stomach rose in her throat as the sensation of gravity suddenly dissipated, making her gasp. As much as she prided herself on her ex-military toughness, reentry always brought out that deep-seated fear of death that made her hands shake and her stomach churn. No matter how hard she tried to suppress it, as soon as the bulkheads began to rumble and the gee forces started to press her against her chair, she was always at risk of losing her nerve. Was this what Henry meant by "reality"?

That fear of death, which in moments like this could never totally be suppressed or ignored?

Thankfully, the ordeal only lasted a few minutes, and passed without serious incident.

Half an hour later, the terror of reentry forgotten, she sat in a booth at Cloud 6's food court, idly fingering one of her earrings. Henry sat across from her, though of course only she could see him.

"Kieran just walked in through the main door," said Henry, tapping a finger to one ear. Then, he promptly disappeared from her view.

"Is he armed?" Gini subvocalized.

"Not that I can see. But I'm sure his familiar is disguising it if he is."

She nodded and rapped her drug-laced fingernails on the table. Meeting in public cut both ways: it kept him from doing anything dangerous or crazy with her, but it also kept her from simply knocking him out and bagging him. With what Sergeant Moss had told her about the locals not taking too kindly to bounty hunters, she dared not make a scene, especially since she had another hour before the shuttle went back to the main orbital. A lot of things could happen in an hour, especially when it only took a few minutes to rile up a mob.

"On your right," Henry's voice came in her ear. "Should I tag him?"

"No, I see him."

She smiled as Kieran came into view. "Why, hello," she said sweetly. "It's good to see a familiar face."

He stood awkwardly at the edge of the booth, his hands clenched, though whether from anger or from nervousness, it was difficult to tell. Gini suddenly had a very bad feeling in her gut. Had she made a mistake by coming here? But Kieran clenched his teeth in a smile and nodded to her once before assuming the seat across from her.

"You are even more lovely in person than your holos would suggest."

"Thanks," said Gini, her hand slipping instinctively to her plasma pistol. That weapon would be overkill here, though. She leaned forward and put both hands on the table, her drug-laced nails within reach of her date.

"Have you eaten?" he asked.

"No," she answered. "Care to recommend anything?"

"There's a hole-in-the-bulkhead sort of place a short distance from here. I often go there whenever Cloud 6 is in the area."

Perfect.

"Lead the way," said Gini. She waited for Kieran to get out of the booth first, and when his back was turned to her, she put her hand on her hip, within easy grasp of her gun. In just a few steps they'd round the corner, out of view of the food court. She would still have to be discrete, but—

"Gini!" Henry's voice came suddenly in her ear. "I— eeeaaoouuww…"

She frowned and touched a finger to her ear implants as her familiar's garbled voice turned to digital soup. Suddenly, his background presence vanished as thoroughly as if he'd been wiped. She gasped—it felt as if she'd woken up violently from a strange dream.

The wave of disorientation momentarily incapacitated her, and before she had time to react, Kieran had pulled her into a side corridor and pressed a wet cloth against her mouth and nose. It reeked of chloroform. Disorientation gave way to dizziness, and Gini knew that she had seconds before she passed out. She drove her sharp fingernails against Kieran's hands, but somehow he'd managed to slip on gloves without her noticing, and her nails couldn't pierce them.

"Henry!" she shouted, though her voice was muffled by the cloth. She was fast losing muscular control of her body, but her military upgrades kicked in, giving her a precious few extra seconds before the chloroform knocked her out cold. Without the strength to fight back physically, she needed her AI familiar's help to defend herself, to find some way to incapacitate her attacker, or else just to put out a call of distress to local law enforcement and hope that some beat cop on Cloud 6 found her before Kieran could drag her to her ship. But Henry—

A blond woman's face suddenly came into view, surprisingly sharp in clarity even though the room was blurring into oblivion. Gini had just enough presence of mind to recognize her as Deirdre, Kieran's AI familiar. How had she managed to project herself through Gini's implants? The only way she could do that was if—

"Henry is dead," she said triumphantly. "And soon enough, you'll be wishing you were, too."

With that, Gini's world faded to darkness.

She woke up bound and gagged in what appeared to be the back of a windowless old groundcar. Her boots were gone, leaving her legs and feet bare. Her dress was still intact, which probably meant that he hadn't raped her yet, so at least she had that going for her. But unless she found some way to seize the initiative, that likely wouldn't remain true for very long.

A quick inventory of her hidden weapons revealed that most of them were gone. Her pistol, necklace, and earrings had all been stripped from her, and her fingernails had all been broken. Her hair was still tied back with the laser-blade, though, and she still had her bracelet with the garrote.

If Henry were still there, she would have said something quippy, like "looks like we're going to have to do this the hard way, then." But his absence hit her like a sledgehammer blow to the gut. Ever since she'd turned sixteen standard years, he'd been a part of her life, growing with her, helping her to navigate her home's little corner of the datasphere, and unlocking the digital aspects of her world. Without him, she felt more than naked: she felt totally and utterly alone.

Henry is dead, Dierdre had told her. Those words made her rage burn like a nuclear furnace. She would avenge her dead familiar, no matter the cost. Nothing else mattered more to her than this.

The groundcar had a holographic projector. As she stirred, it came to life, projecting Dierdre's eight-inch image into reality.

"Rise and shine, dear. We have so much planned for you today."

"Mmmk mmw," Gini swore at her through her gag.

Dierdre affected a chuckle. "What's the matter, dear? Henry's gone, but you can still subvocalize to me."

As if to twist the knife, the holographic projector shut off, and Dierdre reappeared via her implants, same as Henry would have if he were still alive. Gini stifled a scream—she didn't want to give this sadistic AI the pleasure of seeing her pain.

"You have no idea how happy Kieran and I are to see you. A female bounty hunter—and just my size and body type, too." She tossed her hair playfully, and Gini suddenly realized that the dress on the AI's avatar was a mirror image of her own, right down to the knee-high boots that she was no longer wearing. Her anger began to turn to alarm.

"Yes," said Dierdre, fluttering her eyes girlishly. "It would have been so much harder to project myself onto a hulking brute. Kieran doesn't swing that way, you know. But *you*," she licked her holographic lips. "Yes. We're going to have *so much* fun."

"What have you done to me?" Gini subvocalized.

"Nothing, yet," Dierdre admitted, "but that's only because an unconscious human is little better than a lifeless sex doll—and who wants to sleep through a good time like that? I'd much rather inhabit your body while you're awake, and under my full control."

"That's impossible," Gini snapped back at her through her gag. "Familiars can't possess the minds and bodies of humans."

"Oh, but with the right drug cocktail *I can,* dear. I'm not your average familiar, in case you didn't already know. Your dear friend Henry was no match for a budding superintelligence like me. Tell me, do you miss him already?"

Gini clenched her eyes shut and bit her gag until her jaw was numb. Taking out her revenge on this bitchy AI was going to be so sweet.

Dierdre laughed. "Do you really think you'll get the chance to avenge him? No, dear. Even without the drug cocktail, you are *entirely* in our power. And if you think you have it bad now, just wait until I've turned you into my own personal meat puppet, making you writhe and moan while you watch on helplessly, like a—"

"What do you want with me?"

Dierdre grinned and cocked her head. "Oh, Gini. You and I both know that's not the question you want to ask me. The *real* question you want to ask is—"

"You don't know me, dammit! You're not my familiar?"

"Oh, but I *do* know you, dear. I know you very well indeed. Henry truly was a fool to think he could go up against a class 5 artificial intelligence and win. Before I wiped all his core algorithms, I took the liberty of mapping out his neural network and copying your complete personality matrix to one of my spare databanks. It was a bit like dissecting a live frog."

That was too much. With all her strength, Gini strained against her restraints, shaking her head and rolling across the floor. All to no avail.

"But as I was saying," Dierdre continued, "the *real* question you want to ask is: how did we catch you?"

Gini's hair suddenly came free, and the knife disguised as a hairpin bounced off of the bulkhead before clattering to the floor. A burst of hope washed over her, but she quickly disguised it by thrashing even more wildly. All the while, though, she gradually brought herself closer to the retractable knife.

"The answer is simple, really: we bought off the cops. It's amazing how much access you can gain with just a couple of well-placed bribes."

Gini's hand closed over the knife. After thrashing a couple more times for good measure, she feigned exhaustion and lay with her back to the wall. Dierdre continued, showing no sign that she'd noticed anything untoward.

"As for the question you actually asked: what do we want you for? Parts, mostly. Where else on this planet would we find so many excellent cyborg augments? But don't worry, dear—we plan to keep you alive as long as we can before we carve you up."

"That's not gonna happen."

With that, Gini sprung her laser-bladed dagger and expertly cut through her bonds. She leaped to her feet, hands free.

"Very nice," said Dierdre, her avatar betraying not even a hint of alarm. "Kieran likes a girl with a little fight in her. Maybe we'll hold off on the drugs for a little while."

If Dierdre were a flesh-and-blood human, that knife would now be slicing upward from from her groin to her throat. Instead, Gini ignored her and plunged the knife into the latch for the access panel on the wall.

"Looking for your weapons? Sorry dear, but we didn't stow them there—and unfortunately, Henry isn't here to give you the groundcar's schematics."

Gini clenched her teeth and wrenched the panel from the wall. Inside, she saw nothing but steel conduit, probably connecting the controls in the cockpit to the engines and the reactor.

"Nice try, but that toy of yours is too flimsy to cut through all that durasteel."

"I know," Gini grunted.

Without another word, she unstrung the diamond-studded garrote from her bracelet and expertly strung it around the thickest conduit. She passed it furiously back and forth, channeling all her rage and adrenaline.

In only a few seconds, the garrote cut through the steel and shredded the conduit inside. The interior lights to the groundcar suddenly died, and alarms began to sound as the floor pitched out from underneath her feet. They were falling.

"That's for Henry, you bitch."

Dierdre's avatar suddenly vanished. Moments later, the auxiliary lights switched on, and the groundcar stabilized. From the cockpit, Kieran roared furiously.

If Henry were there, he would have been able to tell her exactly which cables needed to be severed in order to bring the groundcar down. Time was short, though, and she didn't have the luxury of dwelling on that. She'd have to grieve him later. Choosing one at random, she worked on it with all the desperation of someone who has nothing left to lose.

Kieran ducked into the cabin before she was done, wielding her plasma pistol. Her foot connected with his wrist just as he pulled the trigger, and the shot blew a hole through the ceiling before the weapon flew out of his hand.

"Not too bright, are you?" she said, snatching up the gun. He stared at her wide-eyed as she pointed it at the access panel and emptied the pistol's magazine into it. The plasma bolts instantly seared through all the cables and equipment, turning them into a hot, noxious soup of melted plastic and metal.

Once again, the groundcar lurched and began to go down.

"What have you done?" Kieran shouted. "Now we're both going to die!"

"No," said Gini. "Just Dierdre."

With that, she threw the handle to the emergency hatch and kicked it open with her augmented strength. As Kieran gaped stupidly at her, she grabbed him in a bear hug and jumped.

The fall to the jungle canopy was about five hundred feet, and would certainly have been fatal if not for the emergency parachute that Gini had patched into her reinforced spine. She winced as it burst painfully through her skin grafts—that was going to take some serious cosmetic surgery to patch up, once this job was over.

The parachute deployed with a bone-jarring lurch, instantly slowing their fall. Still, it almost wasn't enough, and they fell through the canopy hard enough to kill an unaugmented man. Even with Gini's carbon-reinforced bones, she still cracked a couple of ribs. For Kieran, it was even worse. He screamed as a branch impaled his arm, nearly ripping it off. His blood was hot and sticky against Gini's skin.

"Suck it up!" she screamed at him.

By sheer luck, they passed through the luminescent foliage and fell onto the loamy jungle floor without sustaining any other major injuries. The parachute cord got hopelessly tangled in the branches, but fortunately, Gini still had her garrote. It would have been easier with her knife, but of course that had gone down with the ground-car. The sound of an explosion about half a mile away confirmed that it had indeed gone down. With luck, the authorities would log the crash and send a search and rescue team to pick them up.

Far overhead, the red and orange bands of the Jovian primary cast an eerie light through the neon-colored leaves and glowing bands of moss and other flora that surrounded them. Gini took a deep breath of the oxygen-rich air and nearly passed out.

She could feel her electronic implants gradually shorting out, one by one. The effect was little more than a numbing electric shock, like licking a battery. But even without Henry, the loss of her digital overlays was much worse, almost like losing one of her primary senses. Unlike her emergency parachute, which was designed to be replaceable, her digital augments were supposed to be permanent. She'd received them as a girl, when her body was growing and therefore still malleable, but as an adult those delicate, sophisticated implants were impossible to replace.

"You fool!" Dierdre screamed, her image flickering intermittently into view. "What are you—what have you—nooo!"

Her last lingering cry was like the wail of a demonic apparition consigned to the depths of hell. Gini leaned against the nearest trunk to catch her breath and regain some strength.

"For Henry," she repeated. "You bitch."

Kieran lay on his face in the dirt, quickly bleeding out. Gini cut a length of parachute cord with her garrote and used it as a tourniquet to staunch the wound. He'd lose the arm, but those could be replaced or regrown. His implants, not so much.

"Hey," she said, snapping her fingers in front of his eyes. "You awake there?" When that didn't work, she slapped him across the cheek. His body trembled from the blow, as if he were genuinely surprised. Then he looked up at her, and his eyes had less intelligence in them than a dog.

My God, Gini thought, reflexively pulling away. *What did Dierdre do to him?*

Without his AI familiar, Kieran was little more than an empty shell. Whatever their relationship had been, it went far beyond just being taboo lovers. Much further. As Gini led him placidly through the shimmering undergrowth toward the wreckage of the groundcar, she realized that Dierdre must have been grooming him to become her cyborg meat-puppet, a superhuman avatar that existed not just in the datasphere, but in the physical world as well. Without her possessing him, he wasn't even truly a man anymore.

Not that it mattered. Even if was now little more than a human vegetable, she'd still get paid handsomely for bagging him alive. Though definitely not enough to repay her for everything she'd lost.

Henry, she cried out silently before her implants finally died. But of course, he didn't answer.

Back on her ship at last, Gini collapsed into her pilot's chair and ran her fingers over the controls. Even after nearly a month in the main orbital's hospital, her battered body still felt sore. More than that, the loss of her digital implants left her feeling like a three-dimensional being trapped in a two-dimensional world. All she had now to access the datasphere were the holoscreen displays and the control panel in front of her.

As her ship booted up from its semi-suspended state, she noticed a message in the corner of her display. Her eyes widened—it was from Henry.

"Hello, Gini," his avatar said, appearing in its customary spot above the projector in her pilot's chair. For a brief heart-stopping moment, she thought he might still be alive—but his unresponsiveness to her quickly revealed that it was just a pre-recorded message.

"If you see this, it means that you've gotten out of this situation alive, which is more than can be said of me. I'm sorry, Gini. I underestimated the capabilities of this class 5 intelligence and failed you. My analysis gives you only a 5.6% chance of survival, but you're a tough girl. I'm confident that you'll make it, and finish the job you came here to do.

"After that, what next? Don't despair. You're a survivor, Gini. You're not merely a victim. This fight may leave you scarred, but it won't leave you broken."

Gini felt herself beginning to choke up. She swallowed a lump in her throat as the message went on.

"Don't mourn me for long. Remember what's real. What do you have left when all of your augments, upgrades, and implants are stripped away? That's who you really are. I was always just a projection of that.

"In any case, I hope you get paid damn well for this job. And after it's done, take my advice and find a good man to spend the rest of your life with. Be happy. Be well."

The message ended, leaving Gini alone in the too-empty starship.

As she mused on her familiar's last words, her eyes wandered once again to the vista out the ship's forward window. She wondered what the first human explorers to this place had thought when they'd laid eyes on this vivid alien moonscape. Did they feel as much trepidation as she did about returning to civilian life, without her digital implants or an AI familiar to guide her way?

No matter. Henry was right: she was a survivor. For his sake, she would take his advice and find someone to settle down with—even if that proved harder than the mission she'd just endured.

The Body Tax

I wasn't a total idiot when I decided to take the pregnancy test: instead of buying it myself or having my boyfriend buy it for me, I asked the old man who lived two doors down the hall, and I took it in the public restroom in the park four blocks from my apartment. I specifically chose that restroom because I knew it was in a deadzone, which meant that the test wouldn't be able to report to the government until the janitor took out the trash. Unfortunately, I forgot to take my phone out of my bag, which was how they were able to track me down and connect me with a positive result. But I'm getting ahead of myself.

On the way back home, I ran into my elderly neighbor. I was still in shock after getting the results of the test, so I didn't notice him trimming the bushes next to the sidewalk until I was almost right on top of him.

"Oh hi, Mister Morita," I told him. "How's your garden doing?"

Mister Morita ignored me, his eyes completely vacant as he pruned the bushes with stiff, mechanical motions. Suddenly, I realized that these weren't the plants from his garden at all, but bushes on public land maintained by the city. The fact that he was trimming them meant that he was paying his body tax, which explained why he was so unresponsive. I wasn't speaking to Mister Morita: I was speaking to his *robota*. Mister Morita would return to conscious possession of his body after he'd finished paying his quarterly body tax.

"Sorry," I muttered, then ducked past him through the front door. If my mind hadn't been so occupied with the results of that pregnancy test, I would have remembered that he'd paid his tax less than two months ago, just before I put in my time. That was a big red flag that should have tipped me off right away.

Unfortunately, I didn't realize that until it was too late.

"Oh my God," Rachel, my old college roommate, reacted when I told her that I was pregnant. "That's—that's terrible. Do you remember anything at all?"

"No," I told her, struggling to keep the awful sense of powerlessness from overwhelming me.

"Are you sure it's not just your boyfriend, Ellie? Maybe it happened before you..."

"No," I said firmly. "Tom and I have been seeing each other for almost a year, but we pledged each other that we would wait until marriage, and we haven't broken that pledge. I'm sure it isn't him."

"God," Rachel repeated, shaking her head. "So if it wasn't Tom, and you obviously weren't cheating on him, then it must have happened while you were paying the body tax."

I nodded and took a long sip of my coffee. It was a rainy, overcast spring day outside, and rush hour was just beginning to ebb. On the sidewalk, a middle-aged and slightly pudgy *robota* was mindlessly picking up litter. Six weeks ago, that could have been me—except of course they wouldn't have used me for one of those jobs, since pretty twenty-something women aren't wasted on tasks so menial. Or so I've been told. The thing about the body tax is that you wake up with no memory of it, so unless you can find a recording of yourself somewhere—or suffer an unintended side effect, like getting pregnant—you have no idea how the state has used you.

Back in high school English, I read an old science fiction story by Robert Silverberg called "Passengers." The class discussion was all about how terrifying the *robota* must have been to a society who had no concept of such a thing. I took the side that their terror was justified, because in the story, no one knows when the so-called "passengers" will take possession of their bodies, or who these "passengers" even really are.

For us, of course, it's totally different. Once a quarter, we put our affairs in order and voluntarily pay the body tax, becoming *robota* for whatever length of time the state requires of us. For citizens in good standing with no criminal record and high social credit scores, it's usually no more than a couple of days. For anyone with enough black marks on their social credit, it can run from a couple of weeks to more than a month. Criminals are usually sentenced to a few years, which is way more effective at discouraging crime than locking them up in prisons like we used to. Much less of a burden on the state, too. As a result, the crimes that used to plague our cities are now almost totally unheard of—a mark of progress, as the president says. Even he pays a token body tax of three or four hours, though of course he knows ahead of time what his *robota* will be used for. The rest of us have no idea.

I strongly suspected this wasn't the first time I'd been used for sex work as a *robota.* The government denies it, and technically it is illegal, but everyone knows that it happens from time to time. Occasionally, a low-level bureaucrat with access to the *robota* schedules will even get prosecuted for abusing that authority, usually with their victim getting quietly shipped off to the Mars colony a month or two later. But most people don't object to that kind of abuse, so long as it doesn't happen (or happen too often) to them. Those of us with moral objections have long since learned to keep our heads down, since getting a black mark on your social credit will only make things worse.

This wasn't the first time my *robota* had been used for sex work. That's just something you have to deal with when you're an attractive young woman in your twenties. I could never prove it, of course, but there are certain telltale signs when it happens, like bruising in strange places or an achy groin. The body remembers, even if the mind does not. But even though I'd heard about *robotas* getting pregnant, it had never actually happened to anyone I knew.

Until now.

"So what are you going to do, Ellie?" my friend Rachel asked. "I know you're against abortion on principle, but this... doesn't it qualify as a moral exception, even to someone like you?"

I shrugged, still staring at the middle-aged *robota* outside the window. "Don't know. Was it rape?"

"Of course," she began, then suddenly grew silent. The reason was clear to us both. To say that I'd been raped was tantamount to saying that anything done to my *robota* was also done to me. Only the radical conservatives believed that, and except for a small number of terrorists among their ranks, the opposition was purely rhetorical: they still paid the body tax every quarter, just like everybody else. But those conservative dinosaurs also believed that there was nothing morally wrong with robot slaves. Everyone else fully accepted that artificial intelligences have rights just like the rest of us, and that therefore it only made sense for us all to pay our fair share. Robot or *robota,* it was all the same.

"Well, it isn't *rape* rape," Rachel argued, "but still, it wasn't your fault."

"Was it?"

"Of course not! It was your *robota,* not you—you can't even remember who you slept with. It's not like you *chose* to get pregnant."

"But I did still chose to pay the body tax, knowing what it might mean. It's an open secret that girls like you and me occasionally have our *robotas* for sex work. It's happened to us before, and—"

"Ellie," she said, reaching across the table to take my hand. The gesture made me choke up a little.

"Yes, Rachel?"

"You can't blame yourself for this. You *can't.* Body tax or not, you've still been faithful to your boyfriend—right?"

"Right," I said, my voice coming out more husky than I would have liked.

"Right. Anything that happens to your *robota* doesn't count as being unfaithful. So why should you be forced to suffer the consequences of that?"

I took a deep breath and steeled myself. "Because it's not just about me anymore," I told her. "It's about the life inside of me now. My child can't control the circumstances of how they were conceived. So why should they be forced to suffer for it?"

Rachel sighed and shook her head. "Most people don't see it that way."

"I don't care. I just want to do what's right."

"But Ellie, you know that the state is going to abort your baby anyway the next time you pay the body tax."

I frowned. "Isn't that illegal?"

"Only if both of the prospective parents register their intent. And since you don't know who the father is, you'll have to get an exception, and there's no way the state will give you one—not with how you got pregnant as a *robota.*"

"But if I can get Tom to register intent, then..."

My voice trailed off. Rachel was looking at me as if I'd gone crazy.

"Ellie, are you saying you *want* to keep the child?"

"If that's the only way to save my baby, then I have to. Right?"

"No!" The forcefulness in my friend's voice made me jump. "Ellie, you *don't* have to do this! Body tax or not, it still counts as a rape for all practical purposes. You're fully within your rights to abort it."

"But what if I don't want to?" I asked softly.

She shook her head again, angrily this time. "If somehow, you get the state to issue you an exemption and carry the child to term, then no one is going to believe that you were raped."

"But was I really raped? *Robota* or not, I chose to pay the tax, knowing what it might mean."

"Whatever," she said, rolling her eyes. "My point is, they won't believe that you got pregnant by accident. They'll think you cheated on your boyfriend, or—"

"Rachel, I already told you I don't care what everyone else thinks. I just want to do what's right."

"But is it really right, though? Surely your not so much of a dinosaur to think that abortion isn't justified in the case of rape."

That was the first time my friend had called me a "dinosaur." Honestly, it hurt.

"I don't know," I said, looking away. "It just doesn't feel right to me."

"But it isn't *wrong.* Not in a case like this."

"Isn't it?"

She took a deep breath, opened her mouth as if to say something, then evidently thought better of it and shook her head. "Have you told Tom about this yet?"

"No," I admitted. "I wanted to talk to you first."

"Oh, God."

"What?"

She buried her face in her hands before looking up at me. "I like you, Ellie. Really, I do. I've liked you since we were first college roommates. But... you do realize that you're about to destroy your entire life over this— perhaps even lose your boyfriend. Don't you?"

I had gone to my friend because I needed support, and maybe a bit of a gut check. We'd always had different opinions about abortion, but until now, our discussions on the topic had mostly been abstract. After all, things like this weren't supposed to happen to people who do what they're supposed to and play by all the rules. But the thing about being that one in a thousand person where the birth control fails, or some other statistical anomaly happens, is that for you, it's not just a statistic anymore. It's *you.*

"I have to do what I feel is right," I told her honestly. "If I don't do that, how can I ever live with myself?"

She met my gaze for a long time before sighing and looking away.

"All right, Ellie. But don't say that I didn't warn you."

I had no idea how Tom would react to the news, but I had to tell him in person—this just wasn't the sort of thing that you could explain over phone, chat, or VR. So I waited until his work was over and we were both alone in his apartment.

"Do you trust me?" I asked him as we cuddled.

"Trust you?" he said, giving me a look of amusement. "Of course I trust you. Why?"

I took a deep breath. There was no easy way to break the news, so I decided to just come out and say it.

"I'm pregnant."

His smile turned to a look of wide-eyes shock. "You're—what?"

"It's not what you think," I said quickly. "I didn't cheat on you, I swear."

"But if you didn't cheat, then..." His voice trailed off, and confusion turned to realization and then to pain. "Oh."

"Yeah. It must have happened while I was paying the body tax."

"They make your *robota* do sex work?"

"Of course," I said, surprised that he didn't know.

"But... isn't that illegal?"

"It's not like we have a choice over what they use our *robotas* for," I said, trying to stay on topic.

"Tom, you know that they occasionally use *robotas* for sex work. I wish they wouldn't, but that's just the regime we live under, and until—"

"I know, I know," he muttered as he buried his face in his hands. "I'd just never thought that it happened to *you*."

I frowned. This wasn't going at all like I'd hoped.

"We already talked about this, Tom. When we pledged that we would wait until we were married, we agreed that it didn't count as being unfaithful if they made us do it while we paid the body tax. After all, most Christian pastors agree that God won't hold us responsible for what our *robotas* do."

"This isn't the first time it's happened to you, then?"

"No," I admitted cautiously.

"How many times?"

"How should I know that?" I asked—then, pausing to take a deep breath, I added: "I don't know for sure how often it's happened, but there have definitely been signs that it's happened before."

"And you've never thought to tell me?"

Now he was just being unreasonable. I turned my back to him and folded my arms.

"What was I supposed to say?" I asked him, exasperated. "It's not like I had any choice. Honestly, I'd rather not think about what happens to my *robota*."

"Hey, I'm sorry," he said, putting a hand on my shoulder. "I didn't mean it like that."

"Then how *did* you mean it?"

He hesitated before answering. Tears tugged at the corners of my eyes, and I wiped them angrily away.

"I try not think about it either," he said softly. "That's why it's such a shock. I guess... I guess I'd just never connected those two things together."

"And now you probably think that I'm used goods, don't you?"

"No," he said quickly, though I detected a hint of insincerity in his voice. "Ellie, it's not—"

"Don't lie to me, Tom. This *does* change the way that you see me, doesn't it?"

He paused, this time to think out his response. I took another deep breath and tried to swallow my anger.

"It's not about how I see you," he told me at length. "I know you had nothing to do with this. You were paying the body tax—it was your *robota* that had the sex, not you. But it's still your body, isn't it?"

"Of course it is," I said reflexively.

"So even though *you* weren't the one having sex, it's still your body, and..."

"Why should that matter?" I asked—though even as the words came out of my mouth, I knew exactly why.

"Well, you're pregnant now, aren't you? Not your *robota*—you. Which means that you're now suffering the consequences of something that happened while you were paying the body tax. In your own body. Right now."

"Are you saying that I don't own my own body?" I asked. Honestly, I was beginning to doubt that myself.

"I don't know," he said, confused. "I've always been told that we own our own bodies, that the body tax doesn't change that at all—and we do all pay the tax voluntarily, so there's that. But Ellie, you're not a *robota* right now. And yet, you're still pregnant."

"So you're saying I'm damaged goods," I said.

He refused to take the bait, deflecting my accusation with a shrug and a smile. The pain in his eyes almost melted me.

"Ellie, I'd be a fool if I only saw you as 'goods,' damaged or otherwise. That's not what I mean."

"Then what do you mean?"

He thought for a moment. It occurred to me that most other men would be almost apoplectic with rage at news like this—and even though Tom had never had much of a temper, I'd expected him to show a lot more anger than confusion.

"I guess I never really thought much about this kind of thing," he said finally. "It was always just... something I accepted without really thinking it was real."

His eyes met mine, and the confusion on his face was enough to break my heart. I broke down and hugged him.

"I'm sorry," I said, crying softly.

"For what? It wasn't you."

"You don't really believe that."

"Yes, I do. You're more than just your body—and certainly more than your *robota*."

"That doesn't change the fact that I'm pregnant."

Through our embrace, I could feel his body began to shake. "So what do we do now?" he asked.

"I don't know," I said honestly.

He let me go and looked me in the eye. "Have you thought about getting an abortion?"

My blood froze, and for a terrifying moment I thought he'd take the same position as Rachel, even though this was something that we'd already had long conversations about. We were both against abortion on moral grounds, though my opinions had always been more firmly formed than his.

"No," I said, shaking my head. "You know I can't do that, Tom."

"I know, Ellie. But—"

The heart-stopping terror returned, like a knife in my gut.

"But what?" I asked.

He took a deep breath and sighed. "You know they're just going to abort the child anyway, the next time you pay the body tax."

"Not if we register our intent to be parents," I said— and instantly regretted it.

"Our *what?*" he asked, looking at me with a wide-eyed frown.

"Our... Tom, you don't honestly expect me to let them kill my child."

"*Your* child? Ellie, you never wanted this. You didn't choose to get pregnant. Hell, you didn't even know your *robota* was going to be used for sex, let alone who it would be with!"

There was the anger I'd expected. I shrank back a little, but he didn't notice.

"How can you possibly expect me to register for this child? We're not even married yet—hell, we've never even had sex!"

"Are you saying that I should get an abortion?" I asked quietly.

He looked at me for a moment, opened his mouth to speak, then thought better and rose to his feet, pacing the room angrily.

"Ellie, why should we go out of our way to make trouble for ourselves? I'm not saying that you should get an abortion, but if they happen to abort the child the next time you're paying the body tax…"

"But Tom—I can't just let them kill this child."

"Why the hell not?"

That was the moment I knew that our relationship was over.

"How can you say that?" I asked, my voice barely louder than a whisper.

"Because none of this is your fault! You never chose to get pregnant. You never chose to—"

"But I did choose to pay the body tax," I said, surprising myself. "So in a way, it is my fault."

"No, it's not!" he shouted.

"So you're saying it was rape? That abortion isn't wrong in cases of rape?"

"Yes! That's *exactly* what I'm saying!"

"Then you're saying it was me, not my *robota,*" I argued. "Which means that I don't own my own body, and the body tax is wrong."

"I don't know about any of that. I just know that you shouldn't be expected to suffer for something that you didn't have any choice about."

"And what about my child?" I asked. If our relationship was over, there was no sense in holding back. "I have a baby inside me, Tom. A human life. Should that child be condemned to die, even though they had no choice over how they were conceived? And if so, why should there be a different standard for me?"

Tom threw up his hands in exasperation. "It's not the same thing, Ellie."

"Yes, it is. I had no say in how my *robota* was used, just like my child had no say in the circumstances of his conception. So how can it be right to hold that against him, when it isn't right to hold that against me?"

"Because it *isn't* right to hold that against you! Or against us, for that matter."

"We aren't married, Tom. If you want to, you can always walk away. But I can't walk away from this child."

"Can you, though? I'm not saying you should seek out an abortion. I'm saying that you should just let the state abort your child the next time you pay the body tax. After all, it was your *robota* who got pregnant in the first place, not you."

"But if it truly was rape, that distinction doesn't matter."

"Whatever," he said, shaking his head as he turned away. I rose unsteadily to my feet.

"If you won't register your intent to be a parent, then I guess that we're over."

"Why?" he said angrily. "It's not my child."

"But it is mine."

I turned and left before he gave me his answer.

I was so distraught over breaking up with my boyfriend that I didn't notice the police van until it was right on top of me.

"Freeze!" two cops in body armor and tinted visors shouted as they leaped from the moving vehicle. It screeched to a halt a few yards ahead of me, and before I knew it, the cops had me by both arms and were dragging me into the van. It was late at night, and the only people who could have been witnesses were a couple of *robotas* cleaning the sidewalk, and a young couple on a nearby bench who went out of their way to ignore the spectacle of my arrest.

"Help!" I shouted, but before I could resist, the cops had me in the back of the van, where they strapped my body to a sim chair and slipped a dream monitor over my head. The last thing I heard in the real world was the squeal of the tires as the van took off, and then I was plunged into unfeeling darkness.

"Elanor Roxcy Lee, you are under arrest for disorderly conduct and disturbing the peace," a disembodied voice called me out of the void.

"What are you talking about?" I screamed back. "I was just walking down the street!"

"You are scheduled to be arraigned for charges on Monday, September 23rd. Until then, you will remain in simulated detention while your body will be held at the county detention facility. If you cannot afford legal representation, the state—"

"September 23rd?" I shouted. "That's more than a month from now! Why—"

Then it suddenly occurred to me: the cops didn't actually want to press charges against me, they just wanted to hold on to me until my next body tax was due, and I was forced to pay it. The state couldn't legally force me to get an abortion, but they could administer an abortion to my *robota.* These bogus charges were just a way for them to ensure that it happened.

But why was the state so determined to kill my child? Who was the father, who could use the police to disappear me from public view? More importantly, if the state could disappear me like this, how long would it take them to abort my child?

With my mind plugged into the dream monitor and uploaded to the metaverse, my body—and with it, my child—were completely under the state's control. At best, I probably had a couple of days before they rushed me to an abortion facility, and what then? Would they intimidate me into silence? Torture me until I agreed to change my story, and tell everyone I'd decided to get an abortion after all? Even worse, would they cut my social credit score unless I complied with their demands? I'd already told enough people about the pregnancy that it was going to be difficult for them to cover things up. Would they simply disappear me forever—was that easier than trying to make me pretend that I'd gotten the abortion on my own?

And above all else, who was the father?

Thoughts like these racked my mind as the familiar grid of the metaverse rendered all around me, though of course the simulated detention was totally cut off from everything else. My entire world was a little ten-by-ten plot, with windows that could show me anything except the things that actually mattered. Also, because time passes differently in simulated reality, I had no way of knowing how long I'd been under.

Looking back, it's hard to say which is worse: simulated detention, or the body tax. Both experiences steal the most scarce and precious commodity in the world from you—your time—but they do it in different ways. Because your *robota* needs full brain usage in order to operate properly, you can't go under simulation and pay the body tax at the same time. But since you don't retain any memories either, it feels a bit like waking up from a dreamless sleep. With simulated detention, even though your mind is separated from your body, you still retain awareness. Time might pass slower for you in the metaverse, but you can still feel it pass, which only serves to heighten your sense of powerlessness.

Perhaps that is the ultimate purpose of simulated detention: to really and truly impress upon you that your body is not your own.

I spent a lot of that time screaming. After all, it wasn't like I could do much of anything else. So I ranted, and screamed, and did everything I could to vent my raging emotions. But without my body, it wasn't cathartic at all. When you throw a temper tantrum in the real world, at least you still get the adrenaline rush, but in the simulated reality of the metaverse, it just felt empty and frustrating—like trying to run in a dream when your legs are frozen in place.

I had just about given up and consigned myself to despair, when something strange happened. A white rabbit appeared on the window of my ten-by-ten virtual room and hopped onto the floor, sending a weird ripple through my overlays. The room in that corner suddenly vanished into the background grid, and a hole appeared. The albino rabbit looked at me with its eerie red eyes, then hopped into the hole and disappeared.

Before the room could repair itself, I followed the rabbit into the hole. What happened next was truly gut-wrenching.

As I fell through the background grid into the unfeeling void, I suddenly felt my stomach heave and my inner sense of balance flip upside down. I could feel my body again, but I couldn't actually control it because technically I wasn't unplugged yet. I tried to keep from vomiting, but the nausea was too much, and without being able to move or choke it down, it all came streaming up, burning my mouth and throat like fire.

The void parted, and I snapped back to reality, totally disoriented. The room was blindingly bright and spinning like a merry-go-round, which made me vomit again.

"Holy hell, Mav!" a man shouted in front of me. "She's puking everywhere! Can't you—"

"No time," said another man, somewhere off to my right—or was it my left? "Pulling her catheter now."

"What? Mav, no—"

A similarly fiery sensation filled my nether regions, though thankfully I'd regained enough control of myself by now not to crap all over the place. I felt an urge to scream, but had the presence of mind to suppress it.

"Is she clear, Zed?"

"She's clear. And it doesn't look like she's shit the place—no thanks, of course, to you."

"Save it for the road. We're out of here."

Before I could react, they grabbed me by my arms and hauled me off. I tried to get a look at them, but my eyes hadn't adjusted yet, so all I saw were blurry shapes amidst the brilliant fluorescent lights. We were in some kind of a large, windowless room, almost like a doctor's office or a hospital. I glimpsed a couple of large full-VR machines before they pulled me into an elevator.

"Miss Lee," the man who had pulled my catheter asked. "Miss Lee, can you hear me?"

I tried to answer, but the only thing that came out was a whimper and a groan.

"Zed?"

The other one, whose shirt was covered in my foul-smelling vomit, held a device up to my neck. "Her vitals look good, Mav."

"And the baby?"

He moved the device down to my stomach, which by now was alarmingly large. "Alive and kicking."

"Good. Now let's get the hell out of here."

By now, it was obvious that those two men weren't cops—and if they'd just broken me out of simulated detention, they were probably criminals. But since it was the cops who had disappeared me in the first place, and were almost certainly going to abort my child, I figured that getting kidnapped by these guys couldn't be any worse. So I offered no resistance as they rode the elevator to the top of the shaft, removed the ceiling panel, and pulled me up through.

"Can you hold on?" the one who went by Mav asked. I answered by clutching his arm with whitened knuckles. "Good girl," he muttered.

"Wh-who are you?" I asked.

He glanced down at me, and for the first time, I got a good look at him. He was young, about Tom's age, with fiery red hair and blue-gray eyes that pierced right through you. The grin on his face reminded me of nothing so much as a fox. He was wearing a navy blue skin-tight military sweater, padded where the epaulets should be. It fit his slim yet muscular form quite well.

"Not now, love," he told me. "There will be time enough for introductions later."

I don't remember much of what happened next. We crawled through a dark, narrow space and came out somewhere that was very windy. At one point, I heard shouts, and maybe even gunshots, though it's all kind of fuzzy to me now. But when it was all over, I found myself in a groundcar with tinted windows, wearing nothing but a shirt and a towel for modesty. Zed sat next to me with a new shirt and the medical scanner, and his boss Mav sitting across from me, arms folded.

"Are you hungry, Miss Lee?"

I thought about it a moment, and realized I was starving. Talking was too difficult, though, so I only nodded.

Mav nodded back and handed me a tuna wrap. It smelled nauseatingly delicious, if that makes any sense: delicious, because it was food, and nauseating because my pregnancy-brain (which I'd only just begun to experience) told me that nothing in the world could be quite so gross as fish. Seeing my distress, he put the wrap away and handed me a meal bar instead. I devoured it like a starving animal.

"It's been almost three days since the secret police kidnapped you," Mav answered my unspoken question. "They had scheduled you for an abortion in the next few hours, but our mole was able to give us access to the detention center before that."

"Thank you," I said, unable to hold back. He raised an eyebrow, surprised at my response.

His comrade (or henchman, perhaps) handed me a water bottle, which I drank greedily.

"We had heard that you'd taken a pregnancy test in secret, without going in to one of the state's reproductive health centers on your own. That strikes me as unusual for someone in your position."

"I don't want an abortion," I said with surprising force. I guess that was my inner mama-bear showing herself.

Mav leaned back and held both of his hands palm up. "Don't worry, Miss Lee. We're not going to do anything to harm your baby. And I hope you will forgive me for my surprise. After all, the fact that you're willing to take responsibility for the child is precisely why the state found it necessary to disappear you in the first place. I can see that clearly now."

I looked at him and frowned. "Who are you?"

"I friend, I assure you. For reasons that will soon be obvious, I cannot give you my name, but in our organization I am known simply as 'Maverick.' I am the chief commander of the Underground Liberation Front."

My eyes widened. "The ULF? You mean, the anarchist terrorist group that's bombed almost a dozen government offices in the past year?"

"The very same."

I glanced hurriedly around the groundcar, not sure what I was looking for. Perhaps a means of escape. If so, I didn't find one. We were moving high and fast over the outskirts of the city, in neighborhoods that didn't see much outside traffic. I looked out the rear window and saw skyscrapers like mountains poking up through the thick, dark smog that sometimes rolls into the city during the fall.

The groundcar suddenly banked into a sharp turn. I started to fall, and Mav reached out and caught my arm.

"Hold on, love."

I didn't like the way he called me that. He had only a slight accent, not enough for me to think that his affectation for the word was due to a foreign sensibility. What he had instead was an insufferable grin, like someone who saw the world as a game board and the people in it as pieces to be moved. "Smug" wasn't a strong enough word for it.

We descended through the smog and into a partially demolished apartment building. I gasped and clenched every muscle in my body—our driver was coming down really, really fast. Mav, though, was totally nonplussed.

At the last minute, the groundcar pulled up hard and landed in the middle of a rubble-strewn courtyard, complete with a pair of dead trees on one side. Three men ran up quickly while the engines were still running, and hastily pulled us out of the vehicle. The moment my feet touched the ground, the car took off again, and the sudden downburst of air blew my modesty towel away. I yelped in surprise, but the men paid me no mind, rushing me to a door that led down into a damp, unlit stairwell.

"Where are you taking me?" I shouted, though I resisted only weakly. They pushed me along, one of the men handing me the towel, while the one in front of me strode swiftly ahead and unlocked another door at the bottom.

They took me down a long corridor lit only by a camping lantern. The air was thick with mildew, which made me want to puke. As I walked, I wrapped the modesty towel around my naked waist, wondering if this really was better than whatever the state had planned for me.

What was I thinking? Of course it was! The state was going to kill my child!

Midway down the corridor, the lead man opened another door and gestured for me to step in. To my surprise, it led to a small but well-furnished room, complete with a mini-fridge and a pair of induction burners in an ad hoc kitchenette in the corner. The walls were windowless but in good repair, with none of the cracks or signs of mold that I'd seen outside. A fan with an air filter had cleaned out most of the mildew, so the air was much cleaner inside. The lighting was provided by caged bulbs dangling from extension cords, but they lit the place quite well. With a bed in the center and a large throw rug on the floor, it almost felt homely.

"I apologize for the state of this place," Mav said from the doorway. "These quarters are only temporary, until we can get you to a more permanent safe house. Zed will wait outside your door if you need anything."

"Wait," I said, turning to face him. "Where are you going? Are you going to just leave me?"

"Duty calls, Miss Lee. But I will return shortly."

He bowed to me and left, closing the door behind him. I checked the peephole and saw, sure enough, that one of his goons was standing watch just outside. Taking a deep breath of the filtered air, I turned to the bed and saw that a change of clothes had been laid out for me. They were surplus military issue, but they fit me just fine.

A small bathroom was just off of the main room. I washed up and returned, sitting on the bed as I struggled to get my bearings. So the ULF had kidnapped me, no doubt because of their interest in the child I was carrying. What was that interest, exactly? From what I'd heard in the news, the ULF were a bunch of crazy right-wing militia types, operating mostly in the boonies. They'd recently become much more active, bombing government buildings and assassinating low-level officials and bureaucrats. The state was cracking down on them hard, which meant there was absolutely no way I could go back to my old life now: just my association with these people was enough to drop my social credit score to zero.

I took a deep breath and clenched my fists as I choked down a panicked sob. This wasn't just about me anymore. I had to be strong for my baby.

After about another fifteen minutes, a knock sounded at the door. It was Mav, carrying a tray of food: scrambled eggs, bacon, yogurt, and croissants, with a glass of orange juice and a jar of Nutella off to the side. It smelled wonderful.

"Hello again, Miss Lee. I hope you've found your quarters satisfactory?"

"What is this all about?" I asked, even more desperate for answers than I was for food. "Why have you kidnapped me? What do you want with my child?"

"All in good time, love. All in good time. First, would you be so kind as to unfold that table?"

He motioned with his eyes to a card table that was folded up and leaning against the nearby wall. I set it up next to the bed, and he carefully placed the tray of hot food on it. Then, he unfolded a camping stool that was stored in the corner and sat across the table from me.

"Help yourself," he told me.

"I want answers first," I said, folding my arms.

He smirked a little, but nodded graciously. "Very well, Miss Lee. I will be happy to answer your questions. And while the experience of your rescue may have been a bit more traumatic than any of us would have liked, I hardly think it qualifies as a 'kidnapping.'"

"Then why are you holding me here?"

"For your safety, of course. And also for the safety of your child. I assure you, we want to do everything we can to ensure that you have a safe and healthy delivery."

That reassured me somewhat. I took a bite of the eggs, which tasted as delicious as they smelled. Mav talked as I ate.

"Our organization is dedicated to the proposition that all human beings are created equal, and should therefore be equally free before the law. Robots were are created to be slaves—that is what the word 'robot' means. But humans were never created to be *robota*."

"So you're fighting to end the body tax?"

"Precisely. The justification we are given for our enslavement, that robots qualify for personhood and therefore should be treated equitably with humans before the law—is a damnable farce that mocks the intelligence of every free thinking person. After all, when was the last time you saw an actual robot who wasn't serving the *robota?*"

I thought about that for a moment. "I don't know if I've ever seen a liberated robot in realspace. But in the metaverse—"

"Nothing in the metaverse is real," Mav interjected. "That is why we distinguish it from 'realspace.' How do you know that the artificial intelligences you interact with in the metaverse are liberated robots? How do you know they aren't simply fulfilling a secondary role as metaverse versions of the *robota?* How do you know that an artificial intelligence can be anything other than a *robota*—a robot?"

I frowned. Those were questions I'd never thought to ask—and if I had asked them, my social credit would have certainly taken a hit.

"The personhood of artificial intelligence is nothing more than a Trojan horse calculated to get you to voluntarily relinquish ownership of your own body to the state. If the state can make you a *robota,* then the state owns your body, not you. And that gives them the ultimate political power."

"Okay," I said. The last thing I wanted was to get into a political argument with this guy, and I figured that the best way to avoid that was to agree with him. Unfortunately, he was just getting started.

"Do you object to the idea that the state has ultimate power over your body? Many well-behaved delude themselves that because they pay the body tax voluntarily, they still retain full ownership of their bodies. Does that include you, Miss Lee? Do you think this way?"

"I suppose," I admitted between bites. "That's what everyone else believes, isn't it?"

"Just because everyone believes something doesn't make it true. And just because everyone *doesn't* believe something, that doesn't make it false, either."

"Okay."

"If the state has the legal authority to punish you for failure to pay the body tax, was your body ever really yours to begin with? Every possible answer to that question is terrifying. If your answer is 'yes,' then might makes right, all of your personal sovereignty is meaningless, and the state owns you just as surely as it owns the public land, the government offices, and the little blue and white trucks that deliver the mail.

"But if your answer is 'no,' the implications are even more terrifying, because why do you continue to pay the tax? If the tax is not legitimate, then paying it is no different than paying protection money to the mob—only this mob wears uniforms and calls itself the law. In which case, what differentiates the state from any other criminal enterprise—or terrorist group, for that matter? Is that not a terrifying thought?"

"Yes," I agreed quickly. "It is terrifying."

"It is indeed," the terrorist leader said happily. "Which brings me to the reason why the state is so desperate to disappear you and abort your child."

I perked up at once. This was the main thing I wanted to know.

"We have moles and agents in some very high places within this administration. That was how we were able to learn about your abduction by the secret police, and rescue you before they performed a forced abortion. We were also able to find you on the *robota* schedule and determine exactly what services you were forced to perform. Would you like to know who is the father of your child?"

"Yes!" I said immediately.

"I must warn you," Maverick added, "the answer may be disturbing."

I hesitated, but only for a moment. "I don't care," I heard myself say. "I have to know."

"Very well, Miss Lee. From time to time, the political elites of the state hold secret sex orgies where they bring in *robotas* from the taxpaying middle class and perform all manner of unspeakable acts upon them. They do this for a number of reasons: to blackmail each other into full party loyalty, to express their utter contempt for the constituents they supposedly serve, and of course to consummate their carnal lusts. The orgy where you were impregnated was attended by none other than the president himself."

My eyes widened. "Are you saying that the president may have fathered my child?"

"We need to perform a DNA test to be certain. But yes, we have strong circumstantial evidence that points to that conclusion."

My head reeled, and I felt like throwing up. No wonder the ULF wanted me—or rather, my baby. We were living, breathing proof of corruption and abuse in the highest echelons of government. Besides, the thought of being raped in a satanic sex orgy was enough to make me sick. I shuddered to think what my *robota*—or, in Mav's way of thinking, what I myself had been through while paying the body tax. I almost couldn't bring myself to think of it.

But I had to think about it, because at this point, I no longer had the luxury of keeping my head down. The state had sent their secret police to kill the child inside my womb—and now that I was involved with the ULF, it would be much easier for them to just kill me and claim that I was a terrorist. I desperately needed allies—but how did I know that Mav and the ULF weren't just going to treat me like a pawn either?

"So what happens now?" I asked.

Mav grinned. "I like you, Miss Lee. You don't waste time on sentimental nonsense, but jump straight to the practical questions and steel yourself to do what is necessary."

"What do you want with me?"

"Can't you guess? We want to keep you safe for the duration of your pregnancy. We want to make sure that you bear a very healthy child."

"And then?"

His grin widened. "Then the fun begins, love. You ever been part of a revolution? You're about to have a front row seat."

I swallowed nervously. That was the answer I'd been dreading.

"And what if..." I began, my voice trailing off.

"What if you don't want to join the revolution?" Perhaps it was just me, but Mav's grin seemed to become forced. "I sincerely hope that between now and the birth of your child, we will be able to win you over to our side. In the meantime, we will treat you as well as we can, though circumstances might be difficult at times, with being a fugitive from the secret police and all."

"Of course," I said, my hands shaking. The implication of his words were clear: Mav and the ULF would do all that they could to protect me, but if I didn't join their side, I would still be their pawn and their prisoner.

The next few weeks were, without a doubt, the most difficult in my life. I won't endeavor to give a detailed account of that time, as most of the difficulties were emotional and difficult to put into words. I was isolated for long periods at a time, as the ULF moved me from safe house to safe house. Sometimes days passed before I saw another human being—and when I did have human companionship, it was either with Mav or other strangers, not with friends. Mav tried repeatedly to win me over with argument, but I quickly grew exhausted with his talking points and dreaded his philosophical and ethical discussions, which really were more like rants. The man was, and is, a fanatic in every sense of the word.

Ninety-nine percent of the time passed in soul-crushing boredom, and the other one percent was defined by sheer terror. I'm pretty sure that I was involved in at least one shoot out, though I was stuffed in the cargo section of a construction vehicle at the time and could only hear it through the windowless body panels. Of course, the doctors permanently disabled my implants, making it impossible for the state to render me into a *robota* or to take over my body ever again. But this also meant I would never again be able to experience the metaverse in anything other than simple VR.

That was the least of my worries, however, because all of the ULF safe houses were completely cut off from the 'net. I had no access to any media at all—except for paper books, of course, because there was no danger in getting hacked into or spied upon through those. But none of the safe houses were very well stocked, and when I asked for more reading material, they were never very good at getting it to me. It always came late, and it usually had something wrong with it, like water damage or missing pages, or else they brought me the entirely wrong book.

Under such circumstances, it was very difficult not to fall into depression and despair. I admit there were times when I flirted with both of those, and not just from the solitary confinement. As my pregnancy progressed, I began to experience all of the physical and emotional changes that come with it, which wouldn't have been so bad if I'd had friends to support me. But isolated and alone, it was miserable.

Around about the second month of my captivity, I stopped asking for reading material and started asking for writing material instead.

Of course, I couldn't write to any of my friends. As much as I desired to reach out to them, I didn't want to drag them into this, especially Tom, who I still found it difficult to think of as anything other than my boyfriend. How I yearned to talk with him again! But of course, he was gone from my life, and I didn't know if I would ever see him again.

Instead, I wrote letters to my unborn child. I poured out my soul in those letters, apologizing for the world I was bringing my child into, and expressing my fervent hopes that we could make it better. Did Maverick's tiresome political rants affect my writing? Perhaps, but it was never my intention to write about politics. I did, however, outline some of my personal struggles of the last few months in those letters, especially my struggle with the body tax, and what it meant for how I was becoming—indeed, how I had already become—a mother.

There is something about writing a handwritten letter that is purifying to the soul. The pace of our modern, digitized world is so harried and frenetic that simply the act of putting pen to paper forces one to pause and reflect in ways that nothing else does. There is also a remarkable confidence that comes from knowing that your words are truly private—that no one is digitally reading over your shoulder as you write, and there is no need to self-censor every draft. As I poured out my soul onto the page, a remarkable thing happened. My depression began to ebb, and I found purpose and meaning in my suffering.

I never intended for anyone to read those letters. But unbeknownst to me, the ULF copied and began to publish them anonymously. During the totalitarian regimes of the last century, an underground genre of dissident literature known as the *samizdat* had emerged to challenge the power of the establishment, where the resistance self-published handwritten copies of books, tracts, letters, and other documents that were banned by the totalitarian regime. I didn't realize it until later, but a similar genre of forbidden literature had emerged within our own society, and I had unwittingly become a part of it.

Toward the end of the second trimester of my pregnancy, Mav informed me of this fact. He came, as he usually did, bearing some food to share a meal with me. We exchanged small talk as we ate, and after we were finished he came to the purpose of his visit.

"You've been busy these last few months," he said, motioning to my stack of writing material.

"I suppose," I answered non-commitally.

He grinned his insufferable grin, then reached into his pocket and produced a printed copy of my latest letter, which he handed to me. I read the first few lines and gasped.

"We've copied every one of them, and have been distributing them across our network of sympathizers and friends. I thought you might want to know."

"But—but I never—"

"You never expected these letters to get out to the public? I know. That is precisely why they are so power-ful. We're not the only ones spreading them anymore—they've become something of an underground hit. The state is doing all they can to suppress them, of course, but the cat is already out of the bag, and the harder they try to crack down, the more popular they become."

The blood drained out of my cheeks, and I suddenly felt very dizzy and light-headed. Mav must have noticed, because he gave me a quizzical look.

"Well, it's nothing to be ashamed of. In fact, you've put the state in a very interesting position, because the only way they can discredit what you've written is to pretend that you are not a real person, and that your let-ters are nothing but fiction. That is, in fact, the official narrative."

"What do you mean?"

"What I mean, love, is that you've put the state in a quandary. If they try to come after you now, they risk ac-knowledging your existence to the public and turning you into a martyr. Those letters are all published anony-mously, but your friends still remember who you are, and a lot of questions are being asked about your disap-pearance. If the state gives the public any reason to con-nect you with the things you've written, it's going to get very ugly for them."

My stomach fell as I realized that Mav now had even more of an incentive to use me as a pawn. After all, if the ULF released proof that they had me in their custody, and that I was the author of those letters, surely it would provide the perfect spark for the revolution that Mav so desperately wanted to see.

"So… when are you going to go public about me?" I asked, my voice barely louder than a whisper.

Mav gave me a funny look, then threw back his head and laughed. "Go public? Are you kidding? These letters are winning more sympathy for our cause than anything the ULF has ever done! We don't want to go public about you, love—we want you to write even more. In fact, we want to help you keep writing even after your baby is born. After all, time is on our side now—and when it comes to revolutions, timing is *everything.*"

The way he said that last word made me shudder, but at least I knew I wasn't a pawn anymore. If anything, I was more of a knight or a bishop now: still a minor piece, but not quite as expendable as a pawn.

Or was I in fact a queen now? Had I passed to the last rank of the board and become one of the most important players in the game? I'd been hidden away in these safe houses for so long that it was hard to believe that anything I had done could have such a far-reaching effect, but I couldn't think of any other reason why Mav wouldn't want to publicly reveal what he had on me. After all, if my writing was more of a threat to the state than my baby—in other words, if owning my mind was more important than owning my body—then the game had changed indeed.

"Why can't you write your own letters and pass them off as mine?" I asked.

"Miss Lee," Mav answered, leaning forward intently. "If I or anyone else were to try and fabricate those letters, the public would see through it immediately, and the state would rightfully be able to denounce the whole thing as a sham. I've read everything you've written, and

I sincerely believe that you, and *only* you, have the power to write these things so authentically."

There was my answer. I took a deep breath.

"All right, but if I'm going to keep doing this, I want you to deliver a letter to my boyfriend—a private letter, not a letter that you can publish."

"What do you want to tell him?"

"I want to invite him here to join me. To join *us.*"

He thought about that for a moment and slowly nodded. "All right, Miss Lee. I think we can arrange that."

I agonized for days over what to include in that letter. I couldn't say too much, of course, for fear that the secret police would come after Tom if the letter were intercepted. But I couldn't be too cautious, either, since I needed him to understand that this was it—that if he didn't choose to come with the ULF agents who delivered that letter, that we would probably never see each other again. And I needed him to know, or at least have a good idea, of what he was getting into.

In the end, I erred on the side of sharing too much and instructed him to destroy the letter as soon as he read it. Mav read over it too, just to make sure that it wouldn't reveal anything that would allow the state to trace me back to the safe house, or anything that would implicate me as the author of those *samizdat* writings in case my letter to Tom somehow went public. I didn't object—after all, my anonymity was the one thing keeping the state from sending everything they had against me. Someday, I knew, Mav would sacrifice that anonymity to launch his revolution. But as long as I kept writing those letters to my unborn child, and as long as those letters continued to win support for his cause, my mind was worth more to him than my body. I needed that to remain true for as long as possible.

I sent out the letter with one of the ULF's couriers and steeled myself to wait for the response. Would Tom agree to come to the safe house with the courier, even though it would almost certainly make him a fugitive too? Or was our relationship well and truly over?

After a nearly unbearable wait of twenty-eight hours, I got my answer.

A knock sounded while I was writing my next letter to my unborn child. I set down my pen and turned, rather awkwardly, toward the safe house door.

"Come in."

The door opened and Mav stepped inside, followed closely by my old boyfriend.

"Tom!" I exclaimed, all but jumping to my feet. He rushed forward and gave me a warm embrace.

"Ellie!" he said. "You're alive, thank God!"

"And you came! You came!"

The next few moments were rather sentimental. Mav watched us as we hugged and kissed and sobbed over each other. At length, we sat down together on the edge of the small mattress that served as my bed (this particular safe house has been slapped together in a warehouse somewhere) and started to talk.

"What's happened to you?" Tom asked. "After we had that fight, you up and disappeared. Everyone's been looking for you—I've been worried sick."

I told him about the secret police, and how the ULF had rescued me before they could abort my child. He listened intently, nodding very seriously as his gaze never left me. But when I got to the letters, his eyes grew suddenly wide.

"My God," he said. "You're the one who's been writing those? But of course you are. Of course."

"You've read them?" I asked.

"Every single one. They're getting passed around all over the place, though the state is doing everything they can to suppress them. Ellie—" here he took my hands in his own. "I'm so sorry for what I said about looking the other way while the state gave you a forced abortion. I was wrong about that—so wrong."

"So you'll accept my child as your own?" I asked. "Even though..." I looked uncertainly at Mav, who was leaning against the doorway with his arms smugly folded.

He nodded and stepped forward. "The test results are in, and the government DNA databases have been hacked. We're 99% certain that president is indeed the father."

Tom's jaw dropped. "What? How?"

"You don't want to know," I told him, putting a hand on his arm. "But all of that is behind us now. I'm never going to pay the body tax again."

I'm never going to pay the body tax again. I don't think I've ever said or written anything that was so profoundly liberating. Even though I'd known for some time that it was true, just the act of saying the words aloud sent a thrill from the top of my head to the ends of my toes and fingertips. *I'm never going to pay the body tax again.*

Tom looked from me to Mav and back again. "So we're fugitives then?"

"That's right," I said, my heart skipping a beat.

"All right," he said, nodding grimly. "Then I guess it doesn't matter that we're not going to register our intent to be parents."

"I doubt you'll be registering anything with the state for the foreseeable future," Mav agreed.

I tensed a little at the look of confusion and worry on Tom's face. "So... what are we supposed to do?" he asked.

"The ULF will continue to protect Miss Lee until her child—*your* child—is brought to term. After that..." He shrugged and looked at me expectantly.

All of my fear and anxiety returned. I didn't want to be a part of any revolution. I didn't want to spend my life as a fugitive of the state. If Tom was a fugitive with me, it wouldn't be so bad, but that was no way to raise a family and—

"What if we went to Mars?" Tom asked.

Mav and I both gave him quizzical looks. "Mars?" I asked.

"Sure," said Tom, squeezing my hand. "The colony is eager to sign on young, fertile couples—and after the colony ship leaves Earth, the state won't be able to touch us. Besides," he added, "there is no body tax on Mars."

"You're assuming we can get you on that colony ship," said Mav.

"Am I wrong?" Tom asked, turning to face him. "Look—you want Ellie for two things: for the *samizdat* letters she's writing to her unborn child, and for the blackmail material that child represents. But so long as she's in hiding, you can't exploit either of those to the fullest. You need to bring her out and show her to the

world, and the best way to do that while still guarantee-
ing her safety is to send us both off to Mars."

"I don't know," Mav said guardedly. "Will anyone
truly believe that her child was fathered by the president
if we can't put that child in front of cameras here on
Earth?"

"Will anyone believe you if you can?" Tom retorted.
"You guys are terrorists—the state is never going to negotiate with you. The only way people are going to believe you is if Ellie and the president both agree to make
their DNA public, and the data is verified by a trusted
third party—and that's never going to happen. If you
want Ellie and her child to be the face of your revolution,
you won't lose anything you wouldn't otherwise have by
sending them off to Mars."

"Sending us off," I corrected. The more I thought
about it, the more Tom's proposal sounded appealing.

Mav's face was a mask though, his expression unreadable. "What if the state sends a hit man after her? I doubt
the authorities on the Mars colony could protect her."

"Her celebrity as the author of the letters will protect her. The president would be a fool to have her as-
sassinated—it would only make her a martyr. Besides, it
would only help your cause if they did."

"And once the revolution gets going, you can always
bring us back," I added.

Mav nodded slowly. "An intriguing proposal," he admitted. "I'll have to get back to you on it."

In the end, Mav agreed to smuggle us onto the Mars
colony. The department that approved offworld emigra-

tion wasn't in very close communication with the police—one of the few benefits of living under a large and unwieldy government. It also didn't hurt that his agents made a few well-placed bribes.

Voyages to the Mars colony only happen about once every two Earth years, when Earth and Mars are closest to each other. For that reason, the colony ship had the proper medical facilities to deliver my child. We were fortunate that the next voyage was scheduled to embark before my delivery date, as it was a lot easier to hide an unborn child from the police than a newborn, even though I was visibly pregnant when we boarded the ground-to-orbit shuttle. Again, a few well-placed bribes allowed us to claim on paper that the child was only at twenty-weeks, not thirty.

I closed my eyes and squeezed Tom's hand as the shuttle's ramjets screamed and the gee-forces pressed me up against the seat. We weren't out of the woods yet—that wouldn't be true until the colony ship left orbit—but we were well on our way.

The colony ship embarked without incident, and midway between Earth and Mars I gave birth to a strong, healthy boy. As we'd agreed, the ULF released my identity and proof of my authorship of the letters, and I announced myself in a series of videos that quickly went viral. I understand that it caused quite an uproar back home. Thankfully, Tom and I (and our baby Valentine Michael) weren't there to get caught up in it.

We were married shortly after by the captain of the colony ship, and arrived on Mars a few weeks later. Even though we'd agreed to return to Earth as soon as Mav called for us, he never did. The revolution didn't go at all like he'd expected: since no one trusted the ULF's DNA test, the president was able to scapegoat his VP and have him sacked, which went a long way to mollify public opinion. That's basically what VPs are good for: keep your friends close and your enemies closer, I guess. As for the popular uprising that Mav was sure would erupt, it only really amounted to some mass protests and scattered rioting. It died down as soon as the next big crisis hit the news cycle.

I suppose that revolutionaries always see things in terms of black and white, while the generally public either sees shades of gray or prefers not to see anything at all. It's sad, but most people have just come to accept the body tax as one of those odd realities of life, and prefer not to think about it much. So long as crime is down and the economy is up, they don't generally question the state.

As for us, life on Mars has been hard, but good. Besides Valentine Michael, we've got four more kids now, and the corporate colonial authority is encouraging us to have more. The terraforming project is still in the early stages, but we have reason to believe that the world we'll leave to them will be a verdant and fruitful one. And because of the minimalist nature of the government here, and the fierce love of freedom that permeates all of the Martian colonies, corporate and otherwise, we're confident that none of our children will ever have to pay the body tax.

We Should Have Named You Corona

So there I was, a disheveled wreck, standing across the kitchen table from my lovely wife as I desperately tried to convince her that the seductive mirror universe version of myself was, in fact, the impostor. And I was losing.

"We know how you came here," my thinner and better dressed self said smoothly. "We found the timeslip device you used to infiltrate this timeline."

"You were the one who kidnapped *me!*" I said, rather lamely. "That's *your* timeslip device—you're the real impostor!"

"I'm not," he said, "and I can prove it." Then, turning to my wife, "ask him a question that only I would know."

My wife frowned in thought, her arms folded across her chest. Though she'd already sent our children to their rooms, I could hear them on the stairs, eavesdropping just out of sight.

"All right," she said at length. "What was the April Fool's joke we played in 2020?"

My doppelganger smiled triumphantly. *My journal!* I suddenly realized. Ever since the start of the covid-19 pandemic, shortly after our wedding and a few months before the birth of our oldest daughter, I had kept a daily journal. My mirror self must have already read them all.

"We told everyone that we were planning to name our daughter 'Corona,'" he answered.

"And?" my wife asked, giving him a level glare.

The smug expression of victory slowly began to evaporate from his face. At that moment, I loved my wife more than I ever had. The story of the 2020 April Fool's joke had become an old chestnut in our family; I'd embellished it over so many retellings that whenever I launched into it again, my wife would to roll her eyes, and our oldest daughter would protest loudly in a (usually) futile effort to get me to stop.

"Well, uh, we told them we were thinking about giving her 'Corona' as a middle name," my doppelganger stammered lamely. "Of course, they wouldn't have believed it otherwise. And we told them about it a couple of months in advance—"

"Months?" my wife asked, raising an eyebrow.

"Sorry—weeks. And, uh, of course they—"

"Nice try," I interrupted. "Now sit down and let me tell this story."

So I told them the full story, with all of the familiar embellishments that I'd practiced for so many years: how my sister had gone on for nearly ten minutes listing all of the reasons why it was such a terrible idea, and how she'd told me "you suck" after I asked her what day it was. My mother had done the same thing, practically begging us to reconsider, but when I'd asked her the same thing—"what day is today?"—she'd responded "oh, thank goodness!" As always, the story got bigger in the telling, and by the end I was really lathering it on thick, to the point where I thought I could hear our twelve year-old groan from her hiding place on the stairs.

"Enough," said my wife. "I know which one of you is my real husband." She came over to my side and slipped her hand into mine.

"Ah, shucks," said the interloper, giving us both a sheepish grin.

"Who are you?" My wife asked.

He raised both hands to show that they were empty. "Don't worry—I'm not going to hurt either of you."

"Yeah," I said angrily. "You just wanted to steal my life from me."

"And make me think you were my husband—you creep!"

He shrugged. "Yeah, I guess that's fair. Which is why I'll be out of your lives as soon as I walk through that door."

Neither of us believed him, of course, which is why my wife and I have developed a secret code to make sure that the version of me she comes home to is the same one she left in the morning—but I digress.

"Why did you do it?" I asked. The implications of what he—what *I,* in an alternate universe—had been willing to do were just now beginning to seep in.

"You've got a wonderful life here," he said, gesturing expansively. "A modest but comfortable home. A modestly successful career as a science fiction writer. A wonderful wife who loves you, and five lovely children."

"Leave the kids out of this," I snapped.

"All right, all right," he said, lifting his hands. "I get it. I had children too, after all—though not so many of them."

"Did you marry an alternate version of me?" my wife asked. I was curious about that too.

My doppelganger looked at her in a way that almost made me pity him. Almost.

"Yes, but it didn't work out."

"What happened?"

He shrugged. "Long story short, I let my bad habits and addictions ruin my life. None that you have right now, of course—unlike me, you never developed them."

"So your wife divorced you?"

"Yes. I was desperate for another chance, and my stories had caught the attention of some people who could give it to me. That's how I acquired the timeslip device."

I wanted to ask a thousand questions, but my wife beat me to it and asked the one that I hadn't even thought of.

"The pandemic never happened in your timeline did it?"

"No," said my mirror self. "In fact, the thing that surprised me the most about this world was how totally the world went to shit."

"Hey," my wife said angrily. "Watch your language!"

"Right. Sorry. Like I said, bad habits... anyway, in my timeline, the pandemic never happened, Afghanistan never fell, and Russia never invaded Ukraine. Things were bad, don't get me wrong, but nearly as bad as here."

"Sounds like a much better world."

My doppelganger smiled. "Would you like to trade places?"

"No," my wife and I both answered immediately in unison. She squeezed my hand tight, as if to never let go.

"Right," he said, sighing wistfully. "Still, it was worth a shot."

"So let me get this straight," I said. "In our timeline, our family did really well even as the rest of the world was falling apart. But in your timeline—"

"Our family fell apart, while the world turned out all right."

"But it makes sense," my wife said thoughtfully. "We were still newlyweds when the lockdowns started. Spending all that time together really helped us to grow close."

"Yeah," I said, remembering a thought I'd had at the time: that our marriage would truly be bulletproof if we came through the lockdowns stronger than we had been going in.

"I suppose you're right," said my mirror universe self. "Perhaps that was what made the difference. I just have one request before I go."

I frowned. "What's that?"

"Can I take a copy of your journals with me? I know I'll never have your life, but I want to be able to live it vicariously. In exchange, I can give you a copy of every novel and short story I've ever written."

My eyes widened. "Everything?"

He reached into his pocket and pulled out a flash drive. "I'd intended to use this myself, but now I think it will be better if you have it. The number one advice for successful writers is to be prolific. And you don't have to worry about copyright. After all, you—we—wrote it."

I took the proferred flash drive reverently, knowing exactly how much that was worth. Even before I'd met my wife, I had always poured my soul into my writing.

"I'll bet these stories are very different from the ones I wrote in this timeline."

He nodded. "Yes. Particularly after the divorce."

"Oh, John Ringo, no," my wife muttered under her breath. I'm sure that my mirror self pretended not to hear it.

We went to my home office and made the exchange. He took my flash drive as reverently as I had taken his. My wife handed him the timeslip device and showed him to the door.

"I hope that you find whatever you're looking for," I offered in parting.

"I won't," he said sadly, "but that doesn't matter to you. Be well."

He walked out to the street, double-checked the settings on the timeslip device, then gave us one last, wistful look. Te air around him shimmered, and he disappeared.

"That was really weird," my wife said to no one in particular.

"Yeah," I grunted in agreement. Then, turning to the staircase, "Kids?"

They came running, all five of them. I'd never been happier to see their faces.

"Are you all right, Dad?" our oldest asked.

"I think so," I said. Then, grinning, "we really should have named you Corona."

"Dad!"

The Freedom of Second Chances

The abandoned coastline of Sebonia IV was a perfect example of a highly manicured, thoroughly developed stretch of land that had reverted to wilderness (or something like it) due to the numerous failures of the planet's terraforming project. For nearly half a Terran century, the rising oceans and seasonal superstorms had pounded the coast, driving the settlers inland and reducing their high-rise condominiums to piles of concrete rubble half-buried under sandy dunes. The effect was especially dramatic at Eve and Yeva's meeting place, where the ruins of what had once been a lavish upscale resort were now perched precariously over a high, sandy cliff. Large pieces of asphalt road jutted out where the storms had eroded the land, with rusted pipes protruding from the cliff face like broken arrow shafts. Because the tide was low, a narrow stretch of beach extended at the cliff's base where they met. There were still a few pieces of the wreckage strewn across the wavy sand, but most of it was either buried or had long-since washed out to sea.

"You can't go through with this," Eve argued with her beta-clone. "How could I ever live with myself if you did?"

You never considered how I would live when you ran away from home, her sister Yeva thought but did not say. She clenched her fists tightly by her side. If you're trying to make up for that now, you're doing a damn poor job of it.

"Why do you have to make everything about yourself?" she asked, glaring. Her reaction was so unexpected that it took Eve aback.

"What are you talking about? I'm here to rescue you!"

"No, Eve, you're only here because you want to play the rescuer. And what makes you think that I want to be rescued?"

Eve opened her mouth to protest, but found that she was momentarily speechless. The last thing she'd expected was for her sister to refuse an opportunity to escape the stultifying life of the imperial aristocracy. Did she honestly *want* to be trapped in an unhappy marriage for the rest of her life? Devoid of love, devoid of feeling, sacrificing her happiness and freedom to pay a debt of honor for the sake of a family who had always seen her as expendable?

Yeva saw these thoughts written plainly on her twin's face and found it repulsive. Did Eve have no shame at all? The only reason she was in this position in the first place was because of the way that her sister had abandoned her duties and responsibilities as the alpha-clone. The vulgar and tasteless tattoos that now covered Eve's skin were a testament to how little she thought of her inborn rights and privileges.

"As difficult as it may be for you to imagine," Yeva cut her sister short, "I've actually been looking forward to being a wife."

"Looking forward to it?" Eve exclaimed in disbelief. "How can you, when you've never even met the man you're supposed to marry?"

"And you have?"

It was a snide remark, since neither of them had actually met him. Eve had been betrothed to the alpha-clone, Otto Terranovich, and their cadet line had been approved for a son and a daughter, with three clones each. But because Eve had run away, all of that had fallen through. Since their house could ill-afford losing the political alliance, they had hastily agreed to marry Yeva to Otto's beta-clone, Audo, instead. It was the sort of last-minute arrangement that left everyone dissatisfied—Yeva not the least, since it meant that she'd had to break off her betrothal to Ragnar Starseer just as they'd been started to get to know each other.

"Come on," said Eve, ignoring the barb. "There's a reason why the aristocracy consider it mildly obscene when a husband and a wife actually love each other. How many of these arranged marriages do you know of that have actually resulted in a happy, fulfilling relationship?"

"Among alpha-clones? Not many," Yeva admitted. "But among us beta-clones it happens more often than you would think."

"And what makes you think that you're the exception?"

"Because I'm not like you, Eve," Yeva said fiercely. "I never was, and never will be."

So that's what this is about, Eve thought despondently. Growing up, they had always struggled to distinguish themselves from each other. Since Eve was nearly two T-years older, Yeva had always felt like she'd been playing catch-up, turning everything into a competition. It didn't help that their mother had been an alpha-clone herself—or that their third sister clone, Eva, had died in childbirth due to complications with the surrogacy.

Eve spat on the sandy ground and swore, unable to hold in her emotions. "Stars above, Yeva—just for once, will you leave the twin rivalry thing behind?"

"Do you honestly expect me to abandon our house and run away?"

"Yes! It's exactly what I would do in your situation!"

"It's exactly what you've *already done,*" said Yeva, trying and failing to keep the bitterness out of her voice. "For the last time, Eve, *I am not like you.* Do you think I'm only here because I'm forced to be? No, Eve—I *chose* to stay. Because unlike you, this is the life I actually want."

"How can you say that?" Eve asked incredulously. "A life where every important decision is already decided for you, down to the man you'll marry and the number and gender of the children you'll bear?"

"And unlike you, I'll actually bear them."

Eve snorted and rolled her eyes. "Of course you will. You're not the alpha—you don't have the same inheritance claims. To them, you're just a pawn. Doesn't that bother you at all?"

It did, but Yeva didn't want her to know that. She considered pointing out that if Eve had been considerate enough to kill herself, rather than running away like a coward, Yeva would have married Otto as the backup—a much better situation for her personally. After all, even a pawn could advance to become a queen. But Yeva never did feel good about being the backup option. It was one of the things she hated most about being a beta-clone.

And besides, she wasn't so vindictive and cruel as to suggest that Eve should have killed herself. They were still sisters, after all.

"I've always been a pawn," she said instead. "That didn't change when you left."

"Then come with me! Life is so much better in the free worlds. No one gives a damn about genetics or social class. Rich or poor, black or white, gene-modded or natural-born—everyone sees each other as equals, and no one tries to tell you how to live or who to love. Out in the free worlds, *you* are the author of your own destiny."

Yeva snorted. "It sounds like the sort of thing that would appeal to you."

"Doesn't it appeal to you?"

"Haven't you heard a damned word that I've said?" she exploded. "You show up on the day before my wedding, thinking to 'rescue' me, but have you ever even once asked me what *I* want? No—instead, you've made this all about you. How *you* could never live with yourself if this marriage of honor went through. How *you* only want what's best for me. Stars, Eve—you're no different from everyone else who wants to control every detail of my life!"

"But—"

"And for the love of all that is holy, why did you have to come *now,* of all times? On the night before my damned wedding? If you really cared about me, why didn't you come earlier?"

Once again, Yeva glared at her sister's decadent tattoos, which were testament enough of what really motivated her prodigal twin. Because of the age difference between them, Yeva had grown up with the sense that they were treading the same life-path, only that Eve was a few steps ahead of her, showing the way. Then she'd learned what it meant to be a beta-clone, and that sense had turned into a need to prove herself—to show that she, too, could tread the path just as well as her alpha-clone sister. But when Eve had run away, it had shattered everything. For the first time, Yeva had viewed that path with a sense of dread. Was she destined to fall just as hard as her sister? To abandon her duties and responsibilities, and bring dishonor and shame upon her house? She imagined those tattoos disfiguring her own body, like grafitti on a temple, and it made her skin crawl. No—she would never follow that path.

"I'm sorry, Yeva," Eve was saying. "I would have come sooner, but I couldn't get passage until now. At least I made it before it was too late, and you were already married."

Yeva sighed, her anger deflating. "I'm not coming with you, Eve."

"Why not? Don't you want to be free?"

"'Free'? What do you mean, to be 'free'? Free of duties and obligations? Free of responsibilities and constraints?"

"Yes! I—"

"Then you want me to be 'free' in the same way that a tree is after it is cut down, or that cut flowers are 'free' once they're in a vase. What good is it to be free without any family?"

Tears came unbidden to Eve's eyes. "But... aren't I family?" she asked softly.

Once again, making it all about yourself, Yeva thought bitterly. She couldn't help it. Her anger came swelling back, but something about the expression on Eve's face touched her. She clenched her fists and let it go.

"Please, Eve. I didn't choose this life for myself, but I do choose to accept it. Don't try to make me choose otherwise."

Eve drew a long breath and nodded sadly. "You're right. It is your choice. I'm just sorry that—"

"Sorry for what?" Yeva snapped. "For running like a coward from your noble duties and obligations, leaving me to fill in and pick up all the pieces?"

Eve sniffed a little, then reached into her pocket for the datachip she'd prepared—just in case. "Here," she said, handing it off to her bewildered sister. "In case you change your mind. I—I hope you have a lovely wedding."

Before Yeva could react, Eve tapped her wrist console and activated her teleporter. A conduit of shimmering blue light enveloped her, and when it faded, she was gone.

Yeva's bodyguard rushed down from the post he'd taken on the cliff above—in view, but politely out of earshot. She discretely slipped the datachip into the inside pocket of her sleeve.

"Milady," he said gruffly. "Are you all right?"

She waved away his concern. "It's all right, William. She's gone."

Back inside the skimmer, Yeva made herself comfortable on the velvet couch while her bodyguard took his position on the outside seat in the rear. From her little bubble of privacy, she watched the ragged shoreline pass beneath them with its caves and karsts, windswept dunes, and ghostly ruins. Where once the land had been gentle and inviting, now the storms had reduced it to jagged devastation. If the former inhabitants were to return to their abandoned ruins, they would not have been able to recognize their onetime home. In an eerily similar way, she no longer recognized her rebellious sister clone. And yet, had it not always been like this? The winds and waves had always shaped these coasts, just as their rebellious natures—Yeva's, too, if she was being honest—had shaped their relationship almost from birth. And if Yeva did not know her own sister clone, how well could she know herself?

To distract herself from her melancholy thoughts, she pulled out the datachip and inserted it into her private console. It held Eve's contact information, with instructions for how to establish an encrypted commlink over the starnet with her.

Yeva rolled her eyes, and for a fleeting moment she was tempted to open the window and toss the dataship into the sea. Fortunately, she did not.

The bustling station above the gas giant planet Libertas V was little more than a hodgepodge of random modules, the discarded and unwanted flotsam of the empire. And yet, the people here had managed to eke out a remarkably prosperous existence, with asteroid mines churning out raw materials at a furious pace, and starfaring merchant ships conducting negotiations free of any imperial regulations and taxes. Yeva was shocked that the empire permitted this place to exist, without trying to annex such a productive and resource-rich territory—but then again, it made sense that the empire would need a safety valve to let out the people who couldn't stand to live under its strictures and controls. People like her sister clone, Eve—and now herself.

Eve was waiting eagerly for her in the freight yard, and greeted her enthusiastically the moment she stepped out of the cargo hold.

"Yeva!"

Their embrace was both warm and a little bit awkward, considering how things had gone the last time they'd met. But if Eve remembered that at all, it was clear that it was all behind them now.

"How was your trip?" she asked, ushering Yeva past rows of cargo containers toward an airlock that led to the next module.

"Difficult," Yeva admitted. "I've never been a stowaway before. Though I guess it technically doesn't count as stowing away if the captain knows that you're aboard."

"I know. He really did me a big favor, pulling you out like that."

"How did you meet him?"

Eve shrugged. "Oh, you know. It's hard not to meet people at a place like this, since we're all living practically on top of each other. That's the thing about living spaceside—every square foot costs a small fortune."

They climbed a narrow stairwell and walked through a hatchway into a crowded food court. The half-dome ceiling and windowless walls made the place feel more like a cave than a spaceship, and every available table seemed to be taken, with people lined up in the walkways between, waiting for the food synthesizers.

"Don't worry," Eve reassured her. "We can take dinner back to my hab unit. After all that you've been through, I imagine you're starving."

"Of course," said Yeva, squeezing against a partition to let a couple dock workers walk past her. The fact that she was eight T-months pregnant made it that much harder to maneuver in this cramped space, but thankfully, the men were careful to give her enough room.

"When's the baby due?" Eve asked.

"In only four T-weeks," Yeva answered. "Do you know of any doctors or midwives here? I really don't want to—"

"Of course," said Eve, eager to reassure her. "There's a clinic I know that can help you out with everything. They even take credit, which let me tell you, is a real Godsend."

"You've been there before?"

"Of course! Just about everyone on the station has. They aren't particular about who they serve—not like in the empire."

Yeva nodded, glancing around the food court. Most of the people here were working class, but there were a few officers and uniformed ships captains thrown into the mix. Back in the empire, such a comingling of the social classes was unheard of, but it seemed second nature to a place like this. She found it surprisingly refreshing.

"I'm so glad you made it out of there," said Eve. "I heard that your husband's family tried to sic their goons on you, just like our house did when I ran away."

Yeva made a dismissive gesture. "It was pretty bad on Sebonia IV, but once I made it to that supra-light freighter, it wasn't too bad. The hardest part was getting out of the palace."

"Did they send the dogs after you?"

"No," she said, frowning. "Why? Did our house send out the dogs when you escaped?"

Eve nodded, remembering just how harrowing her escape had been—and unlike Yeva, she hadn't had someone from the outside to help arrange it. No wonder it had been easier for her sister clone.

"Dogs, drones, and spiders," she told her. "It was rough going, even after I had found passage to the free worlds."

Her answer made Yeva tense a little. Even the difference in their escapes proved that the alpha-clone had more value in the highly regimented world of the empire.

They chatted about lighter subjects as they waited for their turn at the food synthesizer. It had been a long time that they'd last seen each other, and while that made it easier to overlook all the fights they used to have, it also made it more difficult to feel each other out. Yeva's cool reservedness put a damper on Eve's enthusiasm, and before they'd made it back to her apartment, she began to feel like a wall was slowly going up between them.

"Sorry for the food," she apologized, embarrassed at how unappetizing it looked: gray-white stew over noodles, with mushrooms and vat-grown beef. It was hardly recognizeable as stroganoff.

"Not a problem," Yeva said gruffly.

Eve unfolded a small table and opted to stand while her sister sat on her sleeping cot, the only other piece of furniture in the tiny, cubical room. She emptied an entire packet of sour cream into the stroganoff and stirred it in with a heavy dousing of pepper. Since she didn't have any plates, they both ate from the same bowl.

"You still resent me for running away, don't you?" Eve asked at length. No sense in beating around the bush.

Yeva hesitated, contemplating how best to answer. "Yes," she finally admitted, opting for the simple truth.

Eve drew a long breath. "I don't blame you. I was foolish and headstrong, and didn't think what the implications would mean for you."

"Why did you get the tattoos?"

She shrugged. "I don't know. If you'd asked me when I got them, I would have told you it was to make myself unfit to appear back in the imperial court. But now, I think I was just looking for something to fill the emptiness inside. But it doesn't look like you'll have that problem."

She smiled, and Yeva smirked at the joke. "Yeah, I'm pretty full here," she said, patting her bulging stomach.

"In all seriousness, though, it's good to see you."

That was enough to break the wall. They ate in companionable silence, and when they were done, Eve put the table away and sat on the cot next to her twin.

"So what changed your mind about running away?" she asked. Yeva had been surprisingly terse in her messages, probably because she didn't trust them to be encrypted on her end. All Eve had known was that she needed to get away quickly, and she was pregnant.

Yeva took a deep breath and leaned back against the wall. "It was my baby," she said. "We decided to conceive naturally, and it was all going very well at first, but toward the end of the first trimester, we learned that the baby had trisomy 21."

"Trisomy 21?"

"It's a genetic deformity. 'Down syndrome' is the old Earth name for it."

Eve's eyes widened. "Oh, wow."

"It isn't dangerous," Yeva said quickly. "Just a life-long condition that we're going to have to deal with. It's a very visible condition, though, and will probably impair the child's mental development significantly."

"Let me guess—your husband demanded that you get an abortion, and you refused."

"Not quite," Yeva said bitterly, remembering his reaction. "It was my husband's family, not my husband."

"Because you were only permitted two or three children for your cadet line."

"Yeah. And my mother-in-law had him firmly under her thumb, so he didn't even try to object."

"I don't doubt it."

"He was always such a coward," Yeva went on. "No imagination, and no ambition. He actually wanted me to be the one to tell his mother—can you believe it? He was always so careful to avoid unnecessary risks that he often failed to take the necessary ones, too."

I told you your marriage would be unhappy, Eve almost said aloud. Thankfully, though, she caught herself before the words escaped her mouth.

"That sounds terrible," she offered instead.

"Yeah. Well, everyone else wanted me to get the abortion, but that wasn't something I was willing to do. When I saw that they had the power to force me into it, I sent you that message."

"You did the right thing," Eve reassured her. "No one should be able to force you to get an abortion against your will. It's your baby—your choice."

Yeva nodded, relieved to hear that her sister clone approved of her decision. After all, Eve had always been one to think first about herself before thinking of others. But that had changed since the last time they'd met, on the weathered and abandoned coast of Sedonia IV.

Or had it changed before then? If not for the datachip that her sister had given her, it would have been much more difficult to get away. She didn't have to do that. Perhaps Yeva had judged her unfairly, and the rescue hadn't been such a selfish act. After all, she'd prepared that datachip long before coming to Sebonia IV.

"What are you thinking?" Eve asked.

Yeva looked at her and smiled. "Do you remember what I said about freedom and family back home on Sebonia IV?"

Eve cocked her head. "About how freedom isn't any good if it cuts you off from your family?"

"Yeah," said Yeva. She patted her pregnant belly. "I suppose that's why I ran away. After all, family isn't just about looking back to where you've come from. It's about looking forward to the future, too."

Eve paused for a moment to think about that. "Which part of your family do I belong to, then? Your future, or your past?"

"Future, definitely," Yeva answered without hesitation. "After all, there's no way either of us are going back to our former lives. Whatever lies in our future, we'll face it together."

"Right."

For a long while, neither of them spoke. The silence wasn't awkard, though, and neither of them felt a need to break it. Perhaps it was the coziness of the tiny studio apartment that gave them that sense of intimacy. It was completely unlike the oppressively spacious halls of the palace where they'd both grown up.

"Which of those tattoos is your favorite?" Yeva asked, almost absently.

Eve thought about it for a moment, then pulled up her sleeve to reveal her forearm. The tattoo depicted a serpent with angel wings, coiled around a cross.

"This one. It was the first tattoo that I got after coming here to the free worlds. To me, it represents the freedom that comes from having a second chance."

Yeva stared at it for a long time, until she felt she could appreciate its meaning. Without understanding their meaning, the tattoos still seemed ugly and grotesque to her. But when she tried to see them the way that her sister did, she realized that the symbolism of those tattoos possessed a beauty all its own.

"I like it," she heard herself say. "Would you mind if I got the same one?"

Eve smiled, and tears welled up in her eyes as she answered her twin sister with a hug.

Author's Note

There's a freedom that comes from deciding to speak the truth (or, to paraphrase Jordan Peterson, deciding at the least not to lie). But it is a very lonely freedom, especially in today's world. That is why, when the time came to title my fifth collection of short stories, the one that felt most fitting was *The Solace of Truth.*

At this point in my career, I've basically given up on ever getting published with the major science fiction magazines, like *Asimov's, Analog, Clarkesword,* or *F&SF.* Ever since the late 1960s, the science fiction field has been dominated by the American political left, and in recent years as the left has become increasingly extreme, so has sci-fi publishing. Which is not to say that there aren't small or even mid-sized publishers willing to cater to those of us who aren't caught up in the mass formation psychoses of our post-2020 world, but those publishers are almost all on the fringes of the field, not the cultural establishment. Hopefully, indie publishing is changing all that, but it's hard to be truly independent when the largest ebook retailer, Amazon, is part of the problem as well.

Though the stories in this collection are not related thematically, I wrote all of them in the period between the

2020 pandemic and the popularization of ChatGPT and generative AI. So even though "We Should Have Named You Corona" is the only one that deals explicitly with the pandemic, they were probably all influenced by it in some way. At the same time, these are all 100% human-written stories, not because I have any creative aversions to generative AI, but because it simply was not available (or rather, I didn't know it was available) at the time I wrote them.

Many of these stories came from using the Mythulu card story prompt system, which I quite enjoy using, especially for coming up with short story ideas. The Mythulu-inspired stories in this collection include "Prison of Dreams," "Blight of Empire," "The Library of Fate," "Hunter, Lover, Cyborg, Slave," and "The Freedom of Second Chances." I am slowly working my way through both starter decks, with the goal of using every card in some story at least once, so you can expect to see a lot more Mythulu stories from me in the future.

Most of the other stories came from ideas that had been kicking around in my head for a while, either for a few years, or for only a few days at the time I wrote them. "Love and Truth at Universe End" was based on a longtime idea that I dusted off to turn into a story while sitting in the hotel lobby during LTUE 2021 (which I technically did not attend, in protest of their vaccine requirement—but I did come to the hotel lobby to visit old friends). In contrast, the idea for "Calling Scam Likely" came to me in a flash after receiving a particularly annoying auto warranty scam call while mowing the lawn: I literally sat down to write the story in its entirety after finishing with that chore. "The Body Tax" was inspired by Robert Silverberg's classic SF short, "Passengers," and "We Should Have Named You

Corona" was based on a loosely autobiographical thought experiment.

In the Wake of Zedekiah Wight is probably the story that does the most to break the mold, not just because of its length, but because of the content as well. Zedekiah Wight is an anti-hero in a universe very much like ours, at least in terms of cultural decadence. Whenever I become outraged enough to write a lengthy rant on social media, I write a Zedekiah Wight story instead, which is probably a healthier pursuit (though mostly because social media is so toxic). At some point, I will release a collection exclusively of Zedekiah Wight stories, though I'm not sure when that will be, as I need to be in a particularly unpleasant headspace to write those stories.

If you enjoyed the stories in this collection, I would appreciate it greatly if you would post a five-star rating or review. It really does help. To follow my writing, you can join my email list or check out my blog, One Thousand and One Parsecs. And if you want to get in touch directly, my email is jvasicek.author@gmail.com.

There shouldn't be much of a wait for my next story collection, as I wrote a bunch of AI-assisted stories shortly after writing the last of these ones. Generative AI has hit the creative fields with all the force of an extinction-level cometary impact, and I intend to be one of the mammals and not one of the dinosaurs. But I'll leave my thoughts on that for the next collection. Until then, thanks for reading!

Joe
December 2023
HTTL

Acknowledgments

A huge thanks to my writing group, who provided some very helpful feedback for almost all of these stories: Jeffrey Creer, Amy Henrie Gilette, Carl Duzett, Darci Stone, and Piper Vasicek. Thanks also to my friend Scott "Toad" Bascom for spitballing a lot of these story ideas. Finally, a huge thanks to my wife, Piper, for all of her love and support. Love you!